A Cascade of Secrets

Emma Bradley

That made of earth is also made of life.

ISBN: 978-1-915909-10-7

To all the characters we have loved then lost, never to be forgotten, and to all the readers who miss them.

TRIGGER WARNING: Grief and death in scene.

CHAPTER ONE
LOLLY

The Flora Court glistened in the early morning dew, and Lady Leilania had never been quite so proud of her home as she was in that moment.

A rambling network of iron and glass greenhouses glinted in the morning sunlight, surrounded by lush gardens decorated in glimmering dew, with meadows, valleys and dells beside rushing streams and rockpools amid clusters of forests further beyond. It was glorious, and it was home.

Being next in line to become the Flora Court's lady came with several irritating requirements, all of which Lady Leilania tended to avoid wherever necessary. The title and her name being one she had eschewed early on, as now she was known as Lolly to absolutely everyone except her mother.

Lolly folded her arms across her chest and slouched into the ridiculously flouncy dress she'd been forced to wear.

A chance to host the high society Fae and a neighbouring court didn't come around often. Most of the time, her excitement came from the growth of a new strain of plant or the prospect of harvest season. But only a short while earlier she had been rolled kicking and screaming into the dress, a stiff dark green monstrosity with velvet to hide all the binding bits, that was in her mother's opinion *"perfect with your autumn-leaf hair"*.

Despite being required to present a distinguished front, the moment Lolly's attendant had finished the final curl in her hair, she hurried off to plant some seedlings and managed to snag her hair-ribbon on a particularly affectionate *ridacin* plant. The bulbous root had tugged the forest green ribbon free, which she hadn't minded too much, but then she had to check on the Spikery which left her pulling burrs out of her curls. Now she stood at the front entrance to the castle waiting to welcome their guests and she looked decidedly dishevelled.

"Stop slouching, dear," Lady Flora murmured. "They'll be here soon and you will need to get used to doing things you don't want to when you become lady of the court."

Lolly rolled her eyes as her other mum, the one who resolutely refused to deal with anything remotely court-related, chuckled and gave her a spirited nudge on the arm.

"They won't recognise her anyway," her mum joked.

Lolly grinned as Lady Flora huffed and scanned the horizon again. No sign of the expected guests from the Revel Court, but they would likely arrive with a ridiculous amount of noisy and unnecessary flair.

But our court is something to be proud of. Lolly stood a little straighter.

Lolly sighed as Lady Flora flicked another glance over at her and grimaced at the slide of mud on her hem and a smudge of soil on her cheek. Something always needed doing at the Flora Court, a plant to nurture or prune or sow, or soil beds to rake, or debris to clear away. While her parents dealt with the bureaucracy of the court and minding the people that were part of it, the treaties and trades and tricks, Lolly focused on the actual reason they were called the Flora Court in the first place.

Lolly absentmindedly brushed down the velvet of her skirts, wishing she could be in her normal stretchy jeans and a cardigan with bountiful pockets full of seeds, leaf samples, spare twine and small gardening implements.

"The greenhouses need weeding," she muttered without any hope of being excused.

Lady Flora ignored her, but her mum sent her a weary smile. Lolly continued grumbling under her breath as her oldest friend strolled to her side, dark hair neatly plaited and a floral strappy dress over a pristine white t-shirt.

"Nice try," Petra said. "But my only job so far since being sent here by the queen has been to keep you from running off. The greenhouses will have to wait."

She would do it too, Lolly knew, with a perfect tackle. Petra had always been agile and fast, but her training at Arcanium had only made her more lethal.

I wouldn't make it three paces.

She knew Petra had the ear of the young queen too, part of the reason Lolly trusted the teenage regent enough to speak up in support of her at the Nether Court gathering some weeks back.

A loud bellowing noise filled the air and Lolly lifted her sulking chin with hope rising. While the other court members looked around in confusion, perhaps expecting the Revels Court to have arrived with a bang as was their style, Lolly scanned the rolling greenery for the source of the sound.

A flash of silver flitted between the nearest line of trees and she picked up her skirts, breaking into a run. She knew Petra would be right behind her but with an Arumpus in the woods so close to the court, it wouldn't be wholly unexpected for her to chase it.

"Lolly!" She ignored her mother's irate voice. "LEILANIA!"

Her full name meant she was in serious trouble now, so there wasn't much point stopping and turning back.

Breaking through the boundary of the wood, she hiked her skirts higher and hurdled a fallen tree trunk, wincing at a loud ripping noise as something snagged the fabric. The Arumpus slowed up ahead, huge hooves dancing over the bracken as it skidded to a halt.

"There, steady now, you've done me a favour, mister," she whispered, hand outstretched.

Because of course females Arumpii didn't have the vast spiky spines from withers to ears like this magnificent beast did. His silver coat rippled in the dappled daylight, hints of shimmering greenish-gold reflecting from the canopy of leaves above.

The Arumpii herd roamed wild, save one or two that seemed happy to choose domesticity and plagued the kitchens in the courtyard, but a long time of the court leaving them at peace meant they came close enough to interact with now and then.

The male lowered his muzzle toward Lolly's outstretched fingers and she waited, tense with excitement. She'd rarely come this close to a wild one before.

Something snapped nearby, a hefty twig by the depth of the noise which meant it had been trodden on by a boot holding some weight.

The noble head of the Arumpus shot up, the eyes rolling liquid black. In a stamping of hooves, he wheeled around and charged off into the forest.

Lolly took a deep breath to calm the swelling rage at losing such a rare opportunity, but she couldn't do anything about her clenched fists as she rotated to face whoever had disturbed them.

She stared into the deepest pair of wide, forest-green eyes. Hovering half a head higher than her own, she glared fire and fury into them, and the rugged, masculine face that surrounded them.

"Can you be any clumsier?" she seethed. "Wild Arumpii don't come this close any old time you know, let alone a beautiful male like that one."

She vaguely recognised the young man in front of her but irritation was clouding her memory. She also had to face her mother and a quick glance down proved her once fine dress was entirely torn and dirty now.

A throat cleared nearby and Lolly spied Petra a respectful distance away, arms folded and a smirk threatening to break across her lips. But the young man in front of her didn't turn around to acknowledge Petra so neither did she.

"I'm sorry I spoiled your amusement then," he said, not sounding sorry or amused at all. "We seem to have skipped into the wrong part of your court. We were walking lost through the forest until we saw your mad dash, *Lady*."

That definitely sounded sarcastic, accompanied by his gaze drifting from her face to the muddy boots underneath her spoilt dress. Lolly bristled but Petra was beside them before she could think up a suitable retort.

"Allow me to make the introductions," Petra suggested. "Lady Leilania of the Flora Court, meet Tyren Berell, aide to the Lord of Revels."

Now she recognised him. He was the sour-faced young man who had stood with the Lord of Revels at the meeting of the Nether Court. His expression didn't shift from disbelief as he glanced over her but he bowed low at least, proper enough to recognise her rank, not that she normally cared about propriety.

"I'm actually the son of the Lord's aide," he added. "But I'm sure the titles won't matter if both of us get lost in the woods."

Lolly huffed. "*I* wouldn't get lost. I know these woods better than half the rangers my parents' employ."

Petra nodded, giving the haughty son-of-the-aide-of-the-Lord-of-Revels what Lolly thought was a wholly unnecessary look of placation. Most people thought Petra didn't do faux niceties but Lolly knew better than that. Petra could play nice when she tried, but she preferred not to be in situations where she had to. Here however she seemed perfectly content to play go-between now, relaxing her arms to her sides.

"She does know the entire wood to be fair. But you won't likely be walking any of them, Lolly, when your mother sees the state of that dress."

Heat leapt to Lolly's cheeks but she lifted her chin high, gathered her ruined skirts and set off toward the court.

"Keep up then," she shot back. "I have things to do once this farce is over."

Despite using her sharpest, no-nonsense tone that usually sent the greenhouse helpers scarpering, neither Petra nor Tyren answered her. She stormed out of the woods and toward her irate mother, nervous mum and their assembled guests.

First the oia buds bloomed early, now this. It was always destined to be a bad week.

She put extra stomp in her step as she crossed the grass toward the lavish garden and wide cobblestone-patterned paths that formed the front entrance of the castle. It was more of a large manor house than a castle, with extra corridors and add-ons that rambled sideways and backwards rather than up, especially as every castle in stories and Lolly's vivid imagination had turrets and towers. But she would have chosen her rambling court with its abundance of greenhouses and wide open windows and trees growing through the floors over the grandest of castles in any realm. Perhaps not when her mother was standing in front of it though, with a jovial smile of fakery on her face and blue eyes bright like summer thunder.

"There she is," trilled the Lady of the Flora Court. "Please don't mind her appearance. We had a loose Arumpus and she's always been best at handling them."

A compliment, because anything negative would have shown weakness or at least a severe lack of control. Lady Flora, for all Ladies of the Flora Court for the past however long Faerie history stretched in the records took that name along with the title, would not concede to being weak or out of control in the presence of her own people, let alone a rival court.

Although we're all supposed to pretend we're the greatest of friends and allies now the Holly Queen has called us all together.

Lolly pushed a smile onto her face, letting it curl prettily as she widened her eyes. It wasn't a hardship to pretend to be beautiful and friendly, at least not physically. She imagined herself back in the greenhouses with people she knew around her and reminded herself that the nicer she was, the quicker they'd forget about her and she could flee when her mother wasn't looking.

She managed not to let her discomfort show on her face as the Lord of Revels strode toward her. His black hair curled around his ears in a rakish way, his golden face deceptively ageless. Lolly eyed the shiny black shirt unbuttoned ridiculously low and the flouncy boots that looked twice the width of his legs at the top.

"Hello young Leilania," he boomed, giving her a wink. "We'll liven this place up a bit, don't you worry."

She tensed. The plants didn't need random courts

bursting in with their noise and their ridiculously wide dancing boots and their non-natural party favours. Neither did she.

Tyren appeared beside her before she could drum up a suitably coquettish answer that would appease both the irritating lord and her mother.

"My Lord, perhaps the, um…" Tyren hesitated before mouthing, "*gift*?"

The Lord of Revels threw up his hands with the utmost drama and flair. Lolly wondered how quickly she could get to the Spikery and grab a prickly vine to hit him with. Unable to be rude to a court lord, mainly because she was only the daughter of a lady, she shot Tyren a stiff frown instead. She didn't need him interjecting, although she hadn't actually said a word yet to stand for herself.

"Fetch the gift!"

The Lord of Revels seemed happiest bouncing about, turning to Lolly's parents and rubbing his hands together gleefully.

"These are rare indeed," he said. "I am under the impression it will be something you don't have in your little herb garden."

Petra's hand was on Lolly's wrist before she had a chance to raise it, her Fae connection crackling awake. She wasn't blessed with plant gifts like Petra had been, the ability to grow natural matter an elemental rarity even among Fae. But she had a speed gift, along with strength and a couple of others. His lordship wouldn't even see her move before she got the first punch in, but Petra had a firm hold on her.

"Let go," she muttered.

Petra grinned. "No, I know how long it takes you to calm down and this isn't calm time."

Aware Tyren had one eye on her as the Lord of Revels hurried toward a wooden crate being manhandled across the grass by several attendants, Lolly took a sharp, deep breath.

"I'm calm. If my mothers can resist the urge to smack him into the next realm, so can I."

"And they might even believe you," Petra said. "But I don't."

All eyes fell on the crate as the lord waved his hand impatiently at someone standing ready to open it. The lid was levered off with a flourish and Lolly half-expected an animal to come tumbling out. Craning her neck, aware that even Petra seemed to have loosened her grip a minute amount, Lolly let a gasp tumble out of her lips.

"A *Ruudenera* sapling?!"

Her mother the Court Lady shot a disgruntled glance her way, but her mum, who insisted she wanted no part of court business that wasn't to do with the trading of the plants and seedlings to other realms and courts, was lost.

"Lolly, come see." She held her hand out as she approached the crate. "It's a beauty."

Lolly wriggled out of Petra's now unresisting grasp and managed a somewhat graceful, if speedy, pace to the crate. The delicate golden leaves were reaching from the dark cocoon of the crate toward the light already, the spindly white trunk and stems flexing to accommodate the movement. The noise of the gathered crowd hushed away and Lolly reached out a tentative hand to feel the delicate gold furring on the nearest leaf.

"The central courtyard," she suggested. "It'll get an almost all-round day of light there, plus we have the energy-powered flame-heaters glowing at night for the late bloomers."

Her mum nodded and Lolly noticed a subtle hint of tangling in the otherwise presentable hairstyle. While she'd inherited the future of a court lady from her mother, her auburn hair, blue eyes and stubborn streak were entirely her mum's doing.

"Spot on. Now, grab an end."

Lolly did as she was told with total eagerness, because helping to move the plant which was basically the same size as her meant she didn't have to waste time playing nice with the lord of frivolity and frippery.

She noted her mother casting them resigned looks as they beetled past with the enormous pot in hand, but nobody stopped her from helping. She caught the steady tap of Petra's feet behind them though and guessed escape opportunities would be minimal.

They crab-stepped across the entrance hall and through the wide, open doorway into the first greenhouse. It was more a conservatory, large enough to host balls but often the floor was a dumping ground for plants that needed an airy space. Through the conservatory and another hallway panelled entirely in wood, they reached the central courtyard. The fountain was more a complicated maze for water; sometimes it tinkled gently and other times the water rushed. Today it seemed to have absorbed Lolly's disgruntled mood as it thundered and dashed against the stone sides of the fountain.

"Right here will do," her mother insisted.

They settled the tree in the very centre of the courtyard and stood side by side to admire it. *Ruudenera* trees were rare and grew in warm climates. Their leaves could be used in all sorts of potions and ointments, and Lolly was almost done updating the court's ledger on all known uses of every type of plant they possessed.

"I take it we're going to have to be present more now," she muttered.

Her mum sighed. "Yes. It's important to your mother."

"Well the plants are important to me. I can't skip my duties to lounge around in a dress. Nobody will want to talk to me anyway."

Petra grinning beside her didn't fill her with confidence.

"They might," she suggested. "For certain things."

"Like what?"

"Suitors."

Lolly pulled a face. "Ergh. No. I'm not being paraded around like some exotic bird for eligible court Fae. Not one of them would be able to tell an *oia* berry from nightshade, and those two look nothing alike as it is."

"You might want to consider staying on your mother's good side then," her mum suggested. "She's already decided you need to take more of a role with this visit."

Lolly froze, the chill of her paling cheeks the only sign she was still with them for several seconds.

"What do you mean, a role? I've already planned tonight's welcome party, what more can there be?"

"Ah, I thought she'd discussed it with you."

Lolly folded her arms across her chest. "Discussed what with me? What is she expecting me to do?"

Her mum grimaced and took a step back. Lolly recognised the tell-tale signs of someone about to flee, not only because it was something she did herself on regular occasions. She was considering doing it right now, except Petra's arm was already hovering behind her back ready to stop her.

"She might have told everyone that you're the one hosting the joint revel in her stead," her mum explained. "This gathering of the Court of Revels, the upcoming celebration of Fae visiting from around Faerie, the open day, all of it."

Lolly wanted to sit down. No, she wanted to run screaming. Throw a tantrum. Hide.

That's why mother has been on at me about napkins and who sits where lately. She never bothered me too much about it before.

"I can't!" she squeaked. "I'm not ready for people. Plants yes, animals, fine. But not people. It's my worst nightmare!"

Petra patted her shoulder, although given the firm clamp of the fingers straight after, she was preparing for the inevitable 'run away into the woods' scenario. Lolly had several camps set out around the court boundaries, some so well hidden that nobody would ever find her. She knew how to mask her scent from most and how to deal with a lot of animals, which to hide from, which she could tame.

Her mum seemed to be in full retreat as she issued her warning shot.

"It's alright, darling. That nice young man you came out of the woods with has been tasked with assisting you. I'm sure you're great friends already."

She was already through the door to the conservatory when the vivid image of Tyren's unimpressed face finally registered in Lolly's mind.

Lolly feinted at top speed, dodging left then right on pure instinct. Petra's hand slithered from her shoulder and she thought in that moment she would be able to make it.

The unerring weight of Petra's arm anchored around her middle and pulled her off her feet. They fell to the ground, Lolly landing with a startled 'oof'. As she blinked away the jarring sensation in her head, she looked up to find an unimpressed face staring down at her.

Arms folded, hip tilted off centre and shoulders tense with irritation, Tyren Berell didn't look like he was any more pleased about the situation than she was.

CHAPTER TWO
TYREN

They wanted him to babysit and placate a spoilt brat.

Tyren followed the ladies of the Flora Court into their home at his lord's hissed insistence. Normally his father would take over such a task, or coordinate the process at least, but he'd been sent on some kind of random assignment in the far-flung reaches of the Revel Court's realm, a task that apparently only he was capable of undertaking.

Tyren hadn't expected much when the Lord of Revels nominated him to be their court's eyes and ears instead. His task was clear and simple: chaperone and monitor the young lady who would one day take over the Flora Court. But after finding her dishevelled and pouty in the woods, then following them inside to see her having a tantrum about being made to host her guests, his expectations for a simple few days of dealing in empty charm had dribbled away to nothing.

Now he stood over her with the firm knowledge he should be fawning over himself to help her to her feet, but he had the absolute reluctance to do it.

She was pretty of course in a wide-eyed, wild-haired way. No doubt foolish men vying for her favour would be writing sonnets about hair the colour of burnished apples and eyes as bright as jewels of the sea or some nonsense. She looked healthy too, strong amid a surprising amount of soft curves for someone who no doubt worked outside given the dirt under her nails and the scuffs on her knuckles.

And she's going to think I'm ogling her because I'm standing here doing nothing.

He reached out to help as she elbowed her friend away and leapt to her feet. She gave his outstretched hand a dirty look of disbelief and folded her arms across her chest.

"I've been told you're supposed to assist me, so you'd best not get in the way," she said.

Charming.

He straightened up, relieved that while she was fairly tall, he was taller and wider. Being considered large and somewhat clunky by Fae standards, especially in a court like Revels which was more suited to acrobats and dilettante rogues with all the cultured charm, he often felt out of place.

No chance of that at the Flora Court though; weight and solid foundation had been built into every aspect of the place, from the sturdy pale stone pillars to the rigid iron of the mid-castle conservatory and the greenhouses outside. But the one-day-to-be-Lady of the Flora Court was still giving him a disgusted look, and he wasn't going to be taking that from someone who'd just thrown a tantrum on the floor.

"I have no intention of getting in the way," he said. "The Flora Court is hosting but the Revel Court is providing the entertainment. We will need to know where we are to perform, what space we have to work with, and any areas we aren't allowed to use or alter-"

"Alter?! What could you possibly need to alter?"

And she interrupts. Perfect.

He took a deep breath. It wouldn't calm him any, but at least it gave him a second to shake off the jangling echo of her voice in his ears.

"We may need to pin banners. If you'd rather us use ribbons instead of pins then we need to know that."

She glowered at him and he expected some kind of flippant comeback. Which would have been better somehow than her turning her back on him without a word.

"Can't I ask you to handle this?" she asked the other woman, who shook her head.

"Nope. Lady's orders at the queen's command. You're to host and to play nice. Do you need a bribe?"

Tyren snorted loudly before he could check himself. So used to the constant din of the Revel Court, where there was always music and social chatter and clamouring to fill the air, he winced as the noise bounced around the otherwise quiet stone courtyard.

Lady Leilania stiffened but didn't deign to turn and face him.

She's a lady still so I need to mind my manners. Things probably aren't as relaxed here as they are at home.

"I don't need you to bribe me to know my place, Petra," she snapped. "I have so many things that need doing, important things. I can't let the entire court slide simply for the whims of..."

Petra grinned. "...For the whims of the court? Look, nobody's going to expect you to devote your entire life to planning a party. You've already done most of the planning already as it is for tonight at least. Plus, you know I'm good with plants. You tell me what needs doing and I'll pitch in while you're hosting, deal?"

Tyren watched the back of the lady's auburn head as she contemplated her answer. She might even dismiss him from her service, which he was technically now in until they went home, and that would look bad to anyone he sought service for in the future. Being aide to a lord or lady wasn't his idea of a fulfilled life, but it was the one his father wanted for him and the one he'd been trained for.

One I'm failing at considering I've all but insulted her, even if she is a total spoilt pain in the behind.

"Fine," she snapped. "The seedlings in the far greenhouse need measuring when they're leaning to the red-spot, and the *agalea* is sick, so that's six drops of *oia* berry juice daily, in the morning preferably. I've got the handlers up to speed on most of the daily chores but there's a huge patch of the far scrubland which we've been clearing. I'm convinced there'll be bulbs if we can clear enough in time, but we don't have as much help this year as we did last."

Tyren listened to her spouting random plant information with growing surprise. She sounded as though she knew exactly what she was talking about, and on top of that it seemed like she was in charge too.

"I will handle all of that," Petra insisted. "If you promise me not to run, and not to smack anyone when I'm not there to stop you, I'll do it all."

Lady Leilania turned her head just enough for Tyren to see the side of her face, her lips lifting in devilish amusement. She didn't look at him but he got the distinct feeling that the next words out of her mouth were a warning just for him.

"I make no promises, but I will host to the best of my ability. I'll even try to be polite and smile prettily and all the boring things when I have to. Dance on the right toes, that sort of thing."

Petra rolled her eyes. "Fine, that'll have to do. Now I'm sure you're dying to show the place off. You could do a quick tour."

Lady Leilania's expression descended back into the

resolute scowl Tyren now recognised her for. She flicked a look at him and nodded back the way they'd come.

"My mother will be showing your lord around if you'd like to join them."

Tyren fought with his urge to snap back. He couldn't fathom why because usually he could handle any kind of hoity-toity court Fae with dogged diplomacy. There wasn't anyone he couldn't quietly out-argue, or any debate he couldn't calm one way or another. Dredging up a placid look, not quite able to smile because he guessed she wouldn't believe it anyway if he did, he pushed himself to wangle a private audience with her. That was what his father and the Lord of Revels wanted of him, so that was what he would do, snotty lady or not.

"I believe your mother will insist on the proper tour," he said. "Is there a way to see what it's really like here without all the ceremony and fanfare?"

Her eyes narrowed. He held his body steady, relaxed limbs, weight centred, eyes soft and fixed on her face.

Is she arguing with herself over whether she wants to avoid the main tour more or avoid being alone with me more?

He couldn't help wondering.

"What do you know of our court then?" she asked, suspicion in every word.

Relieved to have found an opening so quickly, Tyren relaxed for real this time.

"I know you provide the bulk of all natural produce that Faerie trades with, give or take some specialities local to other realms. I know the people of the Flora Court tend to be peaceful and level-headed." He resisted the urge to say anything contradictory in light of meeting her. "Rumour has it you've also managed to catalogue a lot of the plant-life into an index, which considering the variation of what comes out of here is seriously impressive."

The aide to the Holly Queen had passed on that one bit of information to him in passing: when in doubt, mention of the fabled index. Milo had clearly had interactions with the Flora Court's peculiarities before, as Lady Leilania's face settled from suspicion to natural disgruntlement the moment the word 'index' leapt from his lips.

"I'm almost at the end actually," she admitted.

Tyren's brain hitched. He frowned at her for a moment while the words settled, then surprise tumbled out of his mouth on instinct.

"You're indexing it yourself? As in, you rather than the court in general?"

Back to that withering look of sheer irritation at his mere existence, but she dropped her hands to her sides.

"Of course. My mother runs the court, deals with the people, the boring stuff. My mum runs the trades and the business side of things. I look after the plants themselves and our land. Come on then, I'll show you what it's really like here. My mother insisted on having a *cart* ride with fanfares instead of walking everyone around properly, can you believe it?"

Sadly, he could believe a charmingly decorated cart ride with minstrels playing gaily on the back was exactly the thing to keep his own court lord in good spirits. That and a bountiful vat of wine imported from the Illusion Court.

"My lord will appreciate it," he admitted. "Which is most likely why your mother has insisted on it."

Lady Leilania snorted in a very unladylike way.

"A diplomatic answer, how unrefreshing. Okay. So you've seen our front hall, walked through the conservatory and seen our central courtyard."

She stormed at an astonishing pace through a doorway and Tyren realised her friend had vanished already. Apparently not so worried about the lady doing a runner, but then he realised that was because guardianship of her had now passed to him. If she ran, it would look bad on him. If she refused to play nice, they'd wonder what he'd done to upset her. That left him the unfortunate option of hurrying after her.

"This is our secondary courtyard," she said. "Much the same as the first. If you don't understand plants, you won't need more than a quick glance."

He didn't understand much about plants, but the second courtyard was slightly smaller and somehow chillier than the first, perhaps because of the higher level of the building in that part.

"It's colder here so I imagine it's for plants that prefer more inclement weather," he guessed.

It sounded fancy when he said it but the glance she threw his way could have meant any number of things, probably all equally negative.

"Right, well, through here is the communal area." She opened a door and stepped back so he could peer inside. "We use it as a dining hall for the court and you can see the kitchens at the back."

He frowned. "There are trees growing through the walls."

"So? The kitchens like to have their 'little herb gardens' close by for produce picking. This way."

She whirled around in a flutter of torn skirts and stalked toward a door that led outside. Tyren hurried after her because like it or not, the future he didn't really want was hanging in her hands.

"Lady Leilania-"

"Lolly." She stopped dead and turned to face him. "Everyone calls me Lolly, or Miss Lolly if you're working here, but even then that's only when my mother is lurking around. If you call me Lady, or Leilania, I probably won't answer you."

"Because you don't like me."

She scrunched her face up into a disagreeable expression, a habit with her it seemed.

"I don't know you. But I'm only a lady by birth and nobody calls me Leilania unless I'm in trouble. And *you* aren't likely to cause me any trouble, whether you intend to or not."

Orbs alive, I'm going to end up throttling her.

He tried to keep his expression even, unruffled. She was simply yet another reason he wanted to find a way out of the Revel Court and into some kind of trade or service where he could make his own mark instead of following his father. Away from courts and high Fae and all the requirements that dealing with nobility brought. But for that he needed something to trade on and without any money to his name or a fancy title, he had to make do with either trades, friendships or his reputation.

"All the same, you're a lady and I am not," he insisted. "Calling you by a nickname would be improper."

Calling her a brat to her face probably wouldn't go down well either, even though it was the name that kept coming up in his head.

When her lips twitched, he realised what he'd said.

"You're not a lady? I couldn't tell." Her grin widened. "Fine, call me by title and see how far that gets you."

He didn't want to concede. Technically, by rule of propriety he shouldn't either. But he also didn't want to because that meant she would win. Even though it wasn't a game between them, not on his side anyway.

"Well, if I call you by title you'll refuse to speak to me. If I call you by your nickname, I'm overstepping the boundaries of rank. You win either way."

She shrugged, although he saw the tiniest hint of a smirk lift the corner of her mouth.

"I wouldn't consider being able to choose what people call me a game to be won, but whatever weird stuff you're into, leave me out of it."

Before he could find a suitable retort, she was charging through the door and striding across the grass toward a cluster of greenhouses that dominated the surrounding land. He shouldered through the door and powered after her.

The slight increase in breathing he needed to keep up with her surprising burst of determined speed wafted wonderful scents up his nose. Floral and tangy, fresh and earthy, the air was a cornucopia of beautiful smells. He squinted against the sunshine drenching the court grounds, glinting off droplets of dew on the grass that could only be for effect so late in the morning.

And in the midst of so much astounding beauty was Lady Leilania in a torn dress and wild hair, stomping along like she was going to battle.

"Are all these greenhouses monitored?" he asked.

She slowed enough that he could catch up, a disapproving frown crossing her face.

"We don't have enough people that want to work here at the moment," she admitted. "We're a small realm compared to others, and not a lot of people want to live in a court these days when wider cities are growing with opportunities for independence."

A-ha, the real her. He hesitated, judging what best to

say next to keep the conversation going. *Or the whole thing is the real her and that's what put me off, because she's not got any sense of pretence about her for me to play on.*

That he could work with, although it was a rare thing in Faerie, or at least in the Revel Court where almost everyone was a performer of some kind or out to make a sale in the grand market.

"And you do a lot of it yourself, picking up the gaps," he guessed.

When she glanced at him with uncertainty ruffling her brow, he nodded to her hands.

"The scraped skin, the ragged nails, the massive clod of mud on your cheek. The way you're stomping around on the hem of your dress which suggests you don't wear one often, or only when forced to."

She snorted. "And suddenly he thinks he knows everything about me."

He shook his head as they skirted the edge of the greenhouses back toward the castle. He had no idea why she'd bothered to go outside when she was on her way indoors straight away after, but he didn't know the layout of the place, something he'd need to rectify.

But at least I managed to unseat her confidence a bit.

He followed her through a wide archway and along a stone-floored corridor open to the elements on both sides. The unexpected desire to tease some kind of reaction out of her rippled through him.

"I know nothing about you and it'll stay that way," he said. "I'm here on behalf of the Revel Court to help you host and to make sure we don't accidentally tear down the wrong wall."

She stopped in a doorway with a set of winding stone steps on the other side, her deep blue eyes flashing.

"Tear down one of my walls and I'll tear down your entire court."

"That would be a rather dramatic reaction."

She shrugged, continuing on through the doorway and up the stairs, her fingers clutching at the skirts even as she stepped on them. He made sure to keep a respectful distance on the way up, staying a whole turn of the circular staircase behind her.

"Where exactly are we?" he asked.

"The back of the castle. This staircase leads up to the guest quarters. I've shown you the central parts of the castle, the conservatories, the dining hall and the greenhouses. You've seen the front entrance."

The staircase opened onto a long hallway of pale stone, grey except for the forest green runner trimmed with pale pink. Wide windows let in soft light but it was the unending reel of blessed silence that caught his attention most.

He stood at the top of the stairs to revel in the unexpected peace, until Lady Leilania stopped outside a door nearby and smacked her hand smartly against the wood. She threw the door open and pointed inside.

"Your room. You'll hear a gong for dinner. I have things to do."

He stood between her and the staircase, refusing to step aside.

"Hosting things? I've been tasked with helping you, so I should be allowed to do that."

He was supposed to assist her, and by 'assist' the Lord of Revels meant 'steer'. The two courts were both acting on the word of the young queen, but the lord had his own agendas to fulfil in addition to obeying their regent. And while the lord was the player, Tyren was the pawn being sent onto the board for battle.

"That's really none of your business," she snapped back, lifting her nose in the air.

"It is if it's to do with the upcoming revel. Our courts are supposed to be working together, and you and I in collaboration to host on behalf of our lords and ladies."

Lolly glanced down the hallway, taking her time before stepping around him with what had to be a speed skill, her retort ringing in the empty air as she vanished.

"Good luck with that then."

Tyren eyed the top of the staircase. He could go after her. He could go and tattle to his lord or to the ladies of the Flora Court. He could orb and ask his father for advice. But instead of choosing any of those options, he walked into the bedroom and shut the door behind him.

The same pale stone walls and floor surrounded him but rather than feeling hemmed in, he felt cocooned in the quietness of it, the large windows overlooking the vast swathes of forest and glimmering silver jewels of water that surrounded the Flora Court.

The dark wooden furnishings were all covered with some form of the Flora Court's forest green and pale pink colours, but he could easily imagine making his own room similar when he finally found somewhere he wanted to settle for good.

His hefty travel bag was already waiting on the neatly pulled bedspread, no doubt sent up on arrival by the court's staff.

If I'm going to somehow pull this off, I need to find some common ground between us.

He sank onto the bed with a groan and pulled out an old book with a tattered cover.

"You'd better come up with something I can impress

her with, or this will all be for nothing," he muttered.

The copy of *Faraway Plants of Faerie for Remedies and Ruin* he'd 'liberated' from a pile of dusty relics in the Court of Revels didn't answer.

CHAPTER THREE
REYAN

Three weeks had passed since Reyan's last training session with Kainen. It had been five weeks in total since the insurrection at the Nether Court. Reyan hadn't been back there since, but Demi hadn't exactly given her a chance to spend much time at home either. Three weeks in the grand market of the Revel Court pouring through ancient books had passed excruciatingly slowly, and Kainen's orb messages had been minimal.

She'd been getting restless and irritable up until a few minutes earlier, when Milo, aide to Queen Demerara, had arrived unexpectedly. He insisted he was to take Reyan home to be fitted for a dress ahead of the revel at the Flora Court, and that was apparently her time at the market done.

Reyan wiped a hand over her hair and tucked a few errant golden strands behind her ear as she landed in the main hall at the Court of Illusions.

A flush of happiness rushed through her at the familiar sight. The crowd of the court were creating their usual rumble, a jubilant noise that bounced off the rocky walls. The inner-mountain caverns that housed the court had undergone transformations since Kainen had ruled as Lord of Illusions, with light from outside drifting in through holes in the rock and a vein of lilac now weaving through the charcoal and silver court colours that hung all around the main hall. Even the water pool in the middle rippled with a soft glow of lilac from the surrounding firelit lanterns adorning the walls.

She tensed as heads turned and the courtiers watched her walk among them, but she held her head high and let the relief brush over their scrutiny. Even though most of the members of the court and the staff still treated her with distanced suspicion as their supposed court lady, it was home.

Unable to see Kainen in the crowd, she slowed her pace.

Perhaps I should have skipped into his room, or even his study instead. He won't be expecting me though.

In the last three weeks, tucked away among the alleyways of the enormous market, she'd missed the Illusion Court more and more.

She didn't want to admit it to herself either, but she'd missed Kainen the most. Going from routine check-ins and orb calls then two weeks of training every day to nothing much for three whole weeks hurt.

But she couldn't admit that. The longer she'd had to stay away, the more she began to doubt. He was an actual court lord, not a pretend lady like her. Although the whole of Faerie saw her as Kainen's choice, both she and he knew their engagement was a fake. He wanted to avoid being coerced into a 'convenient' betrothal for the sake of Faerie politics and she'd earned her freedom from servitude and more from the exchange.

A cluster of maids she used to work and serve alongside bowed their heads as she passed, which still unnerved her. She forced a smile and turned her gaze to a less welcoming group of courtiers looking down their noses at her.

A flash of brown amid grey and black drew her attention away from them and her nerves took flight. Reminding herself to at least pretend to be calm, she walked toward the familiar back, broad shoulders and artfully rumpled brown-haired head.

Whoever Kainen was talking to fell silent and he turned. His eyes widened with surprise, something that a court lord who dealt in secrets and trickery shouldn't have shown to the courtiers around him. She wondered if there was even a tinge of delight on his face too, and her heart began to pound as his smile widened. Then he caught himself, the smile turning wicked and his cocky court mask falling into place.

"She returns," he teased. "After all this time. I was about to send out a search party."

She grinned back. "You knew exactly where I was. You could have checked in at any point."

He appeared right in front of her, notching up the nerves fluttering inside her chest.

"So could you."

"Ladies don't chase lords."

She froze as he leaned forward, his lips beside her ear.

"The respectable ones do."

He kissed her cheek, just a gentle brush of lips against skin, and she couldn't help wondering if perhaps that one was for them rather than for show.

"I'm only here to change," she explained. "Milo insisted that I make an appearance at the Flora Court revel, and that he's already spoken to Meri on my behalf. Apparently, she then insisted on me coming here for my dress rather than sending it over to me. Perhaps she's worried it won't fit."

She forced her lips closed over the babbling words, her cheeks burning as Kainen slid his arm around her shoulders.

His gaze flickered across the room and gawkers quickly went back to their business. She sank into the familiar touch of him, taking what little she could without making it too obvious as he guided her past the enormous pool and toward the wide stone staircase that led up to their rooms.

"Milo let me know he was going to see you," he said. "So I told him to bring you home to change."

Her heart began to thud with a scary jolt of hope, but she didn't want to let him see how gleeful his calling her home made her, not when she had no idea yet why he wanted to see her.

"Why? Straight to the Flora Court would have been easier as we're all going to be there anyway for the revel."

Reyan frowned as he swept her up the steps and into the shadowy hallway. His room was the first door on the left and her room was only accessible through his to hide their pretence, but he didn't open his door when they stopped outside it.

"Because I wanted the chance to see you before we go back into the mayhem."

He looked surprisingly serious for the lord of a court known for mischief and trickery.

He's going to tell me he wants to cancel the fake engagement.

Anxiety clawed up her throat. She knew it had to happen someday, but for some reason she hadn't been expecting it so soon.

Was he happy to see me because now he can finally drop me aside? Is there someone else?

She remembered too late that they shared the ability to communicate telepathically with each other, and on odd occasions when she was stressed, he ended up getting a full blast of whatever she was thinking. He started smiling.

Is he smiling like that because he can hear... stop thinking!

She took a deep breath and readied herself for the

dismissal. Even facing the thought of it reinforced the recent realisation; she had feelings for him. Not affection or gratitude, but full-blown 'wonder what he's doing and dream about him most nights before going to sleep' feelings.

"We don't know what will happen when we get to the Flora Court," he said. "Demi's asked me to enquire in a few choice ears I used to know, but I take it she hasn't given you any further instructions?"

Reyan shook her head, her nerves chomping tension through her muscles. Kainen opened the bedroom door then which prolonged the agony. She walked in, soaking up the sight of it.

Firelight flickered against the dark stone walls and she soaked up the delight of the shadows lurking all around the room. In the opposite wall was the multi-way door that would lead to Kainen's bathroom, his study or her bedroom, or anywhere else in the court he chose to open it to. From the enormous four-poster bed to the plush dark green sofa and armchair near the balcony overlooking the main hall, she couldn't shake the panic that this was her home now.

She had no idea if he'd even let her keep her separate bedroom when she wasn't a lady anymore, or if she'd be expected to return to the dorms and service if she wanted to stay. She rotated to face him and he stared back, his eyes widening in alarm.

"What's up with you?" he asked. "You look like you're about to cry."

Stupid face always showing everything.

"What about your face? Reyan?" His eyes narrowed. "Has someone done something I need to know about?"

At least he sounded concerned about her, but she didn't

dare go on a rant about her stupid inability to think when he was around without hearing it.

"I'm fine." She inhaled sharply, pushing down the ache clawing up her throat. "Go on. You were saying Demi asked you to speak to people, and then you're going to say we're dissolving our fake engagement, so I'm guessing-"

"Whoa whoa whoa, what?"

She risked a look and found the most confused man she'd ever seen, his face all crunched and his body tensed in some kind of weird backwards lean. She hesitated and he filled the silence before she could.

"Who told you I was dissolving anything?"

She shrugged. "Nobody, but you say you want to talk to me looking all serious, and Demi wants you to speak to people, which in Fae circles basically means seducing them."

"How are those two in any way connected?" He gawked at her. "Actually, never mind that. I wasn't planning on ending anything, unless you want me to?"

She opened her mouth and froze. She couldn't say no, because that might give her actual feelings away, and she couldn't exactly lie and say it was for any other reason, because it wasn't, not anymore.

"I think we need to start again," he said, amusement filling his face while hers burned with embarrassment. "Welcome home, sweetheart. Meri has a dress ready for you then we'll be skipping straight to the Flora Court to show a united front. How was your time at the Court of Revels?"

Reyan folded her arms and clutched at her elbows.
"Fine."

He chuckled and closed the distance between them.

"Come on, surely you can tell me more than that. Did

you meet anyone I have to fight for your honour?"

"I can fight for my own honour thanks," she muttered. "But no, no need for fighting. It was useful though. Arlen who I was staying with refused to let me read any of the books unless I bought them first, so I had to keep going back and forth with Milo to discuss buying them, then read through them, then pile them up for someone to come from Arcanium and get them. It would have attracted too much attention if Milo turned up and he's really busy. But I was glamoured for most of it anyway."

"And who is Arlen? I don't recognise the name?"

His tone turned silky, edged with something she was sure couldn't be jealousy.

Could it? She hid her sudden delighted smirking beneath an airy tone.

"I'm not sure, but he's trusted by the queen's court I think. He was really kind to me, always bringing me books so I didn't have to go hunting myself, even asked me out for a drink one evening. Is someone who's twenty-one too old for me do you think?"

She knew it was cruel but with the residual panic still kicking through her insides, she couldn't help word-tangling the situation to her benefit. She had no idea if Kainen had actual feelings for her, not like she'd developed for him, and she wasn't risking it until she could be sure. But she'd missed taunting him and flirting with him and now she went for it with carefree abandon.

"Not if he's good enough for you," he said. "Did you go? For the drink?"

She hesitated, drawing out the agony. Assuming there was any agony. He might not care in the slightest. Thoughts of the many women at their court eying him up like a prime cow ready to provide all the goods curdled in her stomach.

"No. He wasn't my type and I very much doubt I'm his."

Kainen frowned. "Why not? Anyone would be mad to say no to you."

He was ignoring the fact she had very little prestige or Fae family lineage to trade on, and even less money or assets, but it gave her ego a good brushing all the same.

"Well, he's gay for a start. Think he had a bit of a thing for Milo actually, but he and Ace are a surer bet than a baby challenging the queen."

She turned away to hide her smile, but Kainen's hand wrapped around her fingers and she squeaked as he pulled her back around.

"That trick was cruel and uncalled for," he said, his grin sparkling with devilishness. "But Meri will be waiting. She let me help design your dress for tonight."

"I… what?"

"Yep."

He dropped her hand and started toward the multi-way door. She stared after him before realising she should be following him.

"Wait, do you know anything about women's clothing? Or revel outfits?"

She hurried after him, slamming a hand on the door handle before he could open it, forcing him to answer her.

"Nope. Not a clue. Not while they're on anyw- *oww!*"

He winced as she swung the door open and conveniently elbowed him in the ribs at the same time. She huffed to see the bathroom on the other side, but she'd forgotten to tell the court which room she wanted.

Kainen's grin threatened to carve his face in two as he slid his hand over hers on the handle, pushed the door shut and reopened it to reveal Meri's study.

"Ah, there you are." Meri rose from her chair. "Welcome home, Lady. I hope your travels were fruitful, but no time for that now. Usual rules apply. Lady, change behind the screen please. You, change here."

Kainen huffed loudly. "Why does she get 'oh, over there please, Lady' and I get 'you, change here'?"

Reyan hurried to the screen and hid behind it.

"Because she has earned some semblance of manners and you haven't. Now change."

Kainen's grumbling filled the room but Reyan was too busy assessing the dress hanging in front of her. In true noble style the Illusion Court colours of charcoal grey and silver had been stuck to, but tiny swathes of lilac were now dancing through the fabric, shimmering over the full-length skirt that flared out with a small slit up one side, and the strapless satin body sprinkled with silver stars.

She de-clothed and slid into the dress, aware they were likely pressed for time. Each court and realm kept different time to the others, but given the sharp directive in Meri's tone, she shouldn't be standing around mooning over her clothes.

Which bit did you design then? she asked Kainen through mind-speak.

His chuckle sounded in her head a moment later. *Come out and I'll point.*

She stepped into the waiting slipper-style shoes and emerged, the slight train on the dress causing the slit to widen to low-thigh and the fabric to trail gently behind her.

Wow. He cleared his throat. "Wow."

She snickered at the sheer wide-eyed amazement on his face. Meri eyed her up and down before giving her a satisfied nod and moving across to check the state of her hair. Given that Kainen didn't seem to need any fussing over at all with his dark grey jacket and trousers cloaking him like sinful magic, he stood staring instead.

"So?" she asked again. "Which bit was your handiwork?"

Kainen shrugged, his gaze still fixed on the dress, or certain more revealing parts of it anyway.

"Oh, he did the whole thing," Meri said, oblivious to the irritated look he then threw at the back of her head. "Barely gave me a chance to suggest anything. There you go. Best keep yourself as natural as possible while you still have the skin for it."

Reyan had forced Milo to give her a scant few minutes in the bathroom at Arlen's book emporium market before he skipped her home, time which she spent silently bemoaning the state of her appearance and doing her best to touch it up with make-up. While a lot of Fae tended to exhaust themselves glamouring appearances, she preferred the hand-drawn route because at least she only had to check it hadn't smudged rather than keep one part of her mind fixed on maintaining the magic.

"Right, off you go both of you." Meri dismissed them from her study like errant children.

Reyan smiled. "Thank you, the dress is beautiful."

Kainen rolled his eyes and moved to take her hands in his, his gaze now settled on her face.

"Anything I need to know before we go?" he asked.

Reyan glanced around to find that Meri had vanished already to another part of the court. Her fingers were tingling from Kainen's touch but she tried to keep her mind on the wider issues and not on the confusing state of her 'possibly-not-actually-love' life.

"I can't remember which bits you know now," she

admitted. "There's been a lot of veiled information flying back and forth."

He nodded. "And things you can't tell me, I'll bet."

He didn't sound even the slightest bit down about that but Reyan wanted to tell him everything, even if just for the excuse to keep on talking to him. The moment they reached the Flora Court he'd no doubt be swept away by a gaggle of Fae wanting to talk and dance and flirt with him, and she wanted to keep him to herself that little bit longer.

She risked a wicked smile, lowering her lashes as she looked up at him.

"Are you saying I shouldn't trust you with our royalty's secrets?" she teased.

His eyes sparkled, a hint of his gift leaping forth and swirling darkness through the brown depths.

"You shouldn't trust me with you in that dress maybe, but I have no intention of betraying our dear queen, or having any intention of re-joining the Forgotten."

She almost shivered at the suggestiveness in his low tone, almost. But she held herself still, keeping her gaze fixed on him, pretending that he didn't affect her anywhere near as much as he did.

"I trust you," she said. "But even if I couldn't, I could probably hold my own in a fight now. I've been training while I've been away."

He raised one eyebrow, the rest of his face entirely still.

"What, with Barden?"

She fought a smile. "Arlen, and yes. Amid many a boring hour trawling through old books about the Prime Realm. There were a few mentions of keys, but nothing to suggest what they might be or where to find them."

Kainen placed one of her hands against his chest and slid his arm around her waist as though they were about to dance.

He has to hear my heart tumbling like a landslide.

"Keys, which I guess I'm supposed to ask about without actually asking."

She nodded. "All the mentions of keys kept referencing natural things and 'pathways', so whether we're looking for a tunnel or perhaps a map, I can't tell yet. But I've reported everything already. I suppose your job tonight is to do what you do best."

"And what is that?"

She sighed. "Flirt shamelessly with half of Faerie in the hopes they'll drop information of course."

He gasped, his eyes dancing with amusement as she realised the bitterness had slipped out in her tone and she'd walked right into an opportunity for him to tease her ragged.

"Jealous, sweetheart? As long as it's only information they're dropping, I'll enquire flirtatiously with the relevant people. Oh, one more thing before we go."

"What?"

He lifted her hand to his lips, his gaze holding her captive.

"Can I have your first dance?"

CHAPTER FOUR
LOLLY

"How could you?!"

Lolly fought to keep her voice down, but somehow hissing her irritation didn't have the same effect as full volume screaming. She glowered at her mother, who gave her a weary look and sank into the comfortable green armchair behind the desk.

Her mother's office looked nothing like the main command centre for a lady of a court that revolved around natural elements. It was full of pictures of family, some painted and others candid, piles of papers and several random objects that had been gathered over the many years. But not a single plant or bloom.

"Lolly, try to be understanding. You hosting sends a clear signal to the rest of Faerie that fresh blood is rising through the ranks. This is your mantle to take up, you know that. We're simply reminding Faerie of the fact. Showing hope in you is also a subtle alignment with the new queen, young as she is."

Lolly bit her lip. She knew several people who didn't want to inherit from their parents. Financially yes, in terms of title and property of course, but not an entire court and the responsibilities that came with it. A lot of the people who frequented many of the courts and higher social haunts in Faerie wanted a life of excess. But Lolly preferred the greenhouses and woods to balls and club houses. Or at least, she used to like balls and club houses in moderation until her mother decided she would be retiring, something previously unheard of in Faerie nobility circles.

"Fresh meat more like," she muttered. "I know I have to start sitting pretty and all of that, at least until I can become lady and make my own rules, but *why him*?"

Her mother laughed. "What's wrong with Tyren? By all accounts he's growing into a fine young man. Attentive and calm, poised and proper."

Lolly would have snarked back but the withering 'unlike you' was already oozing in her mother's tone. She folded her arms instead with the most irritable glare she could muster up.

"It's not like I'm asking you to date him." Her mother sighed. "Or even pay him much attention. Simply work on the revel with him, show him where things should be and leave him to his planning. You might even find him rather charming."

Lolly pulled a face. "Eww. The revel is tomorrow, so how much planning can I actually do with him anyway?"

Her mother smoothed down a wrinkle in her black linen trousers and sat up with determination.

"Enough to get us by without the court looking unprepared. It's an opportunity for Tyren to prove himself too by all accounts, so you should take a few tips from his example. Now, the dinner dance is in an hour and you should be getting ready."

Lolly recognised the dismissal but she was adamant she would have the last word. She might not be able to get rid of hoity-toity Tyren or his court for a couple of days, but if her mother wanted her to start running things, she could start to practice backing down.

"Are we still going with the indoor plan?" she asked.

Her mother rose to her feet and waved a hand down

from her face to her middle, the air around her shivering for a moment until her trousers and blouse were replaced by a fitted floor-length gown woven entirely from leaves. A bright pink bloom curled around her upper arm, and her face had been sprinkled as if with starlight, her blonde hair neatly pinned back.

"Of course. Indoors and relaxed," she said. "A band will be playing the entire time, space for dancing and the usual habit of main meal placed and the starter and dessert as buffet-served-tableside style. Exactly as you requested, right down to the jokes on the place-cards."

The wrinkle on her mother's nose said exactly what she thought about jokes on place-cards, but Lolly had been told to plan the dinner originally and plan it she had.

Now I need to oversee Tyren and tomorrow's revel too.

She didn't want to concede and ask Tyren for assistance, but she didn't know anyone else in the Revel Court who might take his place. Before she could figure out a way to cajole her mother into at least letting her have Petra do most of the communication between courts, someone knocked on the office door.

Her mother cast a weary glance at her, the disapproval clear at the grubby hands, torn dress from the welcome effort earlier and her wild hair. She clicked her tongue and Lolly sagged, resigned. She had a dress hanging ready upstairs, but her mother as lady of the court had the ability to re-clothe her at will, and apparently now instead of a sleeved cocktail dress with glitter on it, she was wearing a dark green strapless one made from petals of velvet.

"Be a love and open that."

It wasn't a request, but where Lolly usually would have argued back, she was already quietly nervous about what to expect for the next two days and she didn't have the energy to argue with her mother anymore.

She threw open the door, confused in one moment to find her mum on the other side, then realising her mum must have knocked because of Tyren hanging about right behind her.

"Found this one wandering the greenhouses," her mum said with a grin. "Oh, you're both changed. I should probably go do that."

Lolly's mother nodded, her disapproval radiating out.

"Yes, you should. You have one hour- no, less than that now."

Lolly slouched past her mum, who gave her an affectionate nudge with her elbow and walked into the office, shutting the door and leaving Lolly stuck in the hall with Tyren.

"What were you doing around the greenhouses?" she asked warily.

Tyren blinked. He looked smart at least, a blood-red suit coat and matching trousers over a silver and black waistcoat, the Revel Court colours. His black hair was slicked back, a couple of strands falling forward around his temples, and in the firelit hallway his eyes looked almost black.

"Nobody told me there were off-limits places," he replied. "After you so charmingly ditched me, I fancied a walk."

She couldn't exactly disagree with him about the ditching, not without lying. But she'd be damned if she was going to tell him that.

"Most of the court will be off-limits for outsiders. There are poisons and carnivorous plants all over the place. One wrong step and you might get eaten. Although the one we have in the dining hall, Arthur, is old and friendly. If you feed her some fish, she might even swallow you and spit you out again. Great fun if you stack up a couple of squishy mats."

Tyren's face didn't even twitch at the mention of a carnivorous plant playing throw with people.

"You have a female plant called Arthur?" he asked. "Did you know in the human world that's a masculine name?"

"Names can't be ungendered now?"

She folded her arms, frowning up at him. All the unspent irritation from the short time with him earlier, and then storming around her chores until she could get into her mother's office, had left her crackling with energy.

She took a deep breath as her Fae connection sparked inside her fingertips, her nose beginning to chill with the tell-tale sign of her main gift erupting.

"Of course they can. I didn't mean any offense." His tone didn't change, indicating that he didn't care whether offense was taken in the end or not. "It was more a conversation starter."

"How's that working out for you?"

He raised one eyebrow, which was something. The complete stillness was beginning to drive her mad. It was like approaching the Arthurs that weren't old and friendly, and one wrong move would suddenly go from still to *SNAP* in the blink of an eye.

"Not great clearly," he said, his tone placid. "I thought it'd be worth getting the bulk of the planning done now though, and that way I'll be less of a drain on your oh-so-important time."

The not-so-veiled sarcasm pulled at her lips and she forced down the urge to smile. She'd gotten to him, which was a relief because she irritated most people on a daily basis and it was something of a worry when she found someone she didn't frustrate. But his plan made sense so she nodded reluctantly.

"I have some ideas. Follow me and keep up."

She set off along the corridor in the direction of the dining hall. The general intention was to stride along as she always did but her mother had put paid to that by binding her in the most ridiculously tight dress known to Faerie.

She managed a few seconds of frantic waddling before risking a look at him. His expression hadn't changed, but something about the spark in his dark eyes or the knitted press of his lips suggested he was laughing at her.

"This isn't going to work." She huffed. "Stay here."

She turned back the way they'd come. A few steps later, he appeared at her side.

"I told you to stay put."

He flicked a quick look in her direction before staring rigidly forward again.

"You might fall over," he suggested.

"I won't."

"You might though."

"I won't though."

While he seemed to be thinking his next response, she contemplated ripping the skirt of the dress entirely and speeding up to her room to change into another one.

"You might."

Insufferable. She scowled. *That's it, I'm going to let one of the plants eat him.*

Without a shred of doubt, she summoned her Fae connection into her fingertips. The chill tingled at the tip of her nose and she mentally redirected it down into her forefinger. Not many people outside of the court knew about her icicle gift, or that she could cast frost on anything she touched.

Her finger went rigid, the skin going pale and freezing over until a sharp point of translucent ice tipped her nail. She leaned down with a glare up at Tyren, daring him to say a single word when she wobbled, but he didn't. His gaze was stuck on her finger as she grabbed the hem of her dress and slit the seam up to mid-thigh.

"Don't get any grand ideas," she muttered. "This is purely for movement, nothing to do with you."

He was still staring at her finger with a frown as she pulled back her gift and the ice thawed from her skin, the chill retreating back inside her body and quelling itself.

Back upright, she tried a few steps. There was a potential hazard for the dress to continue unravelling until it was open right up to her armpit, but she could move at her normal speed now and that would do. Worst case she'd become the main attraction and it would be all her mother's fault.

"Come on then, *now* try to keep up."

She set off back toward the dining hall with renewed purpose. Her mother hadn't given her any shoes but several of the court who preferred to remain indoors often moved around barefoot. Those who ventured outside preferred good sturdy shoes that could survive dropped poison or snappy vines with barbs.

Tyren kept pace alongside her through the halls and across the main conservatory.

"It's calm here," he said eventually.

"Calm? You think so?"

He nodded. "In a lot of the rooms you can hear water rushing, but in others there's nothing at all. Maybe a bit of the wind but no loud parties, no shouting, no hooting or hollering or whooping. No crashing and banging. No…

other noises.”

Lolly's cheeks heated, guessing at what kind of noises might count as 'other' to someone from the Revel Court.

“I suppose to someone from your court it would be. We have our fair share of parties and celebrations though. We have things clashing and clanging. Often a lot of the animals who choose to live around the place will escape, or they come inside to steal fruit and the whole court has to chase them out again.”

“That sounds a lot more fun than the same routine of excess every night.”

Relieved deep down that they were at least able to hold a conversation without arguing for more than two seconds, Lolly smiled as she opened the door to the dining hall.

“We manage,” she said.

She waited for him to step ahead of her through the doorway, but he didn't move, his expression shadowing with awkwardness.

“Before we go inside, I need to give you this.”

He held out his hand, a small shiny object catching the firelight and glinting on his palm.

Lolly stared at it. “What is that?”

“A bracelet.”

Thank you, Lord of the Brains.

“I know what it is,” she snapped. “Why are you giving it to me?”

He grimaced. “Don't worry, I'm doing this very much against my will, and at the queen's command. Anyone wearing one of these bracelets will identify themselves to others who know about it. It's to avoid being fooled by glamours.”

Lolly hesitated. The bracelet was pretty in a sparkly rainbow sort of way, not exactly a weaving circlet of briars and buds like she would have chosen for herself, but it had its own sort of charm.

"It's honestly nothing to do with me," he insisted. "I'm just the delivery boy."

She quite liked the idea of that, much more than him giving her any kind of gift which meant she would owe him a gratitude for it.

"Fine."

She took the bracelet and slid it over her wrist, admiring the rainbow pattern of what looked like glass beads.

As she moved to step aside and let him go through the doorway first as a gracious host, he grabbed the door above her head and moved into the same space to make room for her. She almost crashed into his chest and stepped away in alarm, her back hitting the door.

There was a familiar scent about him but she couldn't place it. Dewberries maybe, or an infusion of *kimpta* leaves without the awfully stinky berries.

I think I'd have preferred him to smell of stinky berries.

"After you," she said, her throat dry.

"No, after you."

"Guests first."

He might have been frowning or smirking, she couldn't tell.

"Ladies first," he countered.

She frowned. "Me being a lady is more of a dummy title as I'm not in charge of the court yet, and I don't think anyone could accuse me of acting like one."

It was definitely a smile, his mouth developing a slight crooked uplift to one side. Unwilling to lose to anyone over anything ever, Lolly folded her arms and stared him out.

"How about you go first, and I won't get dismissed?" he tried.

She shook her head. "How about you go first, and I won't get told off about my manners by my mother."

"How about you go first, and I won't tell your mother. That way, you save your precious dignity and I save myself an actual job."

"Or we stand in this doorway forever. And people think all sorts of really awful things."

"Like what?"

Am I flirting with him? No, that's ridiculous. She pushed the thought aside.

"Like we're so annoyed with this whole thing that you're refusing to go first to be childish."

He pursed his lips as if considering that. All the while, she was aware of his arm stretching up over her head to hold the door open, his dark eyes fixed on hers.

"We are so annoyed with this," he reminded her. "And we are both refusing to go first, so by your reasoning that makes us both childish, *Lady*."

"Oh, how clever. You win, mission accomplished, you can all go home now."

He chuckled, the noise needling over her skin. He still thought he had the upper hand, that eventually she would cave. Or perhaps he thought she was the kind of Fae nobility who would flirt and banter and flatter to get her way.

She wasn't. She argued to win. She took no prisoners along the way either and Tyren Berell was no different.

Luckily for both of them, a loud, excitable noise drew their attention before he could retort.

Lolly turned in the doorway in time to see a multicoloured blur moving fast toward her, Petra hurrying along behind it with two young men at her side.

"There she is!"

"Do we have to curtsey yet?"

"Don't be dim."

The familiar voices surrounded her and she forgot about Tyren. She dashed through the doorway, sinking with a delighted yell into a scramble of flailing arms that surrounded her. She had no idea who exactly she was hugging but it didn't matter, because she hadn't seen her friends in over a year and now here they were.

"Why are you here?" she shrieked. "I mean, yay! But also why?"

She huffed in a strangled breath as the trio finally let her go and she was able to get a proper look at the Eastwick sisters. They looked no different at all after the couple of years they'd lived at Arcanium, the hub for Fairy Deity People who took on assignments for the good of Faerie. It was also now the location of the Holly Queen's court, but the sisters never had been good at any kind of propriety, which was another plus in the young queen's favour, at least in Lolly's eyes. Not so much her mother's.

"We're here on *official* business," Beryl muttered, smoothing down her purple hair.

Beside her, Cheryl had grown her messy green mop incredibly long, and Meryl's was a slightly more vivid shade of blue than Lolly remembered.

"As in, 'reason we're really all here' business?" Lolly asked.

Cheryl nodded. "We've been tasked with assisting the assistants to the assistants of the Revel Court while they assist you in prepping your event."

"When the, um, *powers that be* found out we were originally from the Flora Court's realm and knew you, we were the natural choice," Meryl added quietly.

Lolly grinned, then noticed Petra with the two identical

boys.

"You never said a word. Did you know?" she asked.

Petra nodded. "Figured it'd be more fun to surprise you. This is Hutch and Harvey Hutchinson, by the way."

Both boys stepped forward and dipped into low bows, until Beryl elbowed the nearest one in the ribs. Given his purple hair the exact colour of hers, Lolly realised that must be her boyfriend.

"She's not a proper lady yet, idiot, get up," she hissed.

He gave her a prim look. "But she's higher up in the nobility chain than any of us, and *you* said I should work on my manners more. So there."

"Harvey is Beryl's boyfriend," Petra clarified. "He insisted on accompanying her on her errand. Which then meant Hutch wouldn't let Cheryl go without him."

Lolly grinned.

And knowing Petra would be here already, Meryl insisted on coming along with her sisters too because they're a package deal.

"Well, I don't care why you're here," she said. "Tonight is going to be so much fun now!"

There wasn't a single sound behind her but she could almost hear Tyren clearing his throat in his mind. Manners warred with irritation at him, and at his very existence in her court. When she hesitated, everyone's eyes flicked to him. She turned and flinched to find him right behind her. With an irritated look his way, she waved a lazy hand at him.

"Tyren Berell of the Revel Court, meet Beryl, Cheryl and Meryl Eastwick, old friends of mine and my court. Also... I'm sorry, I'm so bad with names until I know people."

She grimaced in the direction of the two brothers as

Tyren stepped around her, his hand held out.

"Hutch and Harvey. We've met before, don't worry."

The twins shook hands with Tyren, a tinge of solemn respect passing across the group. Lolly wasn't sure if it was because of Tyren, if he had some kind of fearsome reputation she didn't know about, or if they simply didn't know each other well enough to be friendly. But Tyren wasn't her problem, not for more than a couple of days anyway, and she had her friends to help her now.

"Right, now you're here, you can help," she announced. "I'm sure the Revel Court have loads of tricks for creating a big, ostentatious show over the next couple of days, but tonight the Flora Court is in charge. I've planned and prepped everything, but-"

"Damage control, got it." Cheryl rubbed her hands together. "I'm glad to see old Arthur is still kicking."

Everyone turned to face the giant carnivorous plant in the far corner of the room, her enormous seed-like mossy brown pod hanging open and drooling sap onto the rug that kept her roots warm. The rug was stained and singed with holes from the venom she sometimes leaked by accident, but it was the flailing tentacle-like red vines with spikes sharper than knitting needles that needed to be watched out for because she did like tripping people up when she got bored.

"You don't want these five doing damage control," Petra said, her tone disbelieving.

Beryl sniffed. "And why not? We're excellent at damage."

"Causing it maybe."

"No fair! When have we ever caused damage?"

Lolly noticed a few guests hovering in the doorway, definitely guests because she didn't recognise them as members of the court and they were in the kind of draped and cushioned finery that didn't scream Revel Court either. The woman had so much fur cladding her body, including as part of her dress, and several ostentatious jewels at her throat and around her fingers. The man wore a large red hat with feathers but his cane had some kind of carved wooden spikes on it as though he enjoyed using it to put people in their place whenever they passed.

The last thing Lolly wanted to do was go and welcome them personally, but a quick glance around proved neither her mother nor her mum were anywhere to be seen.

She took a deep breath and left the group to continue bickering, although the sound of one of the brothers challenging Petra to a duel seemed like the kind of thing she'd need snacks for watching.

But duty always came first in a court. Sometimes she could convince herself that duty lay in the way she interpreted it and therefore she could interpret it to benefit her, but tonight as host she couldn't interpret any way to leave her guests standing there twisting about like husks on spiderwebs.

"Welcome!" She pinned on her best smile. "Please do come in and make yourself at hom- *comfortable*! We've done a place-setting, all part of the fun to find your places."

She made it up as she went along, babbling nonsense to hide the fact she had no idea who these people were. The man seemed reluctant to acknowledge her, a normal enough attitude in some Fae circles that prized hierarchy over all else. She was a lady in name only and barely considered a grown woman yet, so she was beneath his notice. The woman smiled slowly.

"Thank you for inviting us, *Lady*," she said. "I'm afraid we don't have our glasses though. If you'll show us to our seats, there's a dear."

Lolly caught the subtle gleam of satisfaction on the woman's face, the smugness barely hidden. They all knew Lolly didn't have a clue who they were, and the woman intended to punish her for it.

"Arch Marnin, Archess Marnin, I'm sure you'll agree it's an honour to see you again."

Lolly froze, her entire body rigid as Tyren appeared beside her. She noted his word-tangling, smoothly refusing to say it actually was an honour for him, because given his tone it definitely wasn't. That normally would have lifted him in her estimation but she reigned in the urge to kick him as his hand brushed over her back.

Does he think he's doing me a favour or something here? I could have figured something out.

Not something that wouldn't transfer her own indiscretion onto one of the servers or someone who would get treated way worse than she would by the Arch and Archess no doubt, but still.

"Berell. You really do get everywhere, don't you." Arch Marnin sniffed.

It wasn't a compliment but Tyren didn't waver for a second.

"I have my ways. Allow me to show you personally as I think Lady Leilania has more guests on the way in."

He swished off with the Arch and Archess in tow and it took Lolly all her strength to keep her posture upright.

I'll have to thank him now. Orbs alive, he's the most annoying clod of soil I've ever met.

In that moment, she wished she were human, able to lie without consequence. But lying never did anyone any good if the human-tales were to be believed, Fae or not.

Stuck in her irritable thoughts, she almost didn't notice

her mother and mum hurrying toward her.

"The Arch and Archess Marnin are here already?" Her mother's keen eyes noticed them immediately. "Trust them to arrive early. Any problems?"

Lolly shook her head. "No."

Not thanks to me, but they don't need to know that.

Her mother swept past and made a beeline for the couple still talking to Tyren, now seated with him looming over them.

"Save me a dance then, love," her mum said.

"Okay. I didn't know the Eastwicks were coming back."

"Ahh yeah." Her mum lowered her voice and leaned close. "I had a quick chat with the queen and asked if we could have some trusted sources supporting with the Revels. Trust can only go so far. She agreed which means we're the court in favour at the moment. But that's your mother's arena."

Lolly snorted. "Yeah, you just handle the business, right?"

"Of course. Not titled am I?"

"I wish I could take after you instead, do the business stuff and the Flora stuff and leave the court to someone else. People are such a pain."

Her mum patted her shoulder and cast a devious glance at the group now gathered around the Arch and Archess's table. Tyren was stepping back, giving Lady Flora a chance to talk without him listening in, but Lolly noticed it was him her mum was looking at, not her mother.

"Find yourself a nice partner then who enjoys that sort of thing, I would," her mum suggested. "Someone who can run interference and help you with the people side of things."

She was off across the dining hall before Lolly could do more than squawk in disgust. She wasn't even willing to consider a consort for the court yet, let alone consider taking on someone like Tyren who would be intent on annoying her for the rest of eternity.

She was still muttering under her breath when Beryl appeared beside her.

"We, uh, have a little problem," she muttered.

Lolly groaned. "What kind of problem, and how little is little?"

"Well, Cheryl has the gift of being able to learn anything she reads, right? And she read about how to build foundations for a water feature. So Meryl and I thought, brilliant, we'll build a fountain in the middle of the dance floor."

Lolly turned to face the room. Now she was looking for it, she noticed a small pit about knee-height in the very centre of the dining hall, the space in the middle of all the tables that had been set out as a dance floor. Nothing too abnormal there, except the pit was getting bigger.

Technically it was sinking. And fast.

Beryl hissed through her teeth. "That's the thing, I might have tried to dig the rock underneath a bit, and um… yeah."

Lolly stared in alarm as the pit widened. Her mother was turning around now, no doubt sensing the discord in the fabric her court. The Arch and Archess were glancing at each other with smirks of anticipation.

"Well fix it!" Lolly hissed.

"I'm not sure how! It shouldn't be sinking like that. I just moved some of the sediment beneath the earth and suddenly it's caving in."

Lolly thanked her luck that she'd thought to rip her

dress earlier as she hurried across to the pit. She couldn't think of any reason it would be sinking. There were no tunnels beneath the court that she knew of, maybe a few storage rooms and cellars but nothing this close to the hall.

There aren't even any plants that could have big enough root structures this close, not unless...

She snapped her head up, gaze darting across the room. Tyren appeared beside her but he didn't get a chance to say a single word as she shoved past him and stormed toward the far corner.

CHAPTER FIVE
TYREN

Tyren had felt fear on many occasions. During his mother's illness. After she died. When he had to face a Frost cat before he realised it was a tame one. His first day at school. The first time he had to entertain at the court because nobody else was available.

But for some reason, watching a bratty young lady storm up to a Fae-eating plant twice the height of her had his heart pounding like a herd of galloping Arumpii were stuck in his chest.

She's going to get herself killed.

He was moving before he could think, before he had any time to figure out a plan, the only real skill he had in life.

"Arthur, enough. I know it's you."

Lolly folded her arms and stared up at the huge pod that was three times the side of her head. The pod's jaw opened and mashed together, and Tyren stumbled to a halt a few metres away.

"Don't give me that," Lolly snapped. "I won't let you throw the children when yuletide comes around. If you don't put it back the way it was, so help me, I'll tell them you're off limits. Any night but tonight."

The thick red trunk straightened and the pod-mouth snapped down. Tyren opened his mouth to shout, but Lolly smacked the flat of her hand on the pod, sending it veering upward.

She pointed her finger at it.

"Bad! We don't snap." She jumped up in the air as a

vine whipped at her feet. "No lashing either. I'll stop you completely if I have to."

She advanced and something in her words seemed to register. The plant stilled, the pod inching back away from her. Tyren noticed the finger she was pointing now, ever so slightly glinting in the light.

The ice again. I wasn't sure before but she's definitely got a chill gift. Rare, and unusual for someone from the Flora Court.

The ground shuddered, a few of the guests now gathered were uttering protests. Lolly glanced over her shoulder and stared right through him. Tyren twisted to see the pit shrinking, the ground rising back into place.

Fish. Someone had said something about the mad plant liking fish.

He didn't want to leave her alone but clearly she was handling things way better than he could in the same situation. He scanned the room and found the nearest server decked out in the Flora Court colours.

"She said it likes fish?" he asked. The man nodded. "Can you bring some then?"

Realisation dawned and the man hurried off. Tyren had no idea what he was doing, but Lolly was now talking to the plant in low tones, her hand on its trunk.

Ice maiden and plant whisperer. Shame she's all but intolerable to talk to as a person.

The guests were gathering in droves now, and those that had missed the upheaval were being filled in by those that had witnessed it. Fae couldn't lie, but exaggeration was almost a pre-requisite, and he could see the startled faces dotted about as they watched others wildly waving arms in explanation.

The server reappeared with a huge silver tray, several

raw pale blue fish neatly lined up on it. Tyren grabbed the tray in both hands and fought every single instinct of common sense as he approached Lolly and the plant.

He was almost within reaching distance when the pod-mouth swung to face him. He froze, his hands shaking around the tray.

Lolly appeared beside him and waved a hand in front of his face, but he only had eyes for the plant. The huge, scary plant that was looming closer and closer.

"Good thinking." Lolly's words barely registered in his head. "She's cranky because nobody asked permission to hem her roots in. Beryl should have considered that. They're a million miles lower down of course, but like I said, she's cranky."

She grabbed a fish in each hand and lobbed them upward. The pod zoomed after them, snapping happily.

"Are you okay?" she asked.

The amusement in her tone snapped something inside of him, that potential derision breaking whatever cord of fear had him frozen. He might be afraid of the giant Fae-eating plant, but he wasn't going to let her hold something like that over him.

"I'm fine," he said, wishing his voice sounded stronger than it did. "I'll hold the tray, you feed the thing."

"Thing?! She's not a *thing*. She's a *Barilo Pharanta-Narilapod* and her name is Arthur."

"You can remember that, but you can't remember actual Fae people's names?"

It just slipped out. He had no idea if her chill gift could work in every part of her, but the blue in her eyes definitely iced over at that. Before she could react, he found himself babbling an apology.

"I didn't mean it like that. You said earlier you're not

good with remembering people, that's all."

He flinched as the pod snapped impatiently and Lolly threw another fish for it- *her*.

"If you want to tell me your plan for the next few days, now would be the right time," she said coldly. "Nobody will get close enough to overhear."

Tyren's insides plummeted. She was angry at him, and it was cruel to bring her mistake with the Marnins up. He hadn't intended to, and it wasn't even that big a mistake really, not to him. But court politics was everything and if she was to take over the Flora Court she would need to remember everyone.

"The plan is to widen the net," he said glumly. "We're going to have fairground-style events outside tomorrow, and roaming performances which the Illusion Court and Court of Words have promised to add to."

Lolly nodded, her attention on Arthur.

"That makes sense. More clusters mean more chance of overhearing things, and also splitting up anyone suspected of being involved on the attacks at the Nether Court."

Tyren eyed the tray in his hands, mindful that there were only two fish left on it and the plant didn't seem to be showing any signs of getting full. The dining hall was though given the rising hum of voices and laughter. He cast the quickest glance over his shoulder and noticed that the dancefloor looked as though nothing had ever happened to it.

Lolly's friends, the Eastwicks and Petra along with the Hutchinsons, were standing like guards a respectful distance away, no doubt waiting for her to leave Arthur's danger zone so they could apologise.

"We'll split the list of people to watch between us and your friends," he added. "That's technically why they're here.”

He wanted to say that he could help her with names, but no doubt she'd take that as another insult against her inability to remember them. He considered using the whole 'both courts hosting' as an excuse to tie her to his side for the next few days. Not because he wanted to obviously, but only because his lord had told him to keep an eye on the Flora Court, as they reportedly had the ear of the new queen. But Lolly would rebuff any attempt he made to hang around her now, he knew that much.

"How long has it- he- sh- *Arthur* been here?" he asked, very aware that they were down to the final fish now.

Lolly frowned, but it wasn't irritation for once.

"Longer than anyone can tell me. She was here before mother was born. Her roots run deep and she's part of the fabric of the court now I reckon."

Her frown disappeared and she threw the last fish extra high. Arthur lunged, the trunk straining as a vine whipped out and caught it with deathly accuracy. Tyren took a step back as the fish sailed into the pod's waiting jaws.

Lolly patted the trunk and Tyren forced himself to stay still as she drew closer to him. He guessed the plant probably wouldn't try to eat him while Lolly was there.

"So, who are we after?" she asked. "Is this a 'hush hush' eat the paper after reading it thing? Because I'm probably not going to remember who I'm meant to be stalking. It might be better to start tonight if we can though, to get it over with."

The urge to smile welled up and he shoved his hands in the pockets of his jacket. His father was always sniping at him about slouching and 'hands in pockets do not a confident man make', but he doubted Lolly would care either way. It hadn't taken her long to turn her mistake into yet another thing to snap at him about either.

"Tonight was meant to be a chance for the courts to acclimatise to each other and for us and your friends to meet. Tomorrow, we plan in secret and monitor people at the revel. After that we have to hope we have what we need, or a lead to it at least."

A tiny groove wove between Lolly's eyebrows.

"I was hoping if we're busy planning stuff then they can't make me dance."

He eyed the crowd. Most of them were seated still but now a few were standing with drinks and chatting in clusters around the edge of the room. He recognised several of the young people dotted about from various courts and prominent families, and a lot of them were watching her.

"Dancing not your thing?" he asked.

Maybe I can find some excuse and leave her to fend for herself for a bit. She clearly doesn't want me hanging around, and sucks to be her if I'm the only reason the coyotes aren't falling over themselves to dance with her yet.

He was surprised people hadn't come up to ask her to dance yet with or without him hovering. He might not have a lordly title or a family high up the noble chain, but he had his own ways of making it through the twisted world that was Faerie.

The Flora Court servers rushed around distributing towering platters of gleaming golden rolls, colourful collections of fruit and several meaty-smelling dishes to the tables. Despite the wonderful sights and scents, Tyren knew he wouldn't be able to look at any of the silver trays for a while without thinking of fish and the huge carnivorous plant behind him.

"I love dancing," Lolly huffed. "But most of the time I don't have anyone worth dancing with. Everyone's so boring. They want to talk about their racing ponies or how big their family's estate is, or how fancy their suite is at Gallows Oak, and that's fine, but nobody wants to hear me talk about the plants. Everyone's a talker and nobody's ever a listener."

"They're courting you. Trying to impress you."

"They're rats running the same maze over and over because their families have done it for centuries. At least rats have some intelligence though by all accounts."

The laughter bubbled up and out before he could check himself. A few people at the edge of the room nearest them turned to stare.

"Not a fan of our glorious elite then, even though you're a part of it?" he asked.

Lolly folded her arms, her expression entirely stubborn.

"Only under sufferance. If there's someone here on your stupid list that I should be interrogating, then just point them out and tell me who they are and I will. I'll let them talk and talk and talk and hopefully they'll spill so much we won't have to do any of this any longer."

Tyren saw Lyle Auren approaching fast from their right, and Lolly stiffened as she noticed him too.

"Is he someone I need to be interrogating?" she asked out of the corner of her mouth.

Tyren snorted. "Not likely. As if anyone would ever trust such Loudmouth Lyle with a secret, let alone invite him to be part of one."

Lyle skirted around a cluster of people, his wide eyes fixed on Lolly. It was a testament to her morality, Tyren decided, that she didn't look pleased about the idea of Lyle asking her to dance. He was by all accounts one of the finest looking young men in Faerie with thick dark brown hair and a lofty noble bone structure that made him look fit for lounging in grand ballrooms eating grapes or some other nonsense. He was also a self-absorbed pain with the most annoying laugh, something Lolly clearly already knew.

Tyren flinched as she grabbed his hand in hers, the unexpected chill of her skin radiating through his.

"What are you doing?" he gasped.

She didn't answer, didn't once glance at him as she started toward the dance floor, pulling him along behind her. He didn't resist, too shocked at the sudden contact. Self-preservation filtered through quickly enough for him to recognise the song and remember the steps of the dance, but his hands shook as Lolly rotated him to stand in front of her and they joined in the fray.

"Dare I ask?" he asked anyway.

She rolled her eyes. "You think I'm going to let Loudmouth Lyle monopolise me all evening? Now, point people out to me and I'll try my best to remember who they are."

"What if we give them plant names? You think about what plant they remind you of. Bonus points if their name sounds like the plant's name."

She narrowed her eyes at him, but he was deadly serious and she might have seen that on his face.

"I suppose it could work. Go on then, give me the worst of it."

Surprised, Tyren almost missed a step. The dance was an easy one, useful in that it held couples in front of each other for the whole routine and didn't require any change of partners. Lolly had a natural rhythm to her movements as well which meant he didn't need to worry about her clomping on his toes or having to tow her about like a rag doll.

"See the tall man there, dark hair, bearded, dressed in blue?" he asked. Lolly nodded. "That's Lyle's older brother, Claudius Auren. Nobody knows much about where he's been since his teenage years, but rumour has it he was working for certain people. He may want your social standing, but from what little I've heard the usual Fae flirting won't work on him. Be yourself, but maybe not too- *oww!*"

Her bare foot landed on his toe with shocking sharpness. He wouldn't have felt it in boots, but his father had insisted on him wearing proper dress shoes for the occasion.

"Don't finish whatever you were going to say," she warned. "I've never met him but I can be charming when I need to be."

Oh how I want to finish what I was going to say now.

He looked across the room instead and took note of all the pairs of eyes following their host around the dancefloor.

"He's looking our way," he murmured. "Laugh."

"Don't tell me what to do."

"Um, please laugh? Men like that pay more attention when they think they have competition."

"Men like that are idiots."

He tried to cling onto the remaining shreds of his sanity.

"Maybe, but if you laugh like you find me amusing-"

"Fae can't lie."

Okay, ouch.

He wondered what he could say to get her to at least smile. Claudius wouldn't likely talk to him, and he had no immediate connections to arrange a way to get to the man either. But as their host from a family with a power title in her future, Lolly could hold his interest. Orbs, she could get someone like him on her own merit with her looks if only she'd smile.

He couldn't even remember any jokes to lighten the mood, but then unless the joke was about him she probably wouldn't find it funny anyway…

"Admit it," he tried. "You would have preferred Arthur to eat me."

A tiny smirk flickered at one corner of her mouth.

A-ha.

"Maybe not eat you," she admitted. "Apparently you're meant to be useful for the next few days. Did she scare you?"

"I thought she was going to eat you for a moment, so yes. I had visions of you half in with your legs sticking out being digested. Lots of screaming."

And just like that, she laughed, the sound mingling into the music from the band.

Claudius wouldn't have heard that from where he's standing, but he's definitely watching her laugh.

"Her venom wouldn't be able to digest a whole person," Lolly said. "Not in one go anyway. You might get some sore skin, but for anything to truly cause damage you'd have to be swimming in her mouth for like a week."

Tyren pulled a face which only made her laugh more. Whether she was doing it on purpose because they needed to draw people's attention or he'd actually succeeded in amusing her, he didn't care.

"I'll go back for some more fish then, see if I can make friends with her."

"She'll love you forever. She was clacking her pod at you and that's usually a good sign." Her expression

sobered instantly, so fast he thought for a moment that he'd
done something wrong, stepped on her foot or something.

"Lady Leilania."

Tyren stopped dancing, one hand still on Lolly's waist
as he looked over his shoulder. Claudius Auren had taken
the bait and was standing with amusement playing across
his handsome features. More rugged than his younger
brother, Claudius had his own aura of entitlement. Less
showy, more dark-cloaked and mysterious. But he was still
a lord.

In Fae society, as someone untitled he had to concede
to Claudius, unless Lolly as lady and host refused. Lyle
wouldn't be arrogant enough to interrupt a couple mid-
dance but apparently Claudius was.

Tyren glanced around but he couldn't see any sign of
Claudius and Lyle's half-sister present, or her mother who
was Lady of Words. Although Claudius and Lyle's father
had married the Lady of Words, the two weren't in line for
the Word Court, but their absence at the revel was curious,
because they'd seemed very supportive of the Holly Queen
at the Nether Court meeting a while ago.

"Problem?" Claudius asked.

Tyren tensed at the bite in the tone, along with the
suggestion that he was lingering too long in stepping aside.
He let Lolly go and bowed low.

Lolly inclined her head, higher up the social chain with
a court due to her one day and therefore exempt from
showing any propriety to either of them unless she chose
to.

"Mister Auren. You seem to have interrupted my
dance."

His eyes lit up, a man after a challenge.

Well, we'll luck out if he does have something to do with

the Forgotten, Tyren realised. *She's the perfect obstacle to keep him enticed.*

He shuddered at the thought but neither Lolly nor Claudius seemed to notice.

"Forgive me, Lady." Claudius bowed low and gave her a winning smile. "I'm still re-learning the etiquette of court life. I've been away, you see."

"Where?"

Tyren almost laughed out loud. No smile, no hint that she found Claudius a potential interest in anyway whatsoever. And she wasn't putting it on or playing hard to get, Tyren could read her well enough to know that already.

Claudius's eyes narrowed ever so slightly.

"I've been working in a faraway realm for an employer. I've recently taken on a new role as it happens which will see me around the courts circuit more often from now on."

Wonderfully vague, which means whatever he was doing must have been dodgy.

Tyren's interest in Claudius increased as Lolly eyed him warily.

"Oh," she said, her brow furrowing. "Somewhere with any interesting plants?"

Claudius inhaled, then hesitated.

She's got him unprepped already.

He had to admit that Lolly was something else entirely. Claudius seemed to be thinking the same. After a tense pause, he smiled wide.

"I'm afraid not. My knowledge is woefully lacking, but I'm glad to learn more about the flora of Faerie."

Lolly smiled suspiciously sweet. "We have a plethora of books you can borrow if you're interested, but I'm otherwise engaged at the moment so it'll have to wait. We decided not to have dance cards tonight because it seems like a very outdated system, but perhaps in hindsight it would have been sensible. I'm sorry, Tyren, we seem to have missed the end of our dance. Fancy another?"

Tyren stared at her, torn. The sensible thing would be to bow out and insist that no, of course he wouldn't dream of getting in the way if Claudius wanted to dance with her. It wasn't like he wanted any claim on her himself anyway, even if it was the sensible thing to do in terms of social advancement. But she stood there staring at him with some kind of stubborn, determined pleading in her eyes.

"Of course, Lady, if you wish it." He held out his hand. "I'm sure there's plenty of time yet for dancing. The evening has only just begun."

Claudius nodded, a small smile remaining on his face as he took a step back.

"Apologies, I'll leave you be. But perhaps I can claim the next dance, Lady?"

She nodded. "Fine."

The band started up a raucous reel and Claudius strode away.

"Argh, he's going to annoy the pants off me," she muttered.

Tyren had to hold her waist on both sides to start the dance, and she eyed him stubbornly.

"Ideally keep your pants out of it entirely," he suggested. "But that's up to you. Just be yourself and ask him more questions. Let him talk about himself."

She sighed. "Fine, but if he tries for more than two dances, send someone in to rescue me."

"Is that an order?"

"A plea, an order and I will make your life here unbearable if you don't."

He grinned as she smiled spiritedly back at him, even though he knew she meant every word.

CHAPTER SIX
LOLLY

Lolly figured she would never get the visual of Tyren shaking around a silver platter out of her head. All the more comical because he was tall and broad, with rugged features and that infuriating expression of all-pervading calm. But faced with Arthur, his eyes grew six sizes and his large body started quivering like a child's.

Then she'd seen Loudmouth Lyle steaming toward her and had the bonkers idea to get Tyren to dance with her.

Of course he'd be a good dancer though, he's been at the Revel Court around parties and balls all his life.

Now though their second dance was over and she found herself in the unpalatable position of wishing she could either continue dancing with him to avoid getting snared by anyone else or at least find some excuse to run away and find solitude in the greenhouses. But Claudius Auren was hovering nearby waiting for his dance and her mother would be horrified if she left the party she was supposed to be hosting. The name was familiar too, but for the life of her she couldn't remember where she'd heard of the Auren family from before.

She could have sworn Tyren's lips twitched as he bowed low and stepped away from her.

"Thank you, Lady," he said. "Don't forget you should approve the main course before it goes to the diners."

Lolly stared at him as he nodded to Claudius and swept into the crowd. She had no idea if the Revel Court also had the practice of the host approving the food before it was served or if he'd been inspecting Flora Court customs before arriving. Either way, she'd forgotten all about it and he'd given her an excuse to only dance once with Claudius.

I really hate having to thank him, and he'd better not expect me to owe him for it.

That would be excruciating.

Claudius bowed with his hand already held out to her, another ancient custom. They weren't technically introduced, not that many people bothered about that anymore, so it was another nicety to be observed; she could either walk away and reject the advance in front of everyone, or she could accept and dance with him, showing him favour.

But she'd already agreed and Tyren wanted her to grill Claudius for information. Not that Tyren was calling the shots or anything.

She took Claudius' hand and waited for the music to start.

"You seem unfettered by the normal routine of coquetry, Lady," Claudius said. "I find that refreshing."

She glared at the band until the bass player caught the look and hurried the musicians back into their places. Luckily for them and their entire future at court, they chose the kind of jaunty tune that didn't involve too much close-up dancing.

"I find it boring." She hesitated, remembering the whole reason all these people were in her home. "You must have seen some exciting things, Claudius- can I call you that?"

He smiled, whirling her into a spin. She kept step with him, her mind rootling through potential ways to speed toward the 'getting him to confess all' part.

"You can call me Claus, all my friends do. Claudius sounds so stuffy. It's also my father's name. He's a great-you don't need to hear the boring bits about my family."

"Not if they're boring, no. If you were planning to say he's a great hunter of exotic succulents, or a great pain in the behind who walks around with a duck on his head, then maybe that would be worth hearing about."

They swirled down the waiting lines of dancers and Lolly noticed her mother and her mum standing nearby to watch. Her mother looked like she approved, whether of the dancing or Claus as a partner there was no way of knowing, but her mum was frowning. Lolly almost missed a step and turned her attention back to Claus.

"No ducks and no succulents, I'm afraid. I won't go on about my family, but I will warn you that my brother is set on dancing the night away with you. From what I hear his reputation has only gotten worse since I've been away."

Lolly couldn't find anything nice to say about Loudmouth Lyle so she wisely said nothing for a long moment before swinging the conversation around again.

"And you were extremely vague about where you've been and for who. Makes me wonder why you need to be so secretive about it."

Claus laughed. "It was at the request of my employer I'm afraid, a confidence I have to keep. You needn't worry about my connections and credentials though. My father had the familial need to align us to the noble circuit and saw the benefit of advancement that came with marrying into the Word Court. My brother has always preferred his own interests though, and my sister is increasingly unwell now. As for me, I'm afraid I'll have to remain a mystery, Lady."

Lolly shrugged, recognising the final part of the music coming up. The band had chosen a ridiculously short reel and she wondered if she could find some way of rewarding them after all. Claus hadn't given her anything useful, but at least Tyren had given her an excuse to leave the dance floor.

"Mysteries don't interest me unless they're flora related. People think way too highly of themselves and their secrets. What are your thoughts on the new queen?"

The song finished and Lolly stopped dancing, her gaze fixed on Claus' impassive face.

"I think she'll shake Faerie up right enough," he said. "Whether for good or bad, we'll have to see. But the mountains I was- ah. Let's just say where I've been recently, her initial efforts definitely seem to have helped the regular people there."

So maybe not a raving Forgotten supporter then. Lolly frowned. *But then, he didn't exactly say he supported the queen or her efforts either. Agreeing that she's had a positive impact on the people isn't always going to be a good thing for the kind of elite nobles that align with the Forgotten.*

As Claus bowed low to her, perhaps on the cusp of asking her to dance again, she took a step back.

"I need to approve the food. Thanks for the dance."

Claus nodded, amusement spilling over his lips as he straightened up.

"Of course, Lady. Watch out for my brother trying to catch you. He'll probably propose if you gave him half a chance."

Lolly pulled a face before she could reign the instinct in, but Claus only laughed.

"If he gives you any trouble, I'm happy for you to say you've promised me the next dance, whatever one it may be."

It was barely even a favour but Lolly didn't want to be

owing anyone anything, least of all someone she barely knew who would likely call in anything owed at the worst possible moment. He'd probably noticed his brother hovering at the end of the song, as Lyle was on his way over with a determined smile plastered over his face.

Lolly through an absent-minded greeting for the Lord and Lady of the Illusion Court, then she whirled away in a flurry of excuses and dodged through the people assembling for the next dance, putting some of her speed gift at her heels. She burst into the hallway that led to the kitchens, increasing her speed so that the long corridor took all of two steps' time.

She stopped outside the door, her cheeks flushed. Nobody would have seen where she went at that speed, and any sudden absence could be explained away as her being mixed in with the crowd.

She took a couple of steadying breaths and opened the kitchen door.

"You're certainly popular tonight."

Tyren's voice made her jump. She twisted with a hand on her chest to find him halfway down the hall behind her, her mad breath fluttering in and out.

He couldn't have seen her come this way from the dining hall while she was using her speed gift, and that was annoying because it meant he had assumed she was following his instructions about the food, which technically she was, but only because she had decided to.

She scowled. "Are you checking up on me?"

"Of course not. I wanted to find out if our friend dropped anything interesting."

"Not really. He said something about mountains where he had been, then when I asked him if he supported the new queen I didn't get any serious pro-enemy vibes, but that could be simple word-tangling."

Tyren crossed his forearms over his chest, his fingertips curling around his elbows.

"Doesn't mean he's not one to watch but at least he seems happy to talk to you. Lyle collared me straight after and demanded to know why you were dancing with his brother, as if I knew."

Lolly stared at him. "You did know. It was basically your idea."

"Well he didn't need to know that. Are you approving the food then or waiting for it to grow some intriguing type of mould first?"

Don't smack him. Don't smack him. Don't smack him.

Something about the demanding hint in his tone set her on edge, or perhaps it was his impatience when she was the one who deserved to be irritable with all these random people stomping about her home and demanding things of her.

But she was there to approve the food, so she stalked into the kitchen and decided she would ignore him until she had a reason to talk to him again.

Letting the kitchen door swing back in his face was probably a bit beneath her, but it did make her feel better.

"Hiya, Lol," Mila shouted. "Come to make sure we aren't poisoning your guests? We've been really careful since the *bolouta* bean incident."

Lolly forgot about Tyren and moved through the bustling kitchen with a grin breaking over her face. The vast room rambled an entire corner of the court, several turnings and nooks hiding different areas for food preparation and open windows and arches with access to the herb garden and the greenhouses. The counters shone and several large ovens stood either side of the gargantuan fireplace at the back, the whole system dancing seamlessly to Mila's merry tune.

Mila had been at the court for a long time and insisted she was so much a part of it she'd never die. Her features were deceptively ageless, the greying hair pinned up in one of her riotously coloured headscarves and her sharp hazel eyes noting everything going on around them.

"That was one time," Lolly quipped. "Nobody can hold that against you. I should be approving the main course apparently because it's tradition, so yeah, approved."

Mila chortled. "Nonsense, come have a look. Orbs, have a taste as well, we've made way too much."

It was either that or return to the dining hall so Lolly grabbed a spoon from the holder on the countertop. Then she flicked a grudging look at Tyren.

"You can join in if you want."

He raised his eyebrows. "Very kind of you."

Okay, that was definitely some kind of dig.

She re-firmed her resolve to ignore him and followed Mila around the kitchen. The stews were divinely rich and of course there were no finer platters of deliciously colourful vegetables in all of Faerie, many carved into various floral shapes. Sauces sat in dainty silver serving jugs giving off the most delicious scents, and bread rolls with far too many flavourings for Lolly to taste them all.

"I was worried you were getting a bit too peaky," Mila said with a frown. "All that work, then you nibble."

Lolly shrugged and grabbed a roll.

"Had to fit into the dress."

"That's rot and you know it." Mila huffed even as she held out another roll. "Try the honey one. You've been too busy to look after yourself. Running the greenhouses, learning the court etiquette, scribbling away in that index of yours at all hours.”

She knew Mila was right, but with Tyren standing beside her she didn’t want to run the risk of any pity coming her way. She loved her life as it was. She enjoyed the hard work, the greenhouses and seeing how her efforts helped the plants grow. She liked adding to her index.

The court etiquette I’d quite happily bin, but I can’t have everything.

Mila threw up her hands when Lolly didn’t answer and bustled off toward the servers who were plating up following Lolly’s official approval.

“You take on a lot,” Tyren said.

Lolly eyed him as he settled back against the wooden counter, then she leaned back against it beside him. Again, even talking to him in the kitchen beat being social with others ‘out there’.

“So?” she asked.

He rolled his eyes and closed them, a soft huff of frustration puffing from his lips.

“Not everything I say is an insult you know.”

Relieved that he was at least having as grouchy a time as she was, she relented the tiniest amount.

“Just most of it.”

He glanced at her and chuckled when he saw her smiling.

“Half maybe. I can’t imagine it’s nice to have a load of people storming into your home when you’re not used to it.”

“It’s not nice even when you are used to it. None of these people are here for us. They’re here for social status and scandal.”

He sighed. “I can’t argue with that. I reckon it’s great here though on a normal day.”

"It is. Go through the greenhouses and do morning checks, then maybe work on clearing debris in the woods or pruning sick trees or clearing some of the scrubland. Then the day is our own pretty much for hiking or whatever. In the summer we move the court to the waterfalls so we can swim and relax. Most of it is learning how to prune as you go though, or you'd have huge chunks-"

When she saw Tyren looking at her, the words dried on her tongue. He was really looking at her as though he was actually listening. Like he was maybe interested even.

"Huge chunks…?" Without skipping a beat, he prompted her. "Of what? Don't leave me in suspense like that."

She managed a nervous laugh and looked away.

"Huge chunks of time dedicated to pruning things. Great when you have music or someone to talk to, but it's murder on your back muscles if that's all you're doing all day."

"Ah. Can't be worse than being forced to dance all night because the court doesn't have enough male partners turn up to a bachelorette party it's hosting, surely."

"Yeah that doesn't sound good. Dancing at my own party is bad enough. Although to be fair to him, Claus did say if his brother gets too insistent I can say I promised him the next dance whenever I need to."

Tyren nodded, a simple bob of his chin.

"Claus now is it? That at least is helpful. A permanent dance offer and you barely even smiled at him. He must be smitten."

Lolly snorted. "I doubt it. He'll be exactly like the rest, all here for some nefarious reason. They want the advancement of my title, or they want to align with some of the security it brings. Or they're sent here by other courts to spy and find out our secrets. Which is fine. I have friends who value me for me so I don't need anything else."

Tyren said nothing for a long moment and she knew they should be getting back to the dining hall. If they didn't, her mother would come looking for her and the nagging about being antisocial would be endless.

"You're lucky," Tyren admitted. "To have friends I mean. I have some but a lot of them have moved out of the court now onto other things. New places."

Lolly pushed away from the counter and started toward the hall, throwing a thank you over her shoulder to Mila, who waved a big ladle back in reply. Tyren kept pace with her along the hall, but neither of them seemed in any rush to get there. Lolly had to smother a smirk when she saw their reflection in a window they passed; if anyone saw them, they might look like they were out for an illicit tryst.

I can't imagine anything more ridiculous.

"Is there anyone I should be aiming for other than Claus?" she asked.

Tyren sighed. "Not tonight. If you stomp around interrogating everyone, they'll be on their guard more. Best wait until the *Beast* and wine hangovers kick in tomorrow morning and everyone is relieved they didn't get picked on tonight."

"That means more chance of me having to dance with Lyle though."

"Well, you have your new friend Claus to help with that."

Lolly nodded, squaring her shoulders in determination as they reached the door to the dining hall. She did have Claus ready to dance with her. She could also ask the

Eastwicks to dance with her one by one, then their boyfriends if need be, and Petra. And her mum had asked her to save a dance. She didn't need to be whining to Tyren about being partnerless. She didn't need him for anything.

She stalked into the dining hall, smiling at people she passed and scanning the room for suitable dance victims.

The Eastwicks and the two brothers were at the far end of the hall, apparently about to have some kind of eating contest. Lolly wanted more than anything to join them, to watch at least, but she caught sight of someone else who would do her a favour for nothing and set off across the dancefloor.

"There she is!"

The boy in front of her opened his burly arms and stood ready. He wasn't overly affectionate, she'd learned that early on, but ever since she'd mentioned in passing on an orb call to the queen's court that she was indexing a botanical text, he'd taken great interest in keeping tabs on her. Now, he allowed her to hug him which was, according to his boyfriend, a huge sign of trust.

She squeaked with a laugh as Milo wrapped his arms around her shoulders and hugged briefly before letting go. He'd dressed up for the occasion in a smart black suit, but even with the finery and his brown hair brushed back neatly, she couldn't help but think of him as a huge, cuddly bear. She stepped back, mindful of his space, and grinned at him.

"Is Ace here too?" she asked.

"No, and if anyone asks I'm here by invitation, but I think in reality the queen just wanted me to keep an eye on the FDPs."

He nodded his head toward the group the Eastwick sisters were part of, but his smile suggested it was only a joke rather than an actual fact. She wanted to drag him off and show him her index immediately, because he at least would take a proper interest as the scholar who ran the grand library at Arcanium, but his gaze went past her shoulder and his eyes lit up again.

"Hello, Tyren!"

Lolly stared in amazement as Tyren too received a hug, although she couldn't be sure if hers had lasted longer or his did. But either way, Milo was clearly on very friendly terms with him too.

"This is nice," Milo said with a wide smile. "I'm also here as the warning."

Lolly folded her arms as Tyren frowned beside her.

"What warning?"

"What warning?"

They chorused together then glared at each other. Or in Lolly's case it was a glare, in Tyren's it was more momentary impatience. Milo glanced between them, his smile turning awkward.

"Um, the queen will be here any minute. She decided her presence would rattle any enemies into either taking a swipe at her, or running for very obvious corners to whisper in. Taz isn't impressed but then when is he ever where her plans are concerned?"

Lolly would have smiled at the thought of fussy Milo calling the king consort and previous crown prince of Faerie by his first name so easily, except a huge thrum of panic was giving her trouble instead.

"The queen…" She dragged in a startled breath. "Here? Oh orbs. I'll need to prepare her rooms. I'll get Mila to keep a plate for her as well. Will she want a tour straight away? It's better seen in the morning, but if she's determined…"

She looked around for her mother who was busy chatting to an elderly lady with a huge puff of bright pink hair. She looked for her mum, but of course she would be the lucky one who got to do the final bed-down of the greenhouses for the night.

"She won't need much," Milo insisted.

"That's irrelevant!" she hissed. "We're not going to be the court that couldn't even host a queen at the last minute. The whole of Faerie would laugh at us. Simona!"

She grabbed the sleeve of a passing server, almost dislodging the tray of drinks in her hands.

"Emergency, and it needs to be kept quiet. You know the state room? Have Frankie go and prepare it, fire in the grate, freshened bedding. Have someone on standby to send any bags or cases up. On your way, get Mila to keep a plate aside and hot- no, several plates in case she brings an entourage. The queen is coming but tell nobody else, we don't want uproar before she arrives if she's preparing to surprise everyone."

Simona nodded and let go of the tray when Lolly grabbed it from her. Lolly twirled around and handed it to someone else, who grabbed it without so much as a flinch.

"Right, I'll go up and see the room just in case," she continued. "No, should I be here to welcome her though? Orbs, I can't even see Petra and she's supposed to be helping me."

She had a feeling she should warn the Eastwicks that their queen, employer and the ruler of the court they were part of was arriving imminently, and that they were currently surrounded by the remnants of an ongoing eating contest, but she didn't have time for that.

"She'll be fine, honestly," Milo said, chewing his lip as her anxiety transferred to him. "The fact you're making such an effort will be what matters to her."

Lolly guessed he knew his queen best but she had the pride of her own court to think of. She glanced around the dining hall, groaning when she spotted Lyle on his way over to them.

I can't tell him the queen's coming, he'll tell everyone. But I can't think of a single excuse not to dance with him.

She even looked around for Claus but he was already dancing with the lady of the Illusion Court.

"You've sorted everything already," Tyren said, his voice surprisingly soft. "The room will be prepared, there will be food for them. You'll simply have to welcome her to the court and she will be kind and say not to worry about a tour. Trust me."

In her panicked state she wanted nothing more than to do exactly that, to trust him. But Lyle was almost upon them and Tyren didn't have an entire court to consider.

"Come on." He grabbed her hand. "Safety first."

In any other situation, she'd have pulled away at being manhandled. Shouted or tried to kick him. But it was scarily easy to let herself be whisked onto the dancefloor and flung into a spin.

I will not let him hold this over me.

Instead of focusing on him as they danced, she kept her attention on the room. Lyle hovered on the fringes of the dance floor and she made every effort not to meet his eye. Claus was beside his brother now but he'd been no use when she needed him either. And Tyren with all his helpfulness and turning up at the right moments was entirely too useful and present to be anything other than someone who wanted something from her. It might not be anything more than him being sent to keep an eye on her, or perhaps his lord had asked him to spy on the Flora

Court, but he wasn't here for her.

She twisted her head around as a shiver wavered through the air. In one moment there was a circle in the centre of the dance. The next, there was a queen in the centre of the circle.

Silence fell.

Lolly took a deep breath and detangled herself from Tyren's arms. She'd never spoken to the queen personally before, only in support of her at the Nether Court meeting. But she was hosting so etiquette dictated she welcome the regent.

I bet my mother's saying every prayer or incantation for luck she can think of right now.

The crowd parted as Lolly left Tyren behind and hurried across to the queen, who stood surveying the room. Her black hair was pinned back with several strands of unruly curls already escaping, a sheen of various colours shining over the black and glinting alongside the circlet of silver and holly nestled atop her head. She wore a dress, the silver bodice and velvet skirt simple and elegant, and her arms were left bare. Lolly spied a couple of tattoos adorning the insides of her wrists and her eyes, those blue depths were clear and sharp. Beside her, the king consort wore a suit so dark red it almost looked black in the firelight, the green holly stitched over it woven so intricately it looked a part of him instead, his fiery wings unfurled at his back.

Lolly dropped to her knees in front of them, her head bowed.

"Welcome to the Flora Court, my Queen, King Consort. We have rooms ready for you, and I've also saved food if you-"

She trailed off as the queen waved a pale hand in front of her, a signal to rise. The queen's gaze softened and she smiled. Lolly didn't think about the queen often in her day to day life but knew that she was only a year or two different to her own age and also originally a fairy rather than pure-blood Fae.

"I'm really glad I've finally got the chance to come and see the Flora Court," Queen Demerara announced, loud enough for the whole crowd to hear. "I'd love to see it tomorrow if that's okay, in proper daylight. But the decorations look grea- Oh wow, is that a *Barilo Pharanta-narilapod*?!"

CHAPTER SEVEN
REYAN

Agreeing to give Kainen her first dance at the Flora Court gave Reyan some reassurance as he realm-skipped them there, but they arrived to find the floor of the Flora court's main hall un-sinking itself.

"Looks like we missed the main event," Kainen said.

Reyan nodded. "Either that or this is going to get extremely wild."

"I doubt it can rival our revels," he said, his tone entirely sniffy. "Do you remember the time when-"

Devilish excitement buzzed over her skin as she pressed a gentle hand to his mouth, delighting in how his eyes widened at the touch.

"Don't give away all our secrets now."

He grinned. "Good thinking. Ah, there's our host- oh, no she's gone again."

Despite the filling hall, everyone else looked relatively calm, although several elaborately dressed nobles were gossiping excitedly in small clusters around the room. Reyan let Kainen hold her hand as he ushered her further into the crowd of Faerie's elite. He didn't seem in the slightest bit bothered about escorting her into the social viper-pit, but she'd had to learn the etiquette customs as part of his staff before, and she had also taken some time to look up some rules for court ladies at Arlen's.

Okay, plan. Kainen's voice echoed in her head. *Stick with me until after our first dance. After that, don't dance with too many other people for my sake.*

She smiled, surveying the crowd. *Why, scared someone will whisk me off to another court?*

He dropped her hand and wrapped his arm around her waist instead to guide her further into the swelling crowd.

"They wouldn't dare," he whispered, his words warm against her ear.

She shivered. "They'd have to provide a better court first, and I can't imagine any one better than ours."

She caught the flicker of vulnerability in his eyes but she meant every word. Whether it was the three weeks away from him and home or some unbidden sense of mischief rising, she was beginning to get sick of hiding how she felt.

"My Lord Hemlock!" A strident male voice reached them. "I haven't seen you in ages. Dare I ask you to make introductions with your lovely lady?"

Reyan hesitated. She had no idea who the tall, lithe man with dark brown hair and rugged appearance was, so she couldn't be sure if she should be bowing her head or waiting for him to acknowledge her formally instead. Kainen's arm tightened around her waist.

"Of course. You'll have heard that Reyan is now lady of my court. Sweetheart, this is Lord Claudius Auren."

"Claus to my friends," the man added with a wink. "I think Kainen and I would still call ourselves such, even though I've been away a long while now."

Kainen inclined his head, his confident mask firmly in place.

"We've all been busy, but my focus is now on the protection and wellbeing of my court. Assuming you mean no harm against me or mine, then yes, friends."

Reyan chuckled. "So formal, *love.*"

She played happily into the pretend pet name she'd once

given him, rewarded by the slightest widening of his eyes. While he was apparently shocked into silence, she turned her smile on Claus next.

"If you'll excuse us. Responsibility requires me to gift him the first dance."

Kainen recovered fast and smiled at her, bowing low.

"I did ask rather than insist, which is an improvement surely?"

She gave an airy sigh. "Depends which mood we're in really, doesn't it? Am I leading myself or what?"

Kainen let himself be dragged onto the dancefloor, his palm settling on her waist as he claimed her hand and launched her into the dance, her training from performing for the revels the court held dusting off. He held her closer than necessary and she curved around him with each move more than she had to, her eyes locked with his. When it became a competition she had no idea, but she refused to look away and so did he.

After this, if you get a chance to talk to Claus, do it. His eyes narrowed. *See if he'll be turned by a pretty face. He'll likely want to dance with you considering you're mine, but avoid anyone who you recognise from our court. Waste of time when I can easily interrogate them and some of the highborns won't be kind to you still if I'm not around.*

She considered how to answer that. She had no fears of elite Fae snubbing her or talking down to her; she was more than used to that from years in service.

You think I'm pretty? She shot back with a grin. *My ego is soothed, you can go now.*

He chuckled as the song came to an end but he grabbed her hands and held her in place.

"Claus is on his way over to dance with you," he murmured. "I knew he would."

Reyan took a deep breath and nodded. She froze as Kainen drew her close and brushed a kiss over her cheek, the second since she'd returned to him. She watched him as he walked away, swaying through the crowd, and she wondered if he would dance with others. She pushed aside the pang of anxiety at the mere thought of it.

Claus smiled at her nicely enough as she stepped in front of him, his hand held out. He didn't move in a hurry, no sense of need or desire about him. Unnervingly relaxed and calm.

"Well, Lady, someone has finally tamed the lord of the Illusion Court," he said.

She waited until he'd claimed her hands for the next dance, both of them standing ready as a lively reel started up.

"I don't know if tamed is the right word. But I'm lucky he's been so thoughtful and kind. Many haven't been."

It was easy to be truthful talking about him. Others might not agree, but she saw the good in Kainen and he'd shown her a side of him many others never had the fortune or chance to see.

Claudius chuckled, spinning her in a circle. She didn't weave herself around him as she had done before with Kainen, but he whirled her again and drew her close.

"He's certainly changed directions entirely since the war. Almost a new man. The Kainen we used to know wouldn't have considered taking a girl without family as his lady, or supporting a low-blooded queen so openly."

Reyan forced her body not to stiffen. Low-blooded wasn't exactly a bad term in Fae circles, but she'd decided long ago that it should be. The queen being a fairy, part-human, part-Fae blooded, had nothing to do with how good of a person she was. But in Fae terms, nothing Claus said was technically untrue either.

She faked a bright smile and curled herself ever so slightly closer to him. Temptation to call the queen Demi because they were friends warred with the knowledge she should be keeping her own viewpoint clear to better suss out his.

"Perhaps you never truly knew him. Perhaps the queen's blood proves that there's little sense in those outdated ways. Then again, who knows what the truths really are? We're Fae; trickery and misdeed is everything to our kind."

Claus laughed. "He certainly chose well in terms of temperament at least. I only hope I can be so lucky when my time to choose comes."

"Ah, but who says he got to do the choosing? Who says you will?"

"I'm well known for getting what I want," he countered, his hand brushing lower over her hip.

"And what is that, my lord? Rumours about you are few and far between which in itself could be telling."

She'd never heard of him before tonight, not that she could remember anyway. The surname sounded familiar but she was more unnerved by the positioning of his hand and the constant downward flicker of his eyes.

"What I want is my business, Lady Reyan. Surely Kainen should have taught you at least that a man's business is no place for a lady?"

The urge to kick him somewhere painful swelled but Reyan kept the sweet smile on her face as she twirled away from him and his hand.

"What an antiquated viewpoint." She forced herself to return to him. "I don't need you to tell me anything anyway, but it's interesting to watch how people behave.

I'd be careful though."

His eyebrows rose. "And why is that?"

"Because the last couple of people who tried to touch or proposition me without my consent ended up in rather a lot of pain."

He snorted. "Oh please. What damage could you do?"

"Me?" She grinned. "I have my own assets but a woman's business is no place for a lord. No, turns out Kainen's surprisingly possessive, so I'd watch those hands if you want a shot at keeping them."

His eyes widened and she took vicious satisfaction from it. Kainen had technically defended her honour before, once against one of his guests who tried to buy her from his service, then against an old friend of his who tried to attack her. She didn't want him to have to lose control because of her, but Claus becoming victim number three was looking pretty tempting.

"Besides, this is all in good fun," she added. "I very much doubt there's anything you'd tell me if you were against us, and likely not much you'd be able to tell me if you were on our side either. Keep your pretty words."

Claus smiled again, but the pretence of any charm or warmth had dissipated.

"I imagine our dear Lord Kainen has his work cut out for him against a sharp tongue like yours. But surely we're all still friends?"

Reyan shrugged. "You're a friend of his and our court by his account. As for me, I know very little about you and I'm careful about who I keep as true friends."

"What would you like to know?"

She hesitated, sorting through for the best type of banal chatter that might give them something Kainen didn't already know about him.

"Where did you grow up?"

He frowned. "My family were affiliated with the Court of Words, so I mountain-board extremely well. Not quite as smoothly as my brother who is also here tonight, but enough to make it down in one piece."

"You have a brother? Younger or older?"

"Younger, and an older sister, but she's unwell."

"Oh, sorry to hear that." Reyan didn't have to fake the sympathy for that at least. "So you probably look down on people like me then, family line long out of favour, originally in service to a court rather than patronising it?"

He twirled her around in a tight circle and she bent her body with the slightest dip into the shadows to avoid his hand brushing too far down her back again.

"Everyone has their place," he said. "I agree that noble lines need to be protected, but there are definitely positives to the new way of things too. The queen for example has enabled families to dodge the expectation that the first-born child is forced to carry on the family legacy, which ensures they live on."

Reyan nodded to placate him and tried to guess how much longer the song would run on for. She had no proof he was any part of their enemy, or that he was anything more than a standard Fae noble wanting to cling onto the traditional power granted to the elite by the mere luck of being born.

"I did wonder if the situation with Kainen was all an act," Claus said. "He was so set on following the Forgotten before, now all of a sudden he's changed his entire way of thinking, even to the point of being engaged to someone without fortune or title."

Wild thoughts of Claus referring to their fake engagement had Reyan tensing but she held herself steady.

Nobody knew except for her, Kainen and Demi, and probably Taz by now.

Claus wants to get some kind of dirt on Kainen, she realised.

Giving him a wicked smile, she called the shadows and let them creep over her body. She only wished she could summon Betty, her shadow-snake companion, to wraith her shoulders for added effect.

"I'm sure many people have wondered that. He learned the hard way what following fanatic traditionalists can lead to. But ask him and I'm sure he'll tell you."

Claus inched closer as the last bars of the song trilled over the crowd.

"I wouldn't get anywhere near as much satisfaction dancing up close with him," he murmured.

She froze as he slid all-together too close for comfort, his arms cinching around her waist and his mouth brushing her ear. Unlike Kainen's embraces, this one left her skin crawling and her fighting the urge to shove Claus halfway across the fine dining hall.

"Forget about him," he added. "What side are you on, Lady?"

She refused to answer until he let her go, which luckily coincided with the end of the song. She glanced around the room until she found Kainen, his hands in his jacket pockets and his face set in hard lines as he watched them.

She had her answer then, enough that she knew talking to Claus was a dead end.

"His. And mine. The queen's too, if she continues the way she's been going. She has our court's support."

Kainen appeared beside her before she could get swept up by anyone else, his hand sliding around hers like a blessed weight of familiar comfort.

"At least I know I have my lady's loyalty," he said, his tone far too jovial to be anything other than mutinous.

Claus shrugged. "You can't blame a man for trying, and it's not like you're married yet."

"Not yet, no." Kainen lifted her hand to his lips and sent flutters racing inside her gut. "But she's free to leave any time she likes, and she hasn't left yet."

Reyan rolled her eyes at him. "*She* is still here and capable of answering for herself thanks. Are you planning to dance with anyone else then, or do I have to mind you all evening?"

She turned to face him, blocking Claus out without a second look or an acknowledgement. Manners dictated she thank him for the dance, but she didn't want to.

Kainen grinned wickedly back at her, fully aware she was snubbing his old friend.

"Only you, sweetheart. It took a surprisingly short amount of time to reacquaint myself with anyone worth speaking to."

She sighed. "Fine, if you really can't find anyone else you want to dance with. Or did they all say no?"

"He's gone." He chuckled. "You can stop the character assassination act now."

"Who says it's an act? Besides, where'd be the fun in that?"

She pressed her arm around his neck, her cheek settling on his shoulder. The song was a slow one and perfectly fitting an intimate couples dance.

Any luck? he asked softly. *Other than him getting far too close for my liking?*

So content to be close to him again, she'd almost forgotten the whole reason they were there.

He seems to be playing with the idea of being against

Kainen grinned, taking the song as an excuse to pull her even closer. She wanted him to skip them back to their court so she could change into comfortable clothes and simply relax. She had a book that needed reading and if she was lucky, he'd insist on needing company and they would sit in his room together with their books and something delicious from the kitchens.

"You forget, my lady," he said. "My court is made as much from your decisions now as it is mine."

She couldn't tell if his volume meant the words were for the surrounding dancers and the crowd fringing the dancefloor, or if he meant them. Perhaps the court would see that as true because of the fake engagement, but suddenly she didn't want the answers. She wanted to continue dancing with him for as long as she could, pretending for as long as he'd let her.

As she looked up at him smiling down at her with what she hoped was affection shining in his eyes, she decided to be bold.

"Well then, our court supports the queen. Oh, and while I'm allowed to throw decisions about, I want an outside deck added onto my room."

She grinned but Kainen only shrugged.

"If it doesn't appear, remind me. It might not actually be added on, but I can get you access to one. Oh! I forgot. You mentioned a while back about the staff wanting a deck of their own as well, needing access to the elements. I sorted out the west side for them and they all got little keys to come and go as they like. I think someone was saying they're going to set up a bar as well and have a sort of unofficial set of opening hours."

He looked so delighted with himself that Reyan had to laugh, still astonished he'd remembered her vague suggestion let alone done something about it.

"That's a lovely thing to do."

He shrugged. "Your idea. I just did the running around."

Before she could think of a taunt to hit back with, something to tease and infuriate him enough that he wouldn't want to leave her hanging around while he went and spoke to people, a shiver wavered through the air in the middle of the floor. The crowd, the musicians and the very air in the room paused like a giant single entity as Queen Demerara appeared.

She looks beautiful, Reyan couldn't help the words slipping from her mind to Kainen's.

He smiled. *Not my type, sweetheart. Not anymore.*

Stunned into flustered silence with her cheeks burning up a fire, she turned to focus on Demi as the daughter of the Flora Court's lady stood ready to receive her.

She missed the first part of Demi's speech, but the less than dignified screech at the end couldn't be mistaken.

"Oh wow, is that a *Barilo Pharanta-narilapod*?!"

CHAPTER EIGHT
TYREN

Tyren was still standing beside Milo when the king consort joined them, his gaze fixed on the queen as she followed Lolly toward Arthur's corner.

"She's been practicing that all afternoon," the king consort announced with fond amusement. "Apparently the bara-nara-whatever thing is an ancient part of the court, so she wanted to personalise her entrance."

Tyren hadn't spoken to the king consort before as all dealings had been done by his father and Milo for the Revel Court. He'd heard mostly complimentary things though, and rumour had it that the new royals were both extremely relaxed about the social rules. He still didn't feel entirely confident striking up a conversation however and gave Milo a hopeful grimace.

"Oh, yeah." Milo flapped his hands between them. "This is Tyren Berell, he helps his father deal with the Revel Court's particulars. The king consort needs no introduction these days."

Tyren bowed his head, throwing a bit of shoulder in there as extra deference. He didn't expect the hand that was extended to him a second later, a sure sign of acceptance, but there it was hovering in front of his face. He grabbed the hand and shook, bemused at being treated like an equal.

"Call me Taz, and once the faff is over call her Demi, she won't mind. She'll probably insist on it if she remembers."

Unsure how seriously to take that, although Lolly had

at least given him some experience in the whole 'not disagreeing with the nobility' thing, Tyren nodded to keep the peace. He'd steer clear of names and titles all together if he could.

"We're happy to help the Flora Court host the revel," he offered instead.

They turned their attention back to where Lolly and the queen were now making friends with Arthur. The lady of the Flora Court and Lolly's other mother were on their way over to join them, but all Tyren could think about suddenly was how loud the music was and how flushed his skin felt.

Maybe I can step outside for a few minutes, take a breather. Nobody will notice me missing.

The thought of looking for his opportunity to exit almost distracted him enough to miss a blur of green and burnished red moving through the crowd. He glanced at the queen now standing alone with the lady of the Flora Court and her partner.

"If you'll excuse me." He bobbed his head in the king consort's direction and fled after the blur.

The crowd hemmed in around him but he had the ability to stride fast when he needed to. He pushed through the people, bashing his elbows in his rush to chase after what he could only assume was Lolly with a speed gift.

He slipped through the door at the far end of the hall from Arthur and the dancefloor, the soft brush of balmy night air caressing his cheeks. No doubt the Lady Flora was creating ideal conditions for those visiting her court, but further on past the castle and the firelit grounds, the trees danced in a violent wind.

The air turned chillier with each step he took, but he could see a tiny glow of light now coming from the nearest greenhouse.

He'd heard horror stories about the kind of plants the Flora Court grew in the depths of their greenhouses, and the recent experience with Arthur didn't give him much hope as he pushed open the greenhouse door. He winced in preparation for a creak or whining noise, but the hinges made no sound. He crept inside, keeping a sharp eye out for any foliage that might see him as a potential snack.

Lolly kneeled in front of a low workbench halfway down the greenhouse, a lamp on the bench and something small cradled in her hands. She was murmuring something to it and Tyren inched forward, wondering if she'd found a stowaway mouse or some other small creature.

She stiffened as he approached, her voice drifting away.

"Stalking me, are you?" she asked.

He'd intruded on her when she clearly wanted a moment alone, but she was his unexpected excuse for leaving the rowdy confines of the dining hall. He wasn't going to give that momentary peace up without a diplomatic fight.

"Not exactly. I needed some air and saw the light."

Technically not a lie, considering he had wanted air before seeing her escape and he had seen the light straight after. She turned her head toward him, eyebrows raised.

"Hmm. Do you know what this is?"

He squinted as she twisted and held her cupped hands out to him. With a healthy dose of reticence, he inched closer and leaned forward. A small seven-leafed blob of pale turquoise lay in her palms. He shook his head.

"It's *icalatha*," she said. "They say its semi-sentient like Arthur is, but I've not managed to get any of them responding to me yet. I've tried everything."

Tyren considered that as she placed the plant back into a row of others identical to it.

"Don't let Arthur hear you call her semi-sentient."

Lolly's lips pinched as if she was trying to hold in a smile.

"I won't tell if you won't."

Tyren crossed his arms over his chest. He was beginning to realise that Lolly was so used to people not taking much notice of her, she didn't bother to say much more than flippant comebacks.

"What kind of things do they usually respond to, these Ithacala things?"

She closed her eyes for a moment before turning those sharp green eyes on him.

"*Ica-la-tha.* Think of them like ice plants. I've tried cold, heat, attention, no attention, wet conditions, dry, sun, darkness. Rich soil, nutrient-poor soil, air-growing. I've even-"

She hesitated, her gaze sliding away from his.

"You've even what?"

She shrugged, and he guessed that if they were in full light he'd be able to see her blushing.

"I even tried singing to them."

He grinned. "Lullabies or popular anthems? Are they not fans of *Siren-Sing-Along* then? Maybe you should try telling them jokes instead."

She was up on her feet in a second flat and halfway past him. If it hadn't been for his special sight, he'd have missed her movement entirely.

She gasped as he shot out an arm to block her path, and it was either crash into him or dodge and risk stomping on some of the seedlings. She bashed against his arm and he guided her back in front of him.

"I'm sorry, forgive me." He bit down on the temptation to call her 'Lady' again, because teasing her was too easy and clearly didn't work on her unless she already had the upper hand.

"Let me go."

He did as he was told but continued blocking the path. The seedling trays beside them were spread wide, and she wouldn't be able to hurdle over to the next aisle without crushing something.

"Let me pass."

He eyed her, the petulant scrunch of her face, the wrinkled nose and the furious blue eyes. Her fists were clenched at her sides and he wondered if she was considering the penalties of shoving him.

No doubt she's weighing up the chances of me harming the plants rather than her. Foolish considering she doesn't really know me. Why am I in here anyway?

He shook his head to clear it, sending entirely the wrong message.

"No?" she demanded. "Are you actually refusing to let me leave?"

"Of course not." He found his voice but still he didn't seem to be moving out of her way, and he had no idea why.

She glanced over her shoulder, drawing his attention to the other end of the greenhouse. Where of course there was another door. She wasn't trapped, she was testing him, and he still wasn't moving.

She was frustrating, that had to be why. There was nobody in the realms who could ruffle him, he prided himself on that, and yet here she was being a total pain in the behind.

Although, she didn't ask me to chase her out here.

"Are you sure you haven't tried telling it jokes instead yet?" he asked. "Might be just the thing."

She looked ready to scream, or to slap his face, and he

wouldn't have blamed her. He took a step forward and she took a step back.

Before she could run or he could release whatever temporary insanity had gripped him, a voice echoed outside.

"This is more than far enough. It's freezing in this wilderness wasteland."

Lolly froze but Tyren's adrenalin was already charging and he dropped to his knees. She hissed as he grabbed her wrist and pulled her down beside him, batting him off with a stinging smack to his fingers.

But she didn't leap up again, a minor miracle considering he recognised the voice outside and guessed she might have also.

"You should be keeping better company, brother," Claudius said. "You were always so keen on the idea of family honour in past times."

"I still am. I know which side to fight for. I'm the one that's been keeping the family honourable while you've been off flitting around. I've been shoring up our family's reputation with the right people too, probably higher than you've ever managed."

"You'd be surprised, brother."

"*Claudius and Lyle,*" Tyren mouthed.

Lolly shot him a sharp glare and he turned his gaze down to the hand she'd slapped. The tingles were still burning and the skin was red and puffy.

Almost like frostburns. Ouch, she put her gift behind it. He'd deserved it for grabbing her, he knew that, but still. *Ouch.*

"There's a war brewing, another one." Claudius sounded unconcerned about the idea.

Lyle huffed. "Of course there is. Do you really think the

Forgotten will ever give up? You'd have to obliterate entirely down to the root to get rid of them, and even then the ideals will linger on in the memories of the Fae."

"And what about you? Still crusading? You have extremely chatty lips normally, brother. Nothing you want to tell me?"

Tyren bit his lip. His dress shoes were digging into his feet and his trousers weren't exactly fit for squatting in. Lolly was no doubt used to crouching to look after plants and weed beds and all sorts of active pursuits to keep her fit, so she was balanced without even holding onto anything, her posture entirely still as she listened. He pressed his fingertips against the floor to steady himself, feeling oafish and ungainly beside her.

"Nothing that would change the tide of what's to come," Lyle said. "The queen is getting stronger and support for her reign is growing. The nobility will continue to weather the storm as they always have done – for their own interests. This revel is a cover for many underhanded dealings, but then I'm sure you of all people already knew that."

Claudius laughed. "How disappointing. We should get back before we're missed. I'd give up on chasing Lady Leilania around too if I were you. It's undignified to be slaving after a woman so obviously."

"I have my reasons. Unlike you, dancing with a low-born like the one from the Illusion Court."

"I have my reasons."

Tyren stayed where he was as their voices faded and the muffled thump of their footsteps disappeared. Lolly rose to her feet with all the grace of a noble, but he was beginning to worry that he might not make it if he tried to stand without holding onto something. Either that or he'd split his trousers.

He grabbed the workbench and eased himself up, but Lolly was already balancing on tiptoe with her nose pressed to the window, watching them leave. He wondered how she could be so still in her strapless dress and bare shoulders; he was shivering in a jacket from the wind whistling outside and pressing in on the glass of the greenhouses.

Does her human icicle gift make her immune to the cold? Maybe I should give her my jacket in case, but she'd probably sniff at the offering.

"That's got to be something, right?" she murmured. "Lyle mentioning the revel is a cover for underhanded things. We need to start checking everyone out, follow anyone suspicious. I have free reign so I've got an excuse, and my friends can go where they like."

He inched closer at the same moment she dropped her heels down and stepped back, right onto his foot.

"Ouch!" He hissed through his teeth as her heel crashed onto his toes.

This really was a cruddy day to wear shoes.

Even worse, she was frowning at him instead of apologising.

"What are you hovering behind me like that for? Come on, we should get back or the gossip mill will assume the worst. Perhaps we can break into their rooms and go through their stuff tomorrow, see if there's anything interesting in there."

She dodged around him, nimble on her bare feet, and set off at a sparking pace toward the exit. Tyren tapped his foot to shake some blood back into his poor toes and limped after her. She was right about one thing; the suggestion of the revel hiding evils was something he'd have to keep watch for.

She's also right we don't want the Fae to be gossiping about us. Although...

She grumbled under her breath as he hobbled past her and dodged to block her path again. She folded her arms tight and glowered up at him.

"It's not a bad idea," he said.

"What isn't?"

"The whole letting them think something's going on between us, give the gossips something to focus on so they're all distracted and assume we are too. Less chance they'll notice us asking questions then."

Lolly blinked. Frowned at him. Took a step back.

"I'm sorry, let me get this straight. You're saying you want me to be your fake girlfriend? Can't you get a real one then?"

"It makes perfect sense though, if we- hang on, of course I can get a real one!"

She grinned, a subtle Fae-like impishness sharpening her face, her eyes sparkling in the nearby firelight.

"You don't need to pretend with me, it's fine. I don't care if you can't get a girl to fancy you. But for what it's worth, I think it's a disastrous idea."

"I'm not pretending!" He paused to remind himself that attempting to pulverise her was a bad move. "Besides, it was just an idea. I don't see you coming up with anything helpful, except breaking into everyone's rooms which is madness."

His head was beginning to ache from the sheer hassle of dealing with her. He wanted a hot drink and a warm bed. But even though she was essentially doing his head right in, she was now shivering right in front of him, and both Fae manners and his own morality wouldn't allow him to leave her like that. He shrugged out of his jacket and held it out.

"What's this for?" she asked, staring at it.

He breathed deep and let it tumble out, fighting to keep his calm expression.

"It's a jacket. I wear it to look smart, but you should wear it to avoid the cold."

She frowned. "Because you want me to be your fake girlfriend?"

"Because you're cold, and it's the kind thing to do."

"But then you'll be cold."

Locking her in a room and pretending she'd gone missing occurred to him. Perhaps if he locked her in one of the greenhouses she'd even see it as a favour.

"I'm fine," he tried. "We'll be going inside in a minute anyway."

Again she gave him that disagreeable nose crinkle.

"Then why do I need to wear it?"

He clutched the jacket tight like an anchor in the chaos that was dealing with her.

"Fine, don't. Thank Faerie we're not doing the fake dating idea after all, because you're clearly awful at acting."

She turned her back on him and for a moment he stared at her shoulders, confused. Then he realised she was waiting for him to place the jacket on them. He did so, his mind a-whirl. He'd had a few girlfriends at the Revel Court but nobody had managed to catch his whole heart yet. Love he wasn't entirely sure about, but dating, that he could do.

As Lolly turned toward him with a suspiciously sweet smile on her face, he sent a silent prayer to Faerie and the nether that he didn't have to pretend to be interested in her after all.

"I may be awful at acting but I'm great at creeping around," she said. "Nobody sees me half the time, they're so used to me being wherever. I could be in and out of any room in the castle before anyone even noticed I was gone."

Tyren pulled a face. "Luckily for me, I haven't brought anything of value. Well, except a book or two. But don't tell Milo."

"Ooh, cool. Now I have something to bribe you with on top of everything, thanks."

He groaned and glanced the short distance toward the dining hall door. The guests would party into the night out of sheer spite, knowing that the hosts couldn't go to bed until they left. But he technically wasn't one of the hosts. Leaving Lolly to her fate had a certain petty malice to it, but he guessed his father would expect him to do his duty, and his Lord would be one of the last to roll into bed.

"Well, this has been fun, but I'm turning in early."

It was worth it to see the scandalised horror on her face.

"You can't! If you go to bed, I'll be left to the clutches of oafs like Lyle and Claus and half of Faerie!"

He held the grin back with valiant effort.

"I fail to see how that's my problem. Also, half of Faerie? Someone has a mighty high opinion of herself."

She rolled her eyes, her brow wrinkling in disgust. She was still barefooted in the cold air despite the addition of his jacket, but now he was worrying what people might think after all if they saw her entering wearing it. He could imagine the whispers:

'What is she doing with him?'

'Are they together?'

'Surely not, he's barely even nobility.'

'That'll make her even more desirable to the rest of the rabble though.'

'No doubt all part of her plan to find the right partner.'
'Or her mother's plan.'

It would give them an advantage of bringing all the eligible Fae visiting the court to chase her, but even she didn't deserve that. She hadn't answered him yet, no doubt trying to figure out a way to either cajole or bribe him into not leaving her defenceless on her own.

"Well then." She shrugged off his jacket and held it out. "Feel free to take your lack of problems to bed."

His fingers closed around the jacket before her words registered, but her hair almost whipped his face as she turned on her heel and stalked toward the dining hall door.

CHAPTER NINE
LOLLY

Lolly pushed open the door to the dining hall and slipped inside. If Tyren wanted to go to bed early, she wasn't going to hang around trying to convince him otherwise. It wasn't like she couldn't ask her friends to keep her busy dancing all night so nobody else got a look-in. She didn't need Mister High and Mighty from the Revel Court.

She kept the practiced smile on her face, aware of a few people turning to look at her as she stood and sought out her friends. She feigned ignorance as Tyren appeared beside her, his jacket back over his shoulders.

"Perhaps we should agree a truce," he muttered.

"I thought you were turning in early."

He sighed. "Come on, truce? If you're intent on stealing into people's rooms, you'll need a lookout."

She had a whole host of friends who would be more than happy to help her. She eyed Beryl, Meryl and Cheryl dancing like heathens in the middle of the floor, the Hutchinson brothers joining in with way less elegance, and Petra standing nearby with a hand over her face in disbelief. Lolly choked down a laugh.

Tyren might be the stealthier option.

"I have loads of people I could ask," she hesitated. "But none that will save me from dancing with Loudmouth Lyle. Orbs, you're not going to insist I dance with him next, are you?"

Both of them looked across the room. Lyle caught her eye and his entire body snapped up to attention, his shoulders squaring and his eyes taking on a determined gleam.

"Okay, here's the deal," Tyren said. "We work together. You don't threaten to hold my stuff over me until the revel is over and the crowds have left your court. If you involve me in what you're planning to do, I'll keep Lyle and any unnecessary suitors away from you."

She drew her gaze from the looming figure of Lyle and eyed Tyren instead.

"This isn't another attempt at the whole faking dating thing, is it?"

"No, Lolly, it's not."

He rubbed a hand over his forehead, mirroring Petra so much that she wanted to laugh.

At least he's got the hang of saying my name now.

"Alright, fine, truce. You'll have to help me with morning chores tomorrow though."

She held out her hand and he grabbed it, towing her past Lyle at speed without another word. A sneaky glance back as she turned to face Tyren, and Lyle was almost purple with frustration.

Claus stood watching at the other end of the dancefloor, his expression unreadable. He might be number one suspect on Tyren's list, but she couldn't deny he was good-looking in a traditional, ethereal beauty sort of way. Not that his beauty had any bearing on anything that mattered, and the whole lot of them would be gone in a few days anyway.

On top of that, she'd managed to secure Tyren's help for the morning routine, which meant she'd be done quicker and have more of the day to escape into her own errands. She wanted to ride out across the woods to check on the scrubland and see if the bulbs were breaking through yet; then she could judge just how much time this revel would have set her back by and how hard she'd have to work to get the brush cleared in time.

"Lolly?" Tyren squeezed her hand tight.

She flinched and turned her head to find him frowning at her. She'd been dancing with him but without paying attention. She still had the inane smile on her face, still masked to the watchful crowd, but he'd been shrewd enough to notice her mind wandering.

"Sorry, miles away. Did you say something?"

He shook his head. "Never mind. As much as I can keep you dancing, you know you'll need to chat to people, don't you? And so will I. Then when all this is over, I'll walk you to your room."

She raised her eyebrows at that.

"I'll walk you to yours, actually. You don't know where mine is and I'm going to keep it that way. I don't need a chaperone either."

He snorted and leaned close to her ear.

"I have absolutely no interest in your room, don't worry. It's all for appearances. Besides, it's not a chaperone you need, it's a keeper."

She slid her hand onto his shoulder, gripping tight. A couple booming with laughter swirled toward them, merry faces suggesting an intake of far too much wine, but Tyren swung her out of the way, his hold tightening to keep her steady.

"You're in danger of breaking your own truce," she murmured with a wide smile. "Such a shame. But then I suppose the Revel Court are supposed to be fickle and fair-weather. You may not like me much, but the whole working together was your idea, so don't be mean."

He frowned, but didn't argue. Instead, they danced so

effortlessly that her mind slid away from the dining hall completely, out of the door across the court and past the greenhouses into the woods.

"Do you ride?" she asked as the song ended. "Horses, I mean."

He nodded. "Enough to keep up. Why?"

She led the way across to the refreshment table towering with crystal punch bowls and delicately crafted pastries in the shape of swans or blossom trees. She reached for the nearest crystal ladle but Tyren's warm hand on her forearm stopped her. He filled two cups and handed her one.

"For appearances," he muttered.

"Thanks." She sipped the fragrant citrus wine and closed her eyes in relief. "Tomorrow morning, I need to ride out to the scrubland and check how much needs clearing still. You might as well see some of the actual court, and I'm betting there will be others who insist on going with us. You can ask them lots of questions."

He chuckled. "Is that your sneaky way of avoiding dealing with your guests, 'get Tyren to do it instead'?"

"Well, if it works, why not? You're clearly better with people than I am, and if we're going to achieve this we should make the most of our assets. So, are you interested in riding tomorrow morning?"

"I do want to see more of your court. It was so peaceful before everyone arrived, so I'd like to see the wilder side of it as well. We don't have much access to this style of nature at the Revel Court, and it gets a bit much sometimes."

Lolly couldn't help the surprise filtering across her face. Fae couldn't lie, but he sounded genuine instead of artful, no suggestion that he was word-tangling to impress her.

"What's it really like?" she asked. "I've heard the

market and performance square are enormous."

He glanced around at the dining hall and Lolly caught herself doing the same. Several people were still watching them, her parents included. Her mother was frowning but her mum looked decidedly smug.

"What's what really like?"

Lolly froze, a wave of icy revulsion waking up inside her as the indolent voice echoed to her left. She couldn't snub the Lord of Revels, even though his cool hand landed on her bare arm with an unnervingly firm grip. Tyren might have noticed her expression moments before she turned to face his lord, because he grabbed a large crystal glass of wine and passed it to him at such an angle he had to let Lolly's arm go.

"I was about to tell Lo-*ady* Leilania all the beauties of the Revel Court," he said smoothly.

The lord sank half the wine and laughed loudly, the sound rolling through the air like barrels.

"It'd definitely amaze and awe a country girl, that's for sure," he insisted.

Lolly noted the gems glinting on his fingers, the wide, open-necked black shirt of silk and the artful waves of dark hair around his face. If it weren't for tales of his more debauched behaviour, she would have put him as the star in a swoony romance novel. Like many of the higher nobility running courts, he was deceptively ageless in appearance. To her, he might choose to appear in his late teens or early twenties, and to her mother a middle-aged man.

She wouldn't see the real him, but she wondered if Tyren might have.

I should be asking Tyren way more questions than I have done. But right now I need to play host.

"I wouldn't assume that us country girls don't know a thing or two of our own about amazing and awing, my lord. Then again, what counts as sources of amazement can often vary from opinion to prejudice."

He blinked, momentarily unseated, and she took full advantage.

"If you'll excuse me, my lord. I believe I owe my friend a dance, and if there's one thing us country girls are *amazing* at, it's manners."

She inclined her head and wafted past Tyren, frantically scoping the crowd. She could interrupt the Eastwicks, but they were nowhere to be seen. Neither was Petra. Even her mum seemed to have disappeared.

"My Lady."

She was almost relieved to have Claus appear beside her. She gave him a wary look out of the corner of her eye.

"I won't admit to being without a dance partner," she said. "However, if you were inclined, I appear to have a momentary gap."

"Of course." He bowed low and held out his hand.

This should appease Tyren's plans at least. She shook her head slightly as Claus straightened up. *Not that I care two buds what Tyren thinks.*

His hand settled on her waist as they faced each other and she forced herself not to flinch.

"Can I speak honestly, Lady?" Claus asked.

Lolly nodded. "Might as well. I'm not very ladylike, so you'll get more sense out of me if you do."

"I believe my brother has certain designs on you. I don't want to give you the wrong idea, but consider this a warning."

She stiffened, but he had a firm hold and guided her around the floor without missing a step.

"What kind of warning? He's made it clear I'm on his tick-list of women, but I've got a court coming to me, so who isn't after me for my title in here?"

Claus smiled. It was a smile of spikes and sharpness, no warmth anywhere to be seen.

"I imagine there will be a couple about who aren't interested, but you're wise to be wary. The Lord of Revels is one to avoid, for example."

Lolly rolled her eyes. "Everyone in Faerie knows that. I don't need warnings to stay clear of people, don't worry. This revel, for example. The queen asked us to host and promote togetherness between the courts, but I bet a lot of Fae in here will be hoping for either drama or a chance to conduct their own devious activities."

She left the suggestion hanging, trying not to word herself too similarly to what she'd heard out by the greenhouses.

"A pretty face and a sharp mind." He whirled her in a circle and brought her back to him excruciatingly close. "You'd be wise not to dig too deeply, Lady. Leave the dramas to those that can handle them."

She tried to wriggle out of his grasp, but he clung on with impressive strength and she couldn't free herself without causing a scene. She danced closer instead, glaring at him with her eyes even as she smiled with her lips.

"Don't threaten me. The big, bad, scary Fae look is laughable on you."

He laughed. "Consider it a warning rather than a threat. You'd be wise to keep your guard up around your young Revel Court friend too."

Lolly twisted around as he nodded to Tyren who stood watching.

"Why?"

"Because, Lady, he has his own agenda by many accounts."

She'd guessed as much when Tyren arrived, that he was spy for the Revel Court sent to placate and tail her. The Lord of Revels would be too public a target to go snooping, but of course Tyren would be able to move around, make friends at most levels of the hierarchy, and also attempt to charm her into telling him all sorts.

She smirked. *He's not doing very well on that side though, if he is meant to be charming me.*

"She smiles," Claus said. "I warn her and she smiles. Perhaps you've got your own agenda."

Lolly shrugged as the song ended and she could finally tear herself free of his hold.

"Everyone has an agenda, I just don't make any secret of mine."

His eyes bore into hers, the tiny quirk on the corner of his lips suggesting he was still trying to charm her despite his attempt to either threaten or frighten her.

"And what is yours?" he asked.

"The wellbeing of my court, the advancement of Faerie and the growth of our natural resources. I don't see any of that as a bad thing, so I don't need to skulk behind silly warnings and word-tangling."

He nodded, the smile slipping to reveal a serious expression and a flash of grave darkness beneath.

"Then don't allow me to keep you, Lady. I believe your young man is waiting."

His gaze drifted past her shoulder and she guessed he meant Tyren. Refusing to give in and look, she lifted her chin in defiance.

"Then he can go on waiting. Excuse me."

She set off across the dancefloor with her attention

focused on anyone who might approach her. She still couldn't see any of her friends, but she smiled to anyone who noticed her, nodding and smiling and smiling and nodding and wishing every single one of them was somewhere very far away.

Several of the guests would be staying at court for tomorrow's revel, and she had no idea what exactly the Revel Court would have prepared for them.

I could ask Tyren, but I've run the other way now.

"Lolly!"

She twisted around to find Meryl hurrying toward her, bright blue hair bobbing around her shoulders and the skirts of her jewel blue gown fluttering around her legs.

"Come with me."

Meryl grabbed her arm and tugged, but Lolly was already moving forward.

"Don't need to ask me twice," she muttered. "I'm danced out and peopled out and I'm never hosting ever again."

Meryl laughed. "This may well cheer you up. It's a surprise, but we have your mum's permission."

That sounded interesting and Lolly's anticipation began to run riot on her imagination.

"Aren't you going to give me a clue?" she asked.

"Nope. Oh, hang on. Your mum's condition. Um, you wait in the conservatory. I'll be back in a second."

Meryl all but threw her through the door to the conservatory and shut it behind her. Alone, Lolly closed her eyes and wrapped her hands around the back of her neck with a groan. Her body ached from all the hovering and dancing. She was dehydrated and tired from working so hard on the greenhouses and so late on her index. She wanted her bed, but at least Meryl's surprise would be something good. Her friends had never let her down yet.

Weird that my mum gave them a condition though. Maybe something to do with not abandoning the guests for too long.

She turned back as the dining room door swung open and Meryl hurried toward her.

With Tyren in tow.

"Why not just tell me where we're going?" he asked, his tone placid.

Meryl rolled her eyes. "Because then it won't be a surprise. Okay, it's not a surprise for you as such, but if I tell you, you'll tell Lolly, then it won't be a surprise."

"I wouldn't tell her."

"I don't want him to tell me!" Lolly protested.

Meryl eyed her up and down, then summoned fresh clothing under one arm with a snap of her fingers.

"Nip behind the fountain and throw those on," she insisted. "You too, Tyren."

Lolly took the clothing without protest and hurried behind the stone fountain.

"How do you know these will fit?" Tyren asked.

"I don't, but you're roughly the right size for them. Go on, quick. Lolly knows you won't look."

Lolly snorted. "He better not."

She slid the trousers over her legs, revelling in the freedom of being in comfortable clothing once again. They were hers, as was the sweatshirt she pulled on after wriggling out of the dress and leaving it draped over the ledge of the fountain. Someone might see it and assume the worst, but she couldn't bring herself to care about that when adventure beckoned.

She emerged with a satisfied sigh, giving Tyren a serene grin as he stomped past her.

"Seriously, give me a clue," she begged Meryl.

"Nope."

"Please!"

"Nope."

"Just one?"

"Alright."

"Really?!"

"No!"

She started laughing as Tyren reappeared, his suit over his arm along with Lolly's dress. Meryl grabbed them from him, ignoring his huff of protest.

"I'll just magic these away," she snapped her fingers. "There we go. Come on now, keep up."

Lolly hurried along beside her, aware of Tyren right behind them as they crossed the conservatory and exited through the courtyard to find Beryl, Cheryl, Hutch and Harvey waiting outside.

"What's this about?" she asked.

"We're kidnapping you," Cheryl declared. "We've been tasked with helping the Revel Court set up while everyone else parties, and your mum said she didn't see why you had to miss out on the "punishment" as well."

Lolly grinned. She had expected Tyren to ask her a couple of questions after his statement about taking down castle walls, but being able to actually pitch in was much more her style.

"That is the best news I've heard all day." She turned to face Tyren. "Is this a 'you' thing then? Do you know what needs to be done?"

He cast a glance over the assembled group, his eyes narrowing as he pointed toward Hutch and Harvey.

"Well to start with, those two look far too pleased with themselves, which means something is either going to explode or they've hidden something."

Normally it would have been hard to tell the two brothers apart based on physical features, aside from Hutch being ever so slightly taller. But one had dyed his brown hair the same vivid green as Cheryl's, and the other had copied Beryl's deep purple. Lolly still didn't know which was which, but at least it would keep them sort of separated in her mind.

Tyren folded his arms across his chest as the one with purple hair gasped.

"How can you accuse us of such things?"

The green-haired one tutted. "He doesn't trust us, Harv. After all we've done for him."

Lolly stared back and forth between them and Tyren with amusement. He seemed more relaxed around them than he did her, but then they'd been biting at each other since he arrived.

Tyren shook his head. "Not buying it. Own up. Hutch?"

The brothers exchanged a glance and the green-haired one sighed.

"Alright, we *may* have liberated some of the fireworks for personal use. They weren't in the right place, nobody would have seen them go off from there. We're going to set them off after the main display with a little added flair."

Tyren pressed a hand to his face. Lolly grinned, for all of two seconds until he swung around to look at her.

"This is your party overall. Do they have permission?"

She blinked. Tyren asking her instead of condescending to her?

The roots of Faerie must have burned to ash for such a miracle to occur. She stifled a snicker.

"Are they safe?" she asked. "I'm reluctant to trust anyone who finds these three sensible company."

She flicked a hand to the Eastwick sisters and ignored the round of indignant squawking.

"Mostly. Nobody will get hurt. Might have a few shocks here and there though."

Lolly nodded. "A few shocks is fine with me. Fae always expect something a bit extra."

Tyren's groan suggested she'd made the wrong choice, in his opinion at least, but he was drowned out by the brothers cheering.

"So, what do we need to do?" Lolly asked. "Stand here all night?"

Beryl gave her a not-so-gentle prod in the arm.

"Nope. We're going to the lower meadow to help put up awnings and build the bonfire. Mabon is tomorrow as well, so no doubt there'll be a theme." She eyed Tyren doubtfully. "Is there a theme?"

He returned the look a lot more wearily before straightening up.

"Why don't you come and see?"

Lolly had to hide a yawn behind her hand, and promised herself she'd get a couple of hours sleep before morning chores started.

If Tyren was nice to her for the rest of the night, she'd consider letting him off joining her for morning chores and the ride to the scrubland.

Maybe.

CHAPTER TEN
REYAN

Reyan eyed the beautiful floral bouquets in ornate white vases spread throughout the Flora Court's communal bathroom as she wiped her hands on the plush towel provided. Straight after Demi's arrival, some woman she didn't recognise asked to dance with Kainen and he couldn't exactly refuse. Reyan had stepped aside with jealousy burning in her gut, but rather than be stuck watching him flirt effortlessly with someone else, she'd fled to the bathroom. Perhaps if she timed it right, she could be the one to intercept them the moment the song ended, but she couldn't hear the music anymore to know when to return.

The door to the hall swung open but she stayed by the corner sink, hidden by another enormous floral arrangement.

"I'll be returning soon."

A female voice filled the air and Reyan froze. She recognised both the voice and the snooty tone within it. She dropped the towel onto the counter and inched closer to the giant vase, using it for shelter as she peered out at Lady Blossom, princess of Faerie, Taz's sister and her enemy. Blossom had designs on Kainen which made them at odds with each other, but anyone with a brain could guess that Blossom hadn't renounced the Faerie ways, and Reyan had more experiences with her to prove that fact.

"You can't, not yet." A sharper female voice snapped. "The market is holding for now and your task is to keep the blood-rats busy. Is your glamour holding?”

Reyan couldn’t see whose face was projecting out of the orb hanging from Blossom’s fingers, but given the way the speaker was addressing a princess of Faerie, her money was on Belladonna, the princess that had openly defected and joined the Forgotten during the last war.

“I’m in a bathroom don’t worry, there’s nobody here. But yes, I’m fine holding a simple glamour. Nobody will know I’m here until I officially ‘arrive’ tomorrow.”

“Good. I can’t have you screwing this up, not this time.”

Blossom huffed. “I know what I’m doing. The smoother this goes, the quicker I’ll return and all the better for it because Merle is the only person who can alter shoes to my liking, and I’ve invested handsomely in her stall at the market.”

A moment of silence filled the air and Reyan dredged the shadows around her, dissipating her body until it became an outline of darkness with only her head remaining as a fleshy part able to listen.

“Honestly, when this is all over you can find yourself a thousand Merle’s,” Belladonna said. “Although I’ll admit she does superb work. But shoes are the least of our concerns right now. Have you discovered anything?”

“Not exactly. The queen is here with our brother. The Lady of Words is absent, but her stepsons are here. Kainen is here with that absolute horror-”

“I don’t care about that. Doesn’t matter who’s there.”

“Fine, I was just saying. Claus looks like he’s failing to get Leilania on side so far, which means we may need to find another way to bring them to our cause, and obviously we’ve got no hope of the Illusion Court supporting us willingly. Lord Rydon of the Fauna Court is here, but I think he might need some more determined persuasion from my conversation with him."

"Right, that's enough for now then. Do your job and get back here. You'll need to be seen in the market before making your visible entrance at the Flora Court."

"I will."

Silence fell again and Reyan waited as Blossom slid her orb into the pocket of her jeans, then glamoured herself into a mature woman with black hair and an exquisite gown of white laid with pearls.

Even after Blossom left under her new glamour, Reyan stayed behind the vase, her mind thundering.

It wasn't a surprise the Forgotten would be trying to curry favour and convince the courts to support them, but Blossom being here in disguise was something she hadn't expected somehow.

Only the thought of Kainen wondering where she was guided her out from her hiding place as she took on her normal form and left the bathroom. She almost missed the patter of feet approaching and looked up in alarm as the queen stopped in front of her.

"I'm sorry to do this…"

Every time Demi announced she was sorry, it was always followed by a "but". She trailed off with a grimace but Reyan leapt in before Demi could ask the inevitable favour.

"I have something to share with you actually," she whispered.

Demi nodded and drew her to the end of the hall. While Reyan cloaked the shadows around them, Demi warded them against being heard by unexpected ears.

"Lady Blossom was speaking to someone on the orb, sounded like Belladonna. I didn't see to be sure, but Blossom mentioned returning soon and Belladonna refused to let her. She also mentioned a market and needing to keep the blood-rats, I'm guessing that's us, busy."

Demi frowned. "Blossom's here, under a glamour I'm guessing?"

"Yeah, woman, black hair, white dress with pearls. Also she mentioned Claus, that's Claudius Auren, and how he's not having much luck with Lady Leilania and that they know our court won't support them. Something about the Fauna Court as well needing a more determined approach."

Demi folded her arms across her chest and sighed.

"Worrying but not surprising. I've met Claudius before and I'm not so concerned with him right now, but we need to be on our guard as expected."

"She also said about wanting to be back for the market," Reyan added. "Something about Merle being the only person capable of altering shoes. Could she mean the Revel court? It's the biggest market in Faerie and the most prestigious for elite Fae if you know where to go."

Reyan glanced around them but the hall was completely silent, the shadows still and unruffled.

"I can ask Tyren if he knows a Merle who fixes shoes," Demi said. "That actually ties in very nicely with what I was going to ask you for though. Most of the nobility are here, so I was wondering if you'd visit someone. She's apparently very ancient and twice as cranky, but she hates men so I can't ask anyone else. The Eastwicks won't have the tact and Petra's got her hands full with helping Lolly set up for tomorrow."

Reyan nodded with a weary sigh. "I'll do it. Let me tell Kainen and I'll go now."

"Anything to be out of a dress?" Demi asked with a grin.

"Kind of. Not the dress, but I'm people'd out."

"Oh orbs, me too. I'd give anything not to be queen for a week, which is an awful thing to say I know."

"I imagine it's really stressful. Being a lady of a court has had hardly any responsibilities for me so far and I'm still overwhelmed by it."

"He's treating you okay?"

Reyan understood why Demi wanted to ask given the history she had with Kainen, but even the subtle suggestion of his past now that she knew a lot more of the truth of it, set a possessive irritation inside her.

"Like a queen actually."

Her tone was bordering on icy in an instant, and Demi raised both hands with a surprised chuckle.

"I didn't mean any harm by it. Most court lords have a reputation for many scandalous things, not just him."

Allowing her temper to settle, Reyan managed a penitent smile and tugged at her necklace chain with awkward regret. Queen or not, Fae or not, Demi had been really kind to her so far and here she was snapping at her.

"It's… kind of a mess," she admitted. "But we'll work it out. Right, Revel Court. Where's this woman you want me to speak to?"

Demi eyed her for a moment. "At the north end of the market there's a flower shop that's always closed, and behind it a dusty path leading up the hill. Follow that, pass the charred barn and turn right at the field of bluegrass. You'll find a cottage with a grass roof. We don't have her name, but ask her about the Flow of Origins. We need to know how to get into the Prime Realm. If you happen to see anything Forgotten-related on your way through, well, that's a bonus. Hold still."

Reyan froze, her muscles cramping from the sudden

shock as Demi veered toward her. She couldn't do a single thing as Demi swiped the quickest, lightest kiss on her forehead before stepping back.

"I know your shadows let you travel through the dark, and you have a transmutation gift, but now you can realm-skip anywhere same as Kainen can. If you're ever in any kind of trouble you can get yourself home or to my court, or anywhere without having to exhaust yourself travelling the shadows."

Amazed, Reyan touched the spot on her forehead that was still tingling with the residual Fae magic as it leaked through her entire body.

"Thank you."

Kainen's going to be pissed. She snickered, earning her a bemused look from Demi.

She flinched as the familiar masculine voice echoed right back in reply.

Kainen's going to be pissed about what?

Demi grinned and stepped back, vanishing the sound-protection around them.

"Go, before he starts threatening people," she said.

Reyan laughed and stepped past her, then turned back after a few steps.

"Can you hear… you know? Like thoughts? Mine and his?" She had to ask.

Demi smiled wide. "That would be telling."

Then she vanished, leaving Reyan alone in the hall. The door to the dining hall opened a moment later, letting in a blast of noise and sending the shadows scattering around her. Kainen stalked along the hall, his face set in irritable determination.

"You didn't answer me," he said.

He stopped in front of her, frowning down. She tilted

her head back slightly, smiling up.

"I was talking to Demi. You interrupted."

The frown deepened. "What did she want?"

"She's asked me to go visit someone and ask more about the Flow of Origins."

"Why?"

"Um… because she needs someone to go? Oh, and the woman hates men apparently, so no, you can't go with me."

"Where?"

She folded her arms, amused by the snappy tone and one-word demands. Had he assumed she was locked in some passionate affair with some random person in a dark corner? Would he care beyond for the sake of appearances if she had been?

"Same place as the last three weeks, different person. She gave me a gift too. I can now officially realm-skip at will whenever I need to."

She half expected him to get fussy about losing the excuse to take her places, but his shoulders lowered slightly instead.

"At least I'll know you can get yourself to anywhere that's safe." He sighed. "Fine. I'm due back at the court tonight, but how about you orb me to let me know you're okay this time?"

She grinned. "Or you orb me updates to keep me entertained on my arduous journey."

Her insides flipped when he reached out and smoothed her hair back, his warm fingertips gliding over her cheek.

"Are you sure?" he asked. "You want me to orb you updates? Keep you in the know about where I am? What I'm doing? What I'm thinking?"

She nodded before she recognised the subtle sparkle of

wickedness in his brown eyes.

"I'm going to regret that, aren't I," she grumbled.

"Absolutely. Let me take you back though now, for old time's sake?"

She nodded. "I have to change first. Let me try skipping to the court to make sure I can do it."

He stepped back but she could see his fingers itching to grab hers.

"Imagine yourself there and visualise your body reappearing, the room forming around you," he explained. "It's probably the same as your shadow-merging."

She nodded and closed her eyes. Even as she began to imagine her bedroom at court and set her intention behind the desire to relocate herself, the visual morphed and took shape around her, but it wasn't her bedroom that was tumbling into place. It was his.

Opening her eyes, she let her breathing steady with relief as she looked around at the familiar furnishings and dark walls.

Okay so I ended up in the wrong bedroom but at least I'm in the right court.

Kainen's multi-purpose door flew open, banging back against the wall. She raised her eyebrows as he swept in, his entire body vibrating with tension.

"There you are." He hid his worry badly for one so adept at wearing masks of confidence. "What made you choose my room?"

She shrugged. "I didn't choose it. I thought of my room and ended… well, I thought of mine, then yours popped into my head and I sailed right in."

He leaned back against the post of his bed, a cocky smirk replacing the anxious frown.

"Great. So I can expect you turning up at inappropriate

moments like when I'm changing or in the bath? Although…"

He let that tease land unspoken as she gave him a weary look and swept through the still open doorway that had her room visible on the other side.

"I won't damage your collection of rubber ducks, don't worry," she called back.

"*Secret* collection of rubber ducks." He huffed after her. "I meant it. You're welcome to turn up anytime you like, in any state, even if I'm-"

With a broad grin, she shut the door on him and silence fell. She changed quickly into her comfiest clothes and packed a bag. It didn't sound like such a long journey to take from the instructions Demi had given her, but she couldn't risk it by being careless.

Flower shop, path uphill, charred barn, right at bluegrass, cottage with grass roof.

She repeated the instructions over to herself until they were burned into her brain. Kainen might even be able to skip her straight to the flower shop and save her blundering through the labyrinthine alleyways of the market. With one final check of her bag, full of long-life snacks and two changes of clothes, she glamoured herself into the woman who had spent three weeks at Arlen's.

She'd started with waving long red hair but quickly decided she preferred it shoulder-length, glamoured or not. Her face was thinner and her eyes a bright green instead of hazel-grey, but when she rejoined Kainen in his room, he pulled a face.

"What?" she complained.

"You don't look like you."

"Kind of the point. Wait, how did you know it was really me?"

He sighed. "I'd know you anywhere, sweetheart. Come on. Sooner you get this done, sooner you can come home."

"Aww, miss me bad, huh?" she teased. "You can't live without someone commenting on your awful housekeeping habits?"

He pouted. "Do you want me to take you or not?"

"Of course. Can't have you feeling redundant. I need to get to the flower shop at the very north end of the market to start with."

He grabbed her hand and pulled her close enough that the breath seemed to fly out of her body. She stared up at the shadowy brown eyes inches from her own, wondering madly if he'd finally give in and kiss her properly.

Seconds passed without either of them moving, eyes locked. Reyan almost crumpled with sheer disappointment as the nether folded around them and dissipated to reveal the north end of the Revel Court market.

Even though it had been evening at the Flora Court, and she had no idea what time at their own, the Revel Court was in the hottest throes of midday sun. The air plumed with the incessant smell of food and her stomach growled in protest. She hadn't eaten breakfast before leaving to go back to the court for her dress, nor had she eaten anything from the buffet at the Flora court. Now she'd bounced back and forth between realm-times so much she wanted to sleep for a week.

"Are you okay?" Kainen asked.

He hadn't let go of her hand or stepped back at all, or stopped staring at her. She nodded even though the hunger and the sudden heat made her feel queasy. She pulled her large bag around to her front and rifled inside it until she came up with a sturdy fabric hat that had a brim all the way around.

"I'll eat something on my way up the hill."

His hold on her tightened.

"We'll eat something now, and something proper. There must be restaurants near here that serve lunch."

"We can't be seen. I'm glamoured and you'll draw too much attention when we're supposed to be at the revel still. Go back, play the part. I'll be home before you know it." His moody expression didn't lift, so she tried something else. "If you're lucky, I'll take you for lunch at this really nice place in the market once this is all over."

He raised his eyebrows and said nothing for a long moment. She wondered if he was warring with the idea of her treating him to lunch or thinking of something else entirely.

"I'll hold you to that. Be careful."

"I will. I checked on Betty as well and she's fast asleep in my wardrobe, but if I don't make it back straight away can you just look in on her?"

He frowned. "You can skip at will, so I'm expecting you back at the Flora Court in a few hours, dress or no dress. Worst case skip home and I'll come to you. Any longer than a couple of hours and I'm coming back to get you."

"It might take longer than that."

"Then orb me. I'm serious. And the moment you see the slightest bit of trouble, you skip to me, okay?"

She nodded. "I'll be fine. I'm going to see an ancient lady to ask a question, not going into battle."

He pulled a face. "Could easily be the same thing."

She took a step back, aware he was trying to prolong her leaving.

"You waiting to watch me walk away or what?" she asked, her tone gentle.

He smiled, but it was wistful and somehow sad.

"No, I won't do that. Be careful, and if you can't be careful, come home."

She held still as he swept the gentlest kiss over her cheek and vanished in a plume of glittering smoke.

Alone with only her thoughts and her belongings for company, Reyan dug an energy ring from her bag and munched on it as she set off up the hill. She had no idea what went into them, but the *oia* berry flavour ones were her favourite.

Something that the court didn't often have until Kainen named me Lady.

She set her pace with determination. Kainen was right; the quicker she found the old woman and got what she needed, the quicker she'd get to go home to him.

CHAPTER ELEVEN
TYREN

After several hours of putting up marquees and decorations around a huge bonfire, Tyren fell into bed and passed out without a single thought in his head. He was pretty sure the Hutchinson brothers had hidden their illicit fireworks in the bonfire, but he knew them well enough to trust they'd done it safely.

Lolly had even offered to let him off the deal of morning duties, but he made sure he was awake and moving about at dawn all the same. The chance to see the Flora Court's realm was one that didn't come about often by all accounts, and he wanted to be one of those fabled few. Rumour said it was awash with natural beauty, something that the Revel Court seriously lacked with its tall buildings all crammed in on one another and the constant crowds in the central and outlying markets. He'd ventured outside of the Revel City many times, but the land was flat and full of barren rock and gnarled bushes, aside from the rows of golden and purple fields of the maize and lavender farms.

He dressed smartly in a black shirt and black jeans, glad he could wear his normal boots instead of the dress shoes from the night before.

She won't be able to keep stamping on my foot so easily in these.

He smirked at the mirror and grabbed the coffee that had appeared in his room when he woke, along with some delicate pastries oozing purple jam and a huge platter of various fruits. He thought of the kitchens and the cook he'd met the night before as he left his room.

Lolly seemed on friendly terms with everyone around her, lively and kind. Except him. He'd already decided during the long stint of labour the night before that he would try to be less reactive to her, but it was baffling that she could even manage to ruffle him.

He had no idea where she would be, so he trotted down the stairs she'd shown him the night before and along the corridor to the door outside. The chilly dawn air was fresh and the wind still, the greenhouses cloaked in darkness. He searched for any sign of light or life but it seemed he'd even beaten Lolly.

He stood a while longer to watch the sky pale from inky to lilac, the sun rising over the woods and casting the court in a soft golden glow.

It was the silence that captivated him. Not a whisper from the world or the court behind him, just a soft cocoon of nothing except for the occasional far-off noise from the woods.

"It's best seen in the still hours."

Lolly's voice was hushed with reverence as she appeared beside him. He glanced at her, taking in the tired eyes and her slumped shoulders. All the spark and fight seemed to have settled inside her in view of the peace around them, and he wondered if this was how she often was when guests weren't traipsing noisily around her court demanding things.

"It's beautiful," he agreed. "I want it to stay like this forever."

She chuckled softly. "So do I sometimes. But other times, noise and activity is fun. And necessary. Last chance to bow out of chores. We're short-handed so if you pitch in you'll need to keep up."

"No bowing out. Just tell me what you need me to do."

It might have been a flash of surprise crossing her face, or maybe doubt that he'd be able to keep up. But she only shrugged and started toward one of the greenhouses.

"Lolly!"

The peace was broken by the shout that echoed too loud in the otherwise silent air.

"Crud," Lolly muttered.

They turned back to face the castle and Petra hurrying toward them.

"Nice try, but you can't escape me for long." Petra's dark hair was escaping its long braid and she looked stressed already. "I'm doing your chores this morning- no, don't argue. I can ask for help where I need it from the other workers. You're to get dressed and be seen at the morning meal, then join the rest of the hoity-toities at the revel."

Tyren almost took a step back. If looks could kill, Lolly would have been beaming lethal ice-spikes from her eyes.

"I hate being noble," she muttered. "Hate it. Hate it hate it hate it hat-"

"That's great, but doesn't get you out of doing it. At least Tyren's been thrown in with you."

Tyren blinked. "I'm sorry, what now?"

Petra's unnervingly devious grin didn't inspire him with any hope for the rest of his day.

"The Lord of Revels has um… well putting it bluntly he's out of action because someone slipped him something that makes it *imprudent* to let him leave his room." She pulled a disapproving face. "He has company so he won't mind I'm sure, but when his entourage were asked for a stand-in, your name came out unanimously."

Lolly eyed him warily, but he was too busy panicking

to care about her doubts on his suitability.

"What does standing in involve?" he asked. "Surely not take his place?"

Petra nodded. "Essentially, yes. You'll be a figurehead. Fits perfectly with everything else as you're expected to trail Lolly around anyway. It's just another convenient excuse for you to be seen doing it."

"But-"

"There aren't any specific expectations," she continued. "Oh, except the speech, but you two can sort that between you. I'll be getting along to my chores then."

She made to walk past them but Lolly was in front of her with hands on her shoulders before she could so much as lift her foot.

"I've already prepared my speech! We don't have time to merge them, and he doesn't even have one. Is this my mother's doing?"

Tyren rubbed his hands over his face with a groan.

"I wrote my lord's speech, so I'll stick to that. It'll be fine. If we're hosting though, we should go and change. Argh, I hate wearing dressy shoes."

Lolly wrinkled her nose. "Then don't. Wear boots and say I insisted. This is already the most ridiculous farce in all of Faerie, might as well be comfortable doing it."

She let Petra go and they stood watch her walk away toward the nearest greenhouse.

"Come on then." He sighed. "We'll have to change."

Lolly shook her head and stepped back, looking him up and down with narrowed eyes.

"No need. Any requests? Never mind."

She snapped her fingers, wiggling them in random motions. Tyren flinched as the tingle of magic filtered over his skin, but his bulky sweater became a neat black cotton shirt, his black jeans becoming smarter than the pair he'd been wearing and a blood-red jacket piped with silver falling over his shoulders. She left the boots as they were but with a frown at them and a twitch of her fingers, they shone like new.

He watched her shoulders sag even lower like a sack of tumbling potatoes, but asking if she'd bothered to sleep at all might sound like he was insulting her appearance.

"Thanks." He gave himself a final once-over. "What about you?"

She sighed and clicked her fingers again, sweeping a lazy hand in front of her chest. A simple knee-length dress of dark green velvet with a flared skirt replaced the cardigan and jeans she'd been wearing, her delicate feet becoming bare.

"That's as good as I'm going to get," she said. "Don't let anyone talk to me before I've eaten something."

He frowned and fell in step with her back toward the castle.

"You didn't get the fruit and pastries in your room?"

"Fruit and pastries?"

He grimaced. "Must be a guest thing. Here."

He pulled out the small bag from his pocket that he'd wrapped one of the pastries in along with some napkins. She stared at it as he held it out to her, then at him, before taking it and digging in.

"Wow, they really do feed the guests well." She chuckled. "We usually make our own food here, even my mother does. Everyone else is always busy. Thanks, this is good."

Tyren glanced back at the greenhouses as he held the castle door open for her. It seemed she was so tired she didn't even remember to argue with him about who went through first, and given that she'd been on her way to start her chores when she found him, he wondered how often she forgot to eat.

That thought nagged at him for all of three steps through the castle hall before she whirled around, arms flying out until she anchored them across her chest, a suspicious frown on her face.

"Claus said- well, intimated really, that I shouldn't be trusting you. Not that I do, not blindly, because I don't know you, but why would he say that?"

Why indeed. Tyren hesitated. *I don't know him. He doesn't know me. I doubt my name is known enough even in the Revel Court to make any salacious rumours about me.*

"I have no idea," he said.

Her face scrunched even more. "You don't know him? Or have some hideous secret I should know about?"

The sensible thing would be to reassure her, but having such doubt thrown in his face early in the morning made him feel reckless, especially after she'd admitted she didn't trust him despite him being nothing but open and helpful to her.

"If I did have a hideous secret, what are the chances I'd blurt it out simply because you're glowering at me?"

He'd stunned her momentarily speechless. She blinked at him and visions of her mind whirring and getting repeatedly stuck flickered in his head. Strangely, it wasn't the elated victory he'd assumed it would be.

"So, you do have a secret?"

She rubbed a hand over her face, giving her shoulders and head a rough shake as if to wake herself up.

Tyren grimaced. Now was not the time to be feeling guilty for goading her, but somehow he couldn't help it.

"I don't have any secrets," he confirmed. "None that you should know about anyway."

He twisted the words a little to cover the fact his lord had told him to spy on the Flora Court. He was feeling oddly guilty about that too now that he'd seen the place and met its people.

Her suspicion didn't abate but she turned and set off in the direction of the dining hall. He found it easy to stride at her side this time, regretting needling her already as she ambled along.

"Do you have any secrets?" he asked against his better judgement.

She flicked a glare at him, but it lacked the usual disparaging vehemence as they crossed the conservatory.

"If I did, would I blurt it out simply because you asked?" she retorted.

He held the door to the dining hall open, a waft of chatter and enticing scents from the tables laden with food spilling out. Even though he'd eaten well, his stomach grumbled loudly.

Not mine, hers. He was amazed the sound could have travelled to his ears so loudly. *And Mila in the kitchens said she often forgets to eat.*

"Right, food, come on."

He held his elbow out to her. She stared at it, then at him. He rolled his eyes.

"Take my arm and let me lead you in." He rushed on as she opened her mouth to argue. "No agenda, nothing sinister. As much as you passing out from exhaustion and hunger would get us out of this, we do have a job to do."

She took a deep breath and nodded. Slid her fingers around the crook of his elbow. Then a mask of polite civility fell over her face to hide the tiredness and she dragged him into the room.

She called greetings to people they passed tables, smiled prettily and clung onto his arm like a lifeline.

Tyren allowed her to drag him the long way around the breakfast tables but tilted his body this way and that to guide her toward the buffet table on the far side of the room to Arthur. He knew without asking that the rebellious plant would probably eat straight from the buffet trays if given the chance. Lolly stood with her back to the food while he piled up a plate of pastries and fruit.

"So, I'm going to ask him what he meant," she muttered.

Tyren held the plate in front of her.

"Eat. You mean ask him about me?"

She nodded, grabbing the nearest pastry and pulling tiny bits off to eat. It seemed to be worrying her, or sticking on her mind at least, but he had nothing to hide from her aside from the spying issue. Several embarrassing stories from child and teen-hood he wanted to take to his grave? Definitely. But big secrets that would be of interest to her beyond tormenting him for fun? None at all.

Does that make me boring?

He shrugged.

"Ask him what you like. But our mission today-" He hesitated and leaned close, lowering his voice to a whisper. "Our mission today is to find any people who might be Forgotten-sworn. Then we report back to the queen."

He cast a glance over the crowd but the queen and king consort were nowhere to be seen. The Marnins however, they were on their way over at great speed.

"Look alive," he muttered.

"Thanks." She held the plate out to him.

He put it on the table for her, amazed to realise those

tiny bites she'd been taking had finished off the whole lot.

Feed her and she's more amenable, good to know.

"Arch and Archess Marnin, good morning to you," Lolly said with a serene smile.

Tyren noted the Arch and Archess pretending not to sneer down their noses at her, but it meant they weren't paying attention to him slipping a few pastries into napkins and into his pockets. For safety's sake.

"Lady Leilania, morning." Arch Marnin gave her a stiff nod. "I hope the festivities are going to be of standard today. We're missing the events at Gallows Oak for this."

Tyren stiffened. The insult was for Lolly and her court, but by mentioning the day's events he'd also ringfenced an insult to the Revel Court in that.

Lolly smiled smugly. "I'm sure they will be. The Revel Court is well-versed in throwing parties. Although I understand the Lord of Revels has imbibed a little too heavily, but no matter. Lord Tyren has kindly agreed to act in his stead."

Tyren froze. Then the words tumbled out of his mouth before he could find some other way to pass over the inaccuracy.

"I'm no lord."

Is she trying to insult me with that? Have I offended her? I can't think how. I've been nothing but helpful this morning.

Inadequacy filtered through him. All lords and ladies of courts had certain allowances to petition elevation of their favourites to titles. The titles themselves didn't have to come with any land or wealth, it was more a recognition, but his lord had never bothered rewarding him or his father.

The Marnins looked delighted at the sleight, but Tyren's

heart plummeted. He could hope that Lolly was simply playing the part, but he barely knew her.

She raised her eyebrows without looking at him.

"Oh. That's disappointing. So your Lord of Revels doesn't recognise Fae or fairies who show loyalty or effort to the court. We certainly do, and I know the queen actively encourages it. I'll ask her. But I'm sure, Arch and Archess, that you will be suitably approving of the festivities."

Tyren searched the words for some kind of trap or trick, but he couldn't find one. It wasn't a sleight against him but against his lord. Which was technically supposed to be against his court, which he should defend automatically. The Arch and Archess were waiting for his response, keen faces fixed on him.

"I'm sure that's not necessary, Lady," he said, finding some hint of his previous social smoothness. "I agree that everyone will be impressed by the revel though. Our court will happily live up to its name."

Their disappointment was almost worth it, but he was still perturbed by Lolly's insistence she would speak to the queen on his behalf. She couldn't lie, but then again she'd said she would ask, but not what she would ask. It would be easy to avoid any mention of him at all with that level of vagueness. It didn't dim the sudden wash of warmth kindling inside him any.

"I'm very much looking forward to it."

The queen's voice filled the air and forced all four of them to twist sideways. She wore flowing green velvet trousers and a long-sleeved grey t-shirt with red and silver sparkles on it. Milo and the king consort stood behind her, Milo already flapping around with several pieces of paper and an expression that suggested she'd left her rooms without attending to most of them.

The queen held up a hand before Tyren could drop to his knees, although he noticed the Marnins had already dipped their heads and had no intention of bowing or kneeling. Lolly was already down and he noticed the wash of exhaustion slip across her face as her head bowed.

"No need for that," the queen insisted. "I'm going to put you in another tizz I'm afraid, because Taz's sister has insisted she wants to be here and she'll need a room somewhere."

"Doesn't have to be anything posh," the king consort added. "Room in the barn will do."

Lolly snorted and Tyren shot out a hand before she could show any signs of struggling to her feet. He guided her up and caught the subtlest squeeze of thanks from her fingers before she pulled away.

"We wouldn't room Fae in the barns," she insisted. "The horses wouldn't tolerate it. Neither would the plants so the greenhouses are out. All sorts of beasties in the woods. No, it'll have to be a room at court, of which we have many. Excuse me."

Tyren watched in amazement to see her tip a shy smile to the queen and a tiny bob of a curtsey as she hurried past. He would have given anything to follow her and avoid having to speak to the queen when his mind was already feeling scrambled, but he had no excuse to leave.

"I want to ask you about the Revel Court when there's time, Tyren," the queen added. "Or rather, Taz does. You're covering for your lord today, right?"

He nodded. "I am, my queen. I'm… honoured to be able to represent my court."

She tilted her head and he stood with the sensation that her bright blue eyes were boring right through his soul, digging out any impure thoughts and negativity.

"I don't believe a layman can stand in for a court lord, your majesty," Archess Marnin piped up.

The queen continued staring at Tyren and his brain urged his knees to buckle, to kneel under the sheer emotional and mental weight of her assessment. But he noticed that she had ignored Marnin, and she hadn't asked him to kneel either. So he stood, wishing madly that Lolly was still beside him.

By the time the queen blinked and broke the spell, Tyren felt like he was sweating. His skin chilled the moment her head straightened and her attention turned to the Marnins.

"You're right, Archess Marnin, and I don't have time to start changing old laws," the queen said. "Not right now anyway. I can however award titles where I see fit, lucky me."

Arch Marnin drew himself up to his rather towering height while the Archess gawped in horror like someone had fed her firstborn to Arthur.

"You can't do that!" The Archess clapped her hands to her mouth the moment the words escaped.

She received a withering look, as a determined royal thumb pointed back at the royal chest.

"Queen. I can do what I like. You'd be safest remembering that, especially with your previous allegiances being well known."

Tyren flinched as she turned toward him and her lips twitched, as though she was used to scaring grown men with a single look and found it hilarious. Behind her, Arch and Archess Marnin stormed off across the dining hall, but he couldn't watch them go when the queen was watching him.

"I'm afraid we don't have much time for any ceremony," she said. "Each court does their own variation, but mine isn't so much about the fluff. So I confer on you a lordship title, which you may use amongst the nobility and stuff. Milo will send you an official document with it on at some point, but if anyone challenges you, tell them to come and speak to me. Okay?"

Bewildered, Tyren nodded. A title meant so much in Faerie, and would mean *everything* to his father. And it had come directly from the queen herself.

He knew he should say thank you, drop to his knees in gratitude, but something about Lolly must have been rubbing off on him because he garbled a random question instead.

"Can I ask you one thing, my queen?"

She huffed. "Call me Demi, everyone else does. Well, not everyone. But you might as well."

He couldn't do that but he nodded obediently. When she said nothing, he realised she was waiting for him to ask his question.

"Did Lolly see you arrive? Lady Leilania, I mean. Did she know you were there when she said about me not being titled?"

Demi's face quivered then broke into a broad grin.

"Ah, that would be telling. You should ask her. Now, I think it's time for the entertainment." She lowered her voice so subtly he almost missed it. "If there's anything to report, let Milo know, not us directly unless it's an emergency."

Tyren caught on and nodded. "Of course. We're confident the entertainment will enchant even the fussiest of Fae nobles. Although the Hutchinson brothers were creeping about, so there might be a few surprises even to us organisers."

The king consort appeared beside him with a laugh.

"Brilliant, I'm with you. Her queenliness is intent on talking to some people and Milo is going to strangle her if she doesn't get up to date on her paperwork."

He shot Milo a thumbs up, and Milo seemed to be regretting his life decisions under his breath as he hurried to Demi with the papers a-flap.

Tyren noticed the hall emptying, which meant everyone would be going back to their rooms a while or already following the large arrows leading them to the site of the revel. But he had the king consort to entertain now, and that wasn't a responsibility anyone often got given on a normal day.

"The revel is this way," he said, unnecessarily because the signs were everywhere.

The king consort raised his eyebrows as they started walking away from Demi now squabbling with Milo in hissed tones.

"I figured that. Today I'm not here as any of my titles though. Call me Taz and tell me all the things."

"You're asking me to talk freely," Tyren suggested.

"As freely as you would with Lady Leilania, or anyone at your court, sure."

Tyren snorted. "I don't think talking to Lolly can be termed as 'freely'. It's more like a blood sport you get hijacked into unawares."

They walked out of the hall through the side door and straight into the soft breeze outside. Once again the trees in the woods danced wildly and the greenhouses could almost be seen to rattle, but the court itself and the path down toward the revel location seemed to be encased in a warm, weather-free bubble.

Rumours of Lolly's mother deciding to retire and hand the court to Lolly rather than die in service had done the rounds of all the courts of course. But Tyren couldn't help wondering if this was why Lolly had been forced into hosting on her mother's behalf, because her mother's strength was waning. Courts had a life of their own and Lolly was definitely devoted to hers.

Has the Flora court already chosen a new lady for itself before the current one has died?

"She definitely has a strong streak from what I've seen," Taz said. "She wasn't brought to the royal court to play with the rest of us nobles when we were kids, not often anyway, so I didn't know her growing up. But she took on the entire bunch of them at the Nether Court meeting."

Tyren nodded. "She's got a hard head and even firmer morals I think. Won't let anyone tell her what to think or what to do. Dangerous in the wrong person, but she's good. Absolute pain to argue with, you never win even when you think you have, but she's kind where it matters."

He had no idea how he'd ended up talking about Lolly, but luckily they arrived at the revel before he could dig too deep into how the morning had unfolded. As Taz stopped dead under the revel's entrance banner and stared with his mouth hanging open, Tyren smiled at the familiar sensation of pride.

He might not be anyone fancy and he might doubt his court and his Lord sometimes, but he knew nobody could do events like the Revel court.

Then again, I'm apparently a Lord in my own right now.

CHAPTER TWELVE
LOLLY

Lolly stood with the Eastwick sisters and Petra taking a moment to admire the revel. Fae all around them were gasping at the stalls selling various magical wares and gimmicks, while others stopped to marvel at the performers dancing with elemental trickery or enticing passers-by into stopping for a card game. The grass underfoot had been trimmed and flattened to provide a level place to walk on while still maintaining the illusion of being natural. Everyone seemed enchanted, but Lolly couldn't help looking at the trees made of glass and tipped with gold and silver leaves and comparing them to real trees. It was showy and everything Fae nobility would prize, but she wanted to build a forest of *tangleward* that would give people a true tricky maze experience. She wanted to build a glade of *bloom-blossoms* and have the trees dance their petals like a gentle snowstorm around people. Natural beauty instead of fakery.

But as she saw Tyren stride by with the king consort, looking every inch a noble alongside royalty, she couldn't imagine insulting his court by commenting negatively on the Revel Court's fancies.

"One question," Beryl asked. "This is meant to be hosted by both the Flora and the Revel Courts, right? So where are the Flora court's decorations? Where are the dancing trees and the green and pink banners? Once you step through the entrance, you could be in the Revel court completely."

She's right. Lolly bit her lip.

Looking around, she lowered her voice to a whisper.

"I thought my mother had all this sorted, but it appears not. We should at least have something to represent the Flora Court, but we had hardly any time to prepare before they arrived. We don't have lavish funds like the Revel Court does either. We make enough to survive, not to thrive."

Beryl nodded sympathetically, but Lolly had to fight the burning shame rising over her skin. She couldn't even afford to grow a *tangleward* right now, let alone hire enough people to maintain it to maze standards. The dancing trees that grew nearby were sentient much like Arthur and needed to be compensated for dancing.

The guilt sank like a stone in her gut. Perhaps she should have been focusing on that to better the court rather than sinking into her index every night.

So stuck in her thoughts, she was still staring at Tyren when his head lifted and his gaze met hers. He smiled so she smiled back. This was his court's revel, and she hoped her interference earlier had at least put him on the queen's radar. He was an absolute pain, but good people deserved good things. Even with Claus giving her silly warnings, Tyren seemed like a genuine person in himself.

"Well, I'm in," Cheryl said.

Lolly tore her attention from Tyren. "In what?"

"She wasn't listening." Meryl grinned. "Probably for the best."

Uh-oh. That doesn't sound good.

Lolly eyed Petra, gauging how bad whatever the sisters were planning would be based on how stressed Petra looked. Not at all, which was a relief.

Although, Petra is always stressed about something.

Which means she's actually in on whatever they're plotting.

"You need to go make your welcome speech," Petra said, her tone far too calm for Lolly's liking. "Oh look, Tyren's on his way over. You can go up to the stage together."

Lolly frowned. "What are you plotting?"

"Never you mind." Cheryl shooed her away. "Trust us that we will make sure the Flora Court has its recognition too. Hi, Tyren. You two should go make your speech. Get it over with."

Tyren stopped beside Lolly, his face crinkling into a suspicious frown. He crossed his arms over his chest, refusing to be shuffled off.

Lolly couldn't help admiring his resolve, because she was so tired of all of it she would have happily garbled out a brief speech then fled to the nearest greenhouse.

"You lot look too gleeful about something," he said.

Lolly sighed. "They have a plan."

"Really?" Tyren groaned. "Between your lot and the Hutchinsons on my side, it's a wonder the place is still standing."

"Hey!"

"That's so rude."

"And we were so polite to him yesterday. Kind of."

"Kind of has a point about Hutch and Harvey though."

"And to be fair, that's what they say about you three as well."

"Hey!"

Lolly prodded Tyren in the arm and pointed quietly to the stage. He eyed the Eastwicks now arguing with Petra and held out his arm to her. She didn't even think twice about accepting the gesture and leaning on him. The overwhelming combination of scents from various food stalls wafted over and turned her stomach with a seemingly endless wave of hunger, and the cacophony of crowd noise was so loud. Exclamations of awe and wonder grated on her ears, forcing tightness into her shoulders as her muscles jittered.

"Quick speech, welcome Taz's sister and get lost in the crowd," Tyren said.

Lolly pulled a face. "Can't imagine anything worse. Oh, and it's Taz now? You on first name terms with our king consort?"

"Sort of, but first I need to ask you something."

He turned her to face him, his expression serious. Her insides fluttered, nerves firing up at the thought of what questions he might have.

"You're not going to ask me to be your fake girlfriend again, are you?" she asked.

He eyed her for a moment with an irritable frown and something about his despair at her loosened her anxiety.

"No, Lolly, I'm not and for the sake of my sanity *please* let that go."

She snickered. "What fun would that be?"

"Urgh. Look, I'm trying to say thank you."

"Are you?" She feigned confusion. "You're not doing a very good job of it. Thank me for what?"

"Did you know the queen was standing there when you mentioned the whole me not being a lord thing?" he demanded.

"I didn't mention the whole you not being a lord thing. You did."

He pressed both hands to his temples. "I'm begging you, please just answer the question."

She wanted to tease him more, because it was funny and

the only source of amusement she had with so many people around invading her sanctuary. But Tyren looked tired and irritated too, so she relented.

"Fine, since you begged so nicely. She was standing there the whole time. Not sure when she arrived, but right after they approached us. But I mean, it's nothing untrue. Your lord should have recognised you by now for all you do. I was just fixing it for him. If anything, *he* owes me for managing *his* court's affairs."

"And how do you how much I do? I might not deserve to be a lord after all."

She smiled. "I guessed, but I'm rarely wrong. People aren't too different to animals and plants. They just put a load of unnecessary things on top of themselves to hide the fact they're not different at all."

He seemed stuck for words but she didn't mind that. The fact that his first intention, or demand really, was to thank her for something the queen had done for him was a sweet thought.

"Right, speech then," she said with a sigh. "Shall I do mine then you do yours?"

He was still frowning at her.

"I wrote the lord's so I can paraphrase. You lead, I'll chip in. I'm new to this whole lord thing."

She nodded. "So she did make you one then? Good. Keep the speech short though. Last thing I want is to have the whole of Faerie's elite staring at me for hours."

This time he held out his hand. She stared at it. The process was standard. She had a pair of fancy gloves upstairs ready for this very moment because the thought of the Lord of Revels touching her actual skin had repulsed her. But it wasn't the Lord of Revels waiting to guide her up to welcome their guests.

She slid her hand over Tyren's, her pulse speeding when his warm fingers closed around her cold ones.

You need sleep and quiet. The last thing you need right now is boy trouble, and it would be trouble. He doesn't fancy you and he's sworn to another court.

She jostled around him and led him up the short flight of wooden steps to the ornately carved wooden stage. The front of the crowd noticed them and a subtle hush rippled slowly backward until all eyes were fixed on them.

Lolly took a deep breath, fixed her smile and lifted her voice to reach the entire revel.

"Welcome to the Flora Court, one and all. We're honoured to have you all here, and give our thanks to the Revel Court for hosting alongside us. Lord Tyren and I won't bore you with long speeches, but we also wanted to give thanks to our queens, in particular our patron, Queen Demerara."

Lolly pointed in Demi's direction, and the queen gave an awkward wave. Emboldened by the reaction and reassured that the queen was also uneasy at receiving mass attention, Lolly turned to Tyren next. She'd slipped in his new title on purpose. Let the nobility talk and wonder, let them take interest in him.

"The Revel Court has always been up for a party," he said to a smattering of laughter. "It's getting rid of us or to help with the clean-up after that's usually the problem. But we're honoured to help the Flora Court host the queen and her guests. We have all sorts of amazements for you today, so please enjoy yourselves."

"But keep to the paths and avoid the woods," Lolly added, only half joking. "The Flora Court has its own amazements, and some of them bite."

The laughter and applause almost shattered her

eardrums. A lot of the Fae assembled would be there simply to look for gossip and things to pick at, but they knew how to play the part well enough. Tyren still had her hand in his and she let him lead her off the stage. She sagged the moment the crowd swallowed them and resumed their celebrations.

"Okay, now that's over, can I please go hide somewhere," she begged.

He chuckled. "Afraid not. We need to be seen talking to people. We've got a couple of potential enemy supporters that we need to rattle a bit, see if they then go rushing to their leaders."

She wrinkled her nose and shook her hand free of his fingers so she could fold her arms around her middle.

"You rattle, I'll listen."

"That hardly seems fair. Then again, you'll probably scowl at them and demand they tell you if they oppose the queen and scare them off."

Hardly fair. She hesitated. *Maybe slightly fair, but still.*

"I can be charming when I want to be," she muttered. "I just happen to not want to often."

He grinned, the mild irritability that always crossed his face in her presence wiping away like magic.

"Really? You could have fooled me. Come on, one more day playing lady and then most of this lot will leave. You can go back to the greenhouses and not sleeping or eating enough."

Unnerved by his sudden desire to personally assess her at every opportunity, she fought the urge to shove him and storm away. He was right she didn't sleep or eat regularly enough, but she liked her life the way it was. He had no right to judge her. But she couldn't make a scene, not when the queen was relying on them to get information.

She straightened up, drew from her never-ending well of petty determination and daubed a fake sunny smile on her face.

"Who do we need to speak to then?" she asked. "Or perhaps you can go charming people while I slip away and look for something of actual use."

Before Tyren could answer, the crowd noise hitched and began to buzz. Lolly twisted around until she found a wide circle with a small collection of people isolated inside it.

She flinched as Tyren's hand appeared on her elbow.

"Lady Blossom," he murmured in her ear. "With what looks like a small entourage. One of the girls was a maid to Lady Belladonna before the war too. Be careful what you say around all of them."

She nodded and gulped. Lady Blossom was the king consort's sister and a princess, third daughter of the Oak Queen. She had the same honey-blonde hair as the king consort, gently curling around her shoulders, and she wore a flowing peach dress embellished with gold that befitted a court princess of old.

"You seem to know a lot about her," she murmured.

Tyren sighed. "The princesses used to visit the Revel Court a lot as guests of my lord. I notice things."

"Well that'll come in handy. Here we go again."

She set off through the crowd, aware of him walking behind her. She didn't once turn back to check, even though part of her wanted to, but she could sense him all the same.

Lady Blossom watched her approach and Lolly caught the dismissive glance behind the otherwise open and friendly face. But when her gaze flickered over Lolly's shoulder, a determined gleam flashed in her sharp eyes.

Lolly inclined her head, a Lady to a Lady, and buried her weariness down deep. Tyren's warning had told her all she needed to know; Blossom was someone to watch, princess or not.

"Lady Blossom, welcome to you and yours. We have rooms ready for you of course. Would you like to freshen up, or head straight into the revel?"

Blossom's facial features sharpened, the Fae spite rippling clear for a few moments.

"Do I look as though I need to freshen up?" she asked, her tone sickly sweet.

Lolly faked a jolly laugh. "Most definitely not, but one shouldn't assume. Your brother and the queen are already enjoying the festivities, so I can have them found if you want to say hello?"

That made Blossom hesitate, and Lolly continued taking strength from being in her own court. She was surprised the princess hadn't levelled a sleight at the court itself yet, but she was prepared for it.

"My brother seems to enjoy mixing with the rabble. Leave him be. If I need him, I will have him found myself." She sniffed. "This looks like the kind of meagre entertainment he would enjoy."

Lolly held in her glee with great effort. She hated the viciousness of Fae politics normally, but Blossom made it so easy.

"Oh I'm sure the Revel Court wouldn't do anything by meagre measures," she said. "This is all their handiwork. Someone told me once that you and your sisters frequented the Revel Court, so I am surprised you'd dismiss their efforts. But of course, the Flora Court as a location isn't for everyone. Too much substance and not enough sparkle perhaps."

Blossom's eyes widened slightly, but she'd been no doubt practicing verbal sparring her entire life.

"The Revel Court has every mastery at providing events, of course. I thought I noticed a few hints of Tyren's handiwork. After all, we're old friends."

That forced Tyren to take a step forward and be recognised, but Lolly sensed the stiffness of his arm under her hand.

"*Lord* Tyren, I think you'll find," Lolly added smoothly. "The queen herself saw fit to recognise him. Excuse me, I'm going to ensure my guests are content." She tried not to smile at the sight of badly hidden anxiety on Tyren's face as she slid herself free of him. "Don't forget, we should check on the big finale in about ten minutes."

Giving him a suitable escape route, because there was bound to be some big finale at some point, she gave Blossom one final, confident smile and set off through the crowd. Blossom wouldn't spill a single secret to her but she might to Tyren. Plus, it also gave Lolly a few minutes peace. She needed it. She would creep into the nearest greenhouse and-

"How do you turn this thing o-oh. Hi everyone. Um… my sister has something to announce."

Lolly spun around to see the Eastwick sisters standing on the stage and squabbling over who got landed with a microphone.

"No, you do it."

"Someone has to!"

"Hello my loves!" Harvey Hutchinson's voice boomed across the crowd. "My beautiful girlfriend seems to have had a touch of the nerves-*OUCH,* don't punch!"

Lolly started giggling as a very red-faced Beryl

smacked her hand into his gut. Cheryl, Meryl and Hutch seemed to be wisely hanging back, but now Lolly wanted to stay and see what madness they were about to unleash.

"You might notice a lot of the entertainment provided is courtesy of the Revel Court in their style," Harvey continued.

A cheer went up from those who supported and patronised the Revel Court, but now Lolly remembered the veiled plans her friends had been discussing earlier. While the crowd was focused on Harvey, she scanned the perimeter of the revel. A shiver in the woods went against the flow of the wind, and noticed the subtle tinge of pale colours waving over the top of the stalls.

How… We can't afford it right now!

"But the Flora Court has its own wonders. So we've arranged some guests from the Flora Court to come and perform."

The crowd had noticed the wave of pale-leaved trees approaching now and voices buzzed with excitement. Bloom-blossom trees were rare and to see an entire group of them was a rare delight indeed.

What if people try to steal cuttings though? Lolly's mind rioted. *How are we compensating them for this? Who agreed it?*

She hadn't seen her mum or her mother all morning, and both had been suspiciously absent. This was ostentatious for them, which meant the Eastwicks had arranged it. Tyren appeared at her side, along with Taz, Demi and Lord Kainen from the Court of Illusions.

"This planned?" Demi asked.

Lolly grimaced. "Eastwicks."

Demi nodded, because she knew them and that was all the explanation that the upheaval needed.

"Did you get anything, you know?" Lolly asked Tyren.

He nodded. "A hint, nothing more. But you know your suggestion last night? And no I don't mean the fake girlfriend one, before you start."

She smirked at that, but guessed he meant her idea of breaking into guests' rooms.

"The going into places one?" she asked.

He nodded. "Yeah. We should do that."

"I'm intrigued," Taz joined in, leaning closer. "Which places are you planning on going into?"

Lolly hesitated. "Um… it's not exactly proper behaviour."

"All the better. You have some kind of secret vault or something?"

"No, but we have rooms. People are staying in them and they tend to keep secrets close by."

Taz grinned. "Excellent idea. Start with my sister's." He caught the withering look Demi flicked at him. "What? She's *obviously* in league with Belladonna, who has disappeared off the face of the earth, and she's spoilt enough to assume nobody would dare challenge her. She won't expect anyone to search her stuff."

Lolly waited but Demi didn't seem to have any royal objections, so she took that as consent.

"You should have let Reyan stay to see this," Lord Kainen grumbled.

Lolly had only met his lady briefly the night before, and she barely knew him except by reputation, but they seemed genuine enough and had Demi's trust which said a lot.

"There wasn't time, or I would have," Demi replied. "Sending her to whatever this Wachala woman is was unavoidable sadly."

The air seemed to still around them until roiling black

smoke glittered around Kainen's hands, his face.

"You sent her to the Wachala?" he asked, his voice a quiet hiss.

Demi frowned. "Yeah, we were told-"

"You sent her alone?" Tyren chipped in.

Lolly heard the horror in his voice and understood why. Rumours of the Wachala were numerous from old stories.

"Why, is that bad?" Demi asked.

Even Taz gave her a grave look, his arm tightening around her, perhaps because Kainen looked one step away from disembowelling something.

"The Wachala is said to have haunted many courts and realms over the ages," Taz explained. "She's an ancient, vengeful spirit who took the form of a woman. She um… all the legends agree on one thing, that she steals people's souls."

Demi flinched as Kainen growled, the black smoke pluming. The crowd was still absorbed in watching the oncoming attraction move closer through the trees, but a couple of people were looking their way now.

"If *anything* has happened to her…" Kainen snarled, vanishing a second later.

"I didn't realise," Demi murmured, shocked. "You said she could give us information!" She turned on Tyren next. "You never said anything about danger."

His eyebrows drew together. "I assumed you would have known. The legends tell of her being extremely territorial, and anyone who crosses her threshold has their souls sucked out. I said it in passing but I never thought you'd take my suggestion. I'm sorry, my queen."

Demi rolled her eyes at that, probably out of habit, but Taz had to use both arms to stop her jittering body pacing.

"Should I go after them?" she asked. "With all the

countless boring tales they taught us at Arcanium, why did nobody ever teach us about this?"

Taz shook his head. "Kainen's strong enough to handle himself. Reyan isn't dim either. She's grown around court fables, so she'll likely know about the Wachala."

"But I didn't give her any names, I just said 'a woman', oh orbs."

They fell quiet, still looking at each other. Rumour had it that they could communicate through mind-speak, and given the active expressions on Demi's face, Taz was trying to reason with her.

Lolly bit her lip, anxious now as the Eastwicks' grand event finally arrived. The crowd noise swelled with awed noises as the *bloom-blossom* trees appeared on large pallet trollies, their roots embedded in shallow soil, but thoughts of the lord and lady from the Illusion Court faded instantly.

"Have they lined for water?" She hopped on her tiptoes. "I hope they have. Otherwise they'll be so worn out and reedy tomorrow."

Tyren placed a hand on her shoulder and pointed through the crowd.

"Look, Petra's right there near the front. She doesn't seem the type to overlook something like that."

Lolly sagged with relief. "No, she isn't. I can't believe they managed to get them to perform. They must have bartered something huge. I need to check. I can't let them do that when it benefits the court."

She squeaked as Tyren clamped a gentle hand over her mouth.

"Have you ever seen them perform?" he asked. She shook her head. "Then shush, and watch. We'll sneak off midway through."

She nodded and he released her, but her heart was

pounding and suddenly she felt cold, which didn't happen often. She hadn't bitten him on instinct when he'd grabbed her either, which was worrying.

The trollies were wheeled around the stage and music started as the trees began to dance. Blooms rained down and out over the crowd. Several people stood with arms outstretched to catch the petals and stuff them into their pockets, no doubt assuming they could try to grow fresh cuttings from them. It wouldn't work, but Lolly could appreciate their interest.

She caught Petra's eye through the crowd, and her smile must have been catching because Petra gave her a fond look and a reassuring nod. Petra would have made sure the Eastwicks didn't promise anything the court couldn't pay, Lolly was almost sure of that.

When Tyren tugged on her hand a while later, she was entirely lost in watching the blooms catch the wind and the coordinated sway of the branches dancing them out over the crowd. Even the huge collection of snooty Fae gathered from the oldest families and richest lineages were stuck mesmerised in silence.

She glanced at Tyren and realised it was time to sneak away. Nobody noticed them tiptoeing off and slipping around the edge of a stall.

"That's blown anything the Revel Court have organised out of the woods," he whispered.

Lolly hurried across the grass toward the castle with a tiny smile on her face. She couldn't use her speed skill without leaving him behind, but he jogged along steadily as she guided them around to the far side of the building.

"I've seen individual trees dance," she admitted. "But a whole group of them, it's something most Fae won't ever see. The cost must be high though. I need to ask Petra what was offered."

Tyren sighed. "I would offer to check if we can contribute, but I'm thinking you'll want that to be the Flora court's gift alone."

Lolly hesitated before dashing up the stairs to the corridor she thought of as the royal wing, the one that had the grandest rooms and suites. He was right that she wouldn't want the Revel Court encroaching on her court's gift to the guests, even if it was just financially.

No, I'll have to see what's been agreed and make sure Mum can cover it from the court's yields.

She didn't answer and Tyren didn't press her, but she was aware of him on the stairs behind her.

"Do we know exactly what we're looking for?" she asked.

"How much has your mother told you?"

She frowned. "Next to nothing since the fight at the Nether Court. I know that we're afraid the Forgotten are after something, so we're trying to find that something, but I don't know what that something is. Orbs, my head hurts."

"Stop a minute." Tyren reached out for her arm but she stopped before he could grab her. "I don't know if this is something I'm meant to be telling you, but I'm doing it anyway."

She held in the natural inclination to be flippant, rewarding him with silence instead. His eyebrows rose in surprise moments later.

"No arguments? Wow, you really must be tired."

"Hey!"

"Okay. The Forgotten are looking for entry into one of the realms that has been blocked off for a long time. Prime Realm one is considered to be our origin realm, but we have no proof of that. It's a legend. Most Fae don't even believe it exists. Whatever the truth, the Forgotten are looking for it."

Lolly frowned. She couldn't shake the sensation of being cold, which was odd for her.

Just my luck if I end up ill after all this stress.

Tyren might have been thinking the same thing as he pulled off his jacket and held it out.

"You're shivering," he said.

She shrank into the jacket and buttoned it. "Tired. My frost gift usually keeps my body regulated, but when my system runs low I can get cold like anyone else."

"Maybe you need to carry an emergency sweatshirt around then. So, the Forgotten apparently have information we don't. Perhaps they've found out how to get in but not where to go, or the other way around. We need to find both before they do, but also figure out what they know."

Ignoring the subtle suggestion she needed to look after herself better, she started toward the room that she'd earmarked for Blossom and her group.

Tyren stopped her the moment her hand touched the handle. He dropped into a crouch and peered through the keyhole.

"Looks safe enough," he murmured. "We're checking to ensure the servants have done a proper job."

He straightened up as she gave him a furious glare.

"They always do a great job. I hate that everyone assumes they can just blame people who work for them."

He pulled a face. "And normally I would agree with you, but we need to get this done without suspicion."

Lolly pushed the handle down and swung the door open, hesitating a moment until the soft glow of the lamps flickered on.

"If we're found in here no amount of excuses will be believable."

He sighed. "Better hurry up then. You do that side, I'll do over here."

Lolly ignored his instructions and went straight for the bags on the bed. Blossom hadn't entered the room yet so she wouldn't have had time to unpack. There was a possibility someone from her group had come up to unpack for her, but Tyren's check of the room itself ended almost immediately when he found nothing personal.

Lolly unzipped the nearest bag, a monogrammed holdall of soft black leather. She sifted carefully through the clothing and found nothing, aiming for the toiletry bag next. Tyren opened the smart wooden writing case that founded out into a bed-top desk and hummed as he read through the contents.

"Does this feel wrong to you?" Lolly whispered.

He frowned. "It should. But I know her, and while morally I'm against going through other people's things, I doubt she'd care if she had to go through someone else's things. Although she'd most likely have someone do it for her. Are you suffering an attack of conscience?"

"Nope. Just wondering if you were. How well do you know her then?"

"I think she sort of took a liking to me when she used to visit the court. I'm too far beneath her notice in any serious way, but as a passing fancy she used to pay attention to me."

Lolly gave up with the bag and headed for the hanging wardrobe rail.

"You shouldn't talk about yourself like that," she said. "as 'a passing fancy'. Besides, you're a lord now in your own right. If you wanted her, you could try."

He snuffled a laugh. "No thanks. I'd rather marry Arthur."

"I'll tell her." Lolly grinned. "She's picky though."

"You said she liked me."

"She did. But your roots aren't showy enough."

Tyren glanced down at his feet. "I don't think I can grow my toes anymore. They're clumpy enough as it is. Oh, hang on. Here's something."

Lolly hurried across to stand beside him and he tilted the small notebook he was holding. It looked tiny in his hands and she leaned closer to squint at the scrawls.

"Wait, this is her diary," she hissed. "You can't read her diary!"

"You're happy rifling through her knickers and her personal papers, but her diary is off limits?"

She nodded. "Yes! Diaries are private. Secrets and all the embarrassing thoughts. It's not like reading the odd letter or piece of business."

Tyren stared back at her. Her cheeks flushed at the intensity, but she refused to back down and look away.

My cheeks flushing definitely means I'm sickening for something. They didn't usually.

"Do you have a diary then?" he asked.

Her mouth dropped open. "What does that have to do with anything? It's none of your business."

"Well you seemed very defensive about it, so I figured you must have one too. Look, I've only skimmed a couple of pages and this says that she's worried her sister has taken on too much, and that the human world isn't the one they read about as children."

Lolly warred with her morals as he hesitated. Curiosity won.

"So, does that mean they think this prime realm is the

human world, or in it?"

"The entrance may well be. There's a couple of place names here. Look, memorise them and I will too. We take these to Milo."

Lolly memorised the two words in an instant and opened her mouth to hurry him, but voices echoed in the hall before she could.

"Crud!" she whispered. "Quick, put that back and get behind the clothes rail!"

He dropped the diary back in the writing case and closed it while she checked the bag looked the way it should. Before she could react, Tyren had her hand in his and was dragging her behind the clothing, moments before Blossom swept into the room.

Lolly shook Tyren's hand off and gently teased two hanging dresses apart so she could peek. It wasn't exactly a great view between two swathes of velvet and a puff of netting, but she recognised the person standing in the doorway, and it wasn't Blossom.

"Are we safe to contact her here?" Lyle asked.

Tyren grimaced.

"*Loudmouth Lyle,*" he mouthed.

Lolly nodded. Their only hope was to stay silent and still until Blossom left the room again. She hopefully wouldn't stay long with the revel downstairs and adoring Fae fawning for her favour.

Lolly knew she could get out of the room with her speed gift mostly undetected, but that would leave Tyren undefended. Then Lyle entered the room and closed the door, dashing any chance she had of getting out without being discovered.

I could make it out quick enough even if they did see me, but Tyren wouldn't.

"We'll be fine," Blossom huffed. "Stop worrying at me. It's tiresome. Nobody in courts have the brains any longer. The queen will be interrogating the masses personally instead of ruling over them like she should from a distance. My insipid brother will be tailing around after her with those tacky FDPs running around like untrained pups. It's fine."

Lolly tried not to imagine the Eastwicks and Hutchinsons gambolling about as puppies. She covered her mouth with her hand as nervous hysteria bubbled up. The Hutchinsons would likely be some kind of huge dopey hounds.

The Eastwicks are more like terriers terrorising the village.

Tyren gave her a sharp look but that only made her sudden urge to giggle even worse. She closed her eyes and tried to breathe in slow and deep to calm herself.

"Bella?" Blossom's voice turned hesitant and respectful. "Hello. We're here and so is the queen still. The Flora Court had *bloom-blossom* trees perform so the Revel Court's entertainment will be next. That's when you should strike."

That swept any urge to laugh away.

Strike? Lolly froze. *If they attack, we're defenceless. The Revel Court doesn't have much of a fighting force either. We don't have defences like the Illusion Court does, or places to hide like the Nether Court. We've no real animals to protect us like the Fauna Court, and the Word Court is near unreachable without permission. We're screwed.*

She tugged Tyren's sleeve.

"*I'm going to warn them with my speed gift.*" She mouthed. "*Stay here and take the words to Demi.*"

He shook his head but Lolly dodged his attempt to grab her. She had no hope of surviving this unscathed, but if the Forgotten were going to attack the court, she needed to beg Demi for FDP help to fend them off.

Tyren tried to catch her again and she darted around the rail to the door with super speed.

She saw the somewhat familiar face of Lady Belladonna, the princess who had defected to the Forgotten during the war, projected in pearlescent grey from the orb Blossom was holding.

Then she threw open the door and drew their startled attention.

"It's her!" Lyle shouted.

"Get her then!" Blossom yelled.

Lolly darted through the doorway and off down the hall with the sound of Lyle's footsteps fading behind her as she pushed her speed gift to its limit.

She had to trust Tyren would keep himself hidden, or at least fight until she returned with help if he was found.

CHAPTER THIRTEEN
REYAN

Reyan followed the instructions, the slaying heat bearing down on her. She didn't dare dip into the shadows to rest, and they were too sparsely set out for her to use them for quicker travel. She passed the charred barn and set her sights on the faint haze of muted blue waving up ahead.

Bluegrass, then cottage with a grass roof.

She strode on, sweat pouring over her skin. A Fae living remotely could be completely harmless, but Demi would have given her the ability to skip home for a reason.

She could have given it to me three weeks ago when I came to stay with Arlen, but she didn't. Gifting me now must have a purpose to it.

That meant potential danger. She was both honoured Demi trusted her, and wary about what she might face. Nobody in the market had mentioned anyone living out this far, but she hadn't wanted to risk asking too many obviously prying questions either.

By the time she reached the bluegrass field and could see the cottage ahead, doubt was setting in. Many a tale and legend had been painted of spirits living in picturesque cottages, all of them waiting to gobble up unsuspecting passers-by in some gruesome way.

She smiled. Tales and legends were just that, stories created to entertain kids, or to mould them. But whatever Fae lived inside, it didn't mean she could trust them. She walked under the shade, taking note of the shadows under a line of trees that started opposite the cottage.

Old, the shadows screamed silently. *Hungry.*

Reyan shivered, oddly cold in the shade after the burst of sunshine. She tried gathering the shadows to her but they resisted. Her skin prickled and she cast a protection warding before venturing toward the gate.

"Hello there, dear."

A soft voice filled her ears but she couldn't see anyone. Reyan drew herself up tall, holding her glamour firmly in place.

"Hello. Who's there?"

"The owner of this cottage. And who are you?"

Reyan frowned. "I'm the girl standing at your gate. My name is… actually, in honesty I've been sent to ask for some information, if you have it. I believe I'm in the right place."

She would trade with honesty because word-tangling would likely put her on the wrong side of whoever she was talking to. Something she'd learned fast from Demi was that most Fae weren't used to dealing with blunt honesty and it worked at least half of the time.

"Ah. Come inside, dear. It's hot out."

Reyan put her hand on the gate but a subtle resistance sucked at her strength from behind.

Hungry. Hungry! The shadows urged.

She hesitated. "No thank you. I don't want to be rude but I've learned not to trust people I don't know and can't see."

A soft chuckle rolled through the garden. Now she took another look from under the brim of her hat, she could see bees in a hive by the far corner of the cottage but no sign of vegetation other than weeds and overgrown grass. Perhaps the woman couldn't go outside much.

"Well then, how do you expect me to give you

information?" the voice asked. "You are a shadow-merger, how could I hurt you, child, before you faded away?"

Posed as a question to hide what was no doubt a real and very dangerous answer.

"With the voice I can hear very clearly from here," she replied. "I've been sent to ask about the Flow of Origins. I'm a messenger only."

"For the queenling," the voice scoffed. "She sends the Lady of the Illusion Court to beg for information instead of coming herself."

Reyan clutched the gate tight. A quick look down and her glamour was still in place, but she'd never once heard of anyone who could see through a glamour, except maybe one of the Queens.

"Who are you?" she asked again, fighting to keep the fear from her voice.

"Ah, that is a very long tale and contains little of the information you have requested."

Long flattery or rude directness? Reyan weighed up her options.

"I would listen, if I had time. I'm thinking I probably don't though. We need-"

"You need to find the keys to the Prime Realm, yes, yes, I do keep up with Fae events," the voice grumbled. "But either way it is a long story. Come inside and I shan't lay a finger on you."

Doesn't mean she can't harm me in other ways.

She thought of the books now in Kainen's library at the court, some ancient fables he'd collected after she'd teased him a while back about only having factual books. He'd insisted on teasing her about reading them aloud, reciting several lines in his least soothing voice.

Faint memories of old tales, older than most, of spirits

who stole souls that crossed their thresholds filled Reyan's head, almost like Kainen was yelling the words at her again.

"So you do have the answers we need?" she pressed.

If the voice belonged to a Fae, the answer couldn't be a lie. But if somehow it was a malevolent spirit then lies were likely to be no problem at all for them.

"I do. Come inside."

Reyan caught the slight, impatient demand in the tone that time, and a wave of heat prickled against her warding.

A compulsion. Still doesn't confirm Fae or spirit, but this is ancient power.

"I'm okay here," she said cheerfully, making her decision.

Demi had asked her to come and enquire but hadn't said anything about putting herself in danger to get the information. If need be, they could come back with half of Demi's FDPs to get the voice to comply.

"Then I shan't tell you anything," the voice said sulkily.

"Well, that's a shame." Reyan shrugged and made a show of pushing away from the gate. "I didn't even get a chance to ask you if there was anything you wanted to trade for info. Not me, I'm not coming over your boundaries. We all know that'd give you some kind of power over me given how keen you are for me to approach."

The voice huffed. Reyan searched the dark windows around the cottage door, but still couldn't see any sign of a face. The only movement in the air other than her uneasy breathing, was the steady waver of the bees humming around the hives.

"I would like company a while."

Reyan frowned. "I can't provide that. Not myself and

not without asking other people. But I can talk to you a while here. Do you have anyone coming in to check on you?"

"I'm no frail old woman, child." The angry tone buzzed through the air. "I can care for myself. I don't need checking on. Come in a while and see for yourself."

Reyan couldn't help laughing. "I'm fine right here. But if that's the only thing you'll accept, then there's not much else I can do. We have people combing the books anyway for mentions of the Prime Realm and the origins, although to be fair those are just legends."

She hoped to play on the woman's vanity, perhaps tug some thread that would have her spilling self-righteous promises about being able to tell everything they needed to know.

"Just legends?!" Even the bees seemed to still at the shock in the bodiless voice. "My girl, myth, legend, history, they all contain truths and lies. Stories are simply where truths go to hide themselves when people don't have the guts to face them. All that is to be found can be found if you know where the words are stored."

Silence descended. Reyan hesitated, then realisation dawned.

"All record of legends are stored at the Court of Words, aren't they?" she asked.

Silence.

"I'm right, aren't I?"

Silence.

"We need to visit the Court of Words. And considering you've been excessively chatty up until now, your silence is your way of telling me that."

Silence.

"Thank you. Are you really lonely? I can't promise to

come back, but I'll ask if there's anyone willing to if you like. Would you harm them in any way?"

A subtle hum that turned into a derisive sniff. "It depends on your definition of harm, child."

"So basically, yes. If I get the chance, I'll try and send someone unworthy this way."

She held her warding firm as a subtle tingling descended around it, then a resigned sigh filled the air.

"You are very sweet. I can tell you for nothing also that stories aren't always formed of words, think on that on your search for the Prime Realm. Now, there is honey on the table there. Take a jar for your trouble."

Reyan eyed the table with a frown. "No tricks? No magic honey that zaps me inside the jar or turns me into something else, or sends me somewhere or makes me pass out or lose my mind or anything?"

The woman began to chuckle as more bees joined the hives.

"Not this time, no. A gift of simple, un-magic food and nothing more. You are wise, and wisdom must be rewarded somehow."

Reyan held her protection with everything she had, letting her glamour drop. The woman already knew who she was anyway. She approached the table and risked darting out a hand to grab one of the many honey jars.

The jar lay warm in her hand, glass with no label on it, but nothing unexpected happened.

"Go, child. Your young man is waiting. I will look forward to the unworthy visitor you mentioned for me to toy with one day."

Reyan hadn't promised and knew no debt would stand against her, but thinking of various people she'd met through court over the years, she had one or two faces in mind.

"Thank you, no promises but I'll try. Wait, what do you mean my young man is waiting?"

There was no answer, a clear enough dismissal. She held the honey to her chest with one hand and started down the path toward the market. As she reached the turning by the lavender field though, she looked back.

A figure appeared in the garden, the form of a human shadowed against the sunlight, wavering not from the haze of the heat or the breeze, but the form of it; a person shaped by an enormous swarm of bees.

Reyan waved and carried on down the hill at a smarter pace, her pulse pounding. She remembered one of the fables well from her childhood, of a swarm-spirit turned Fae as punishment. Many of the retellings insisted the spirit hated men, but Reyan had heard an older telling that suggested it was a hatred of all Fae, not just male ones.

She walked faster. If her memory was right, she'd just walked away from the Wachala unharmed and with a free jar of honey as a gift. And that was unheard of in *all* tellings of the legend.

Her legs felt like jelly as the market came into view. She wanted to drop in on Arlen first to ask if he had any links to the Court of Words they could use, although Demi likely had her own as queen anyway. She also had the whole 'spy on Lady Blossom' side-quest, but then Blossom would likely be at the Flora Court still.

Reyan squinted against the glare of the sun, slowing to a halt as she noticed someone running up the hill. Not in a 'out for a gruelling jog in ridiculous heat' way, but a panicked dash with limbs flailing.

Kainen lifted his head when he was a short way from her and skidded to a halt.

"You're… okay," he panted.

She nodded. "What are you doing here?"

"They didn't tell… you, the Wachala…"

He doubled over with his hands on his knees. Even though his cheeks were tinged pink, he barely looked out of breath. If she hadn't known better, she'd have assumed he wasn't winded at all aside from the body position.

"Oh yeah, I met her. Figured it out eventually. I'm fine."

He lifted his head again, his gaze scanning over her as if he didn't believe it. She held her arms out.

"I am, promise. She even gave me a jar of honey because she said wisdom should be rewarded. I have info I need to tell Demi as well."

Kainen straightened up and she squeaked as he flung one arm around her waist and pulled her against him and held her tight, surrounding her in the scent of sweaty heat and faint shampoo. She winced as the honey jar pressed against her chest, but smiled into his shoulder as he huffed lightly onto hers, regaining his breath.

"I was worried," he mumbled.

She grinned. "Clearly."

"Come on, I'll skip us back to the Flora Court. Oh, before I forget."

He let her go just enough to reach into his pocket and pull out a circle of rainbow beads.

"Demi insisted we all wear these, identity tags kind of."

Reyan held still as he slid the bracelet over her wrist, the glass beads glinting in the sunlight.

"It's a clever idea. Nobody would think of it unless they knew. Does this mean we're trusted now?"

Kainen grinned, relief still washing over his face. He held up his wrist to show her a matching bracelet in place there.

"Yep, even me. Fancy that. What's wrong?"

He noticed her staring at her wrist, the realisation she'd had several times in the past weeks falling over her again. She faked a smile.

"Nothing. Still getting used to not having my court-sworn tattoo."

She'd not noticed the absence of it after Kainen gifted her freedom from the court, not at first. But the swirling tattoo of shadows in the shape of ribbons had slowly disappeared.

Kainen frowned. "We can replace it if you want? You don't have to swear to the court or anything, we'll just have the tattooist come by to re-ink it."

"It's okay." She smiled honestly that time, touched by the suggestion. "One day I'll be able to replace it myself. Until then this rainbow one will have to do. So, back to the Flora Court?"

"Yeah. If we're quick, you might even catch the end of the *bloom-blossom* performance."

She relaxed against him as the nether gathered around them.

"You'd better stop stalling then," she teased.

In a moment she'd have to let go, to resume her lady role and go back to being guardedly social with half of the Fae elite. But in that moment, his behaviour had told her everything she needed to know.

CHAPTER FOURTEEN
TYREN

The sheer pounding in Tyren's chest must have drummed across the entire court when Lolly zipped toward the door of Blossom's room. He held himself still, knowing he'd be found at any moment, and formed a protection warding around him, willing his breathing to calm so that Blossom wouldn't hear and find him.

Visions of Lolly being caught by Lyle, maybe even tackled and tormented, filled his head and his stomach twisted with nausea.

I never thought to ask if she can even protect herself. He cursed his carelessness. *All those stupid questions about who should go through doors first and whether I could get girlfriends or not, and I should have been making sure she would be safe if something happened.*

"She wouldn't be in here alone. Come out."

Tyren resisted the strong wave of compulsion to obey Blossom's command as it battered against his warding. She tutted and he prepared himself to fight with little more than super-strong sight and his fists. His father had wanted to earn him more gifts than that, but court Fae didn't give gifts easily because it required sacrifice, unless you were royalty and could gift at will.

The clothing rail ripped away from him and he tensed, ready for whatever Blossom tried to throw. Her eyes widened slightly when she saw him.

"You?" She frowned. "But you're... I would have thought..." Her confusion cleared, to be replaced by cold malice. "I see. The flower girl got to you. Fancy her, do you?"

Tyren wondered if he could keep her talking long enough for Lolly to get help. She had a speed gift, so he probably only needed to distract for a few minutes at the most.

"I admire her morals but no, she's not my girlfriend if that's what you're asking."

"Nicely dodged. But that tells me all I need to know."

Dodged? I don't fancy her, I basically said as much.

"You think what you like," he said. "But I don't know why that's an issue or even a consideration for you. I'm not vain enough to say you ever had any designs on me."

Not vain enough to say it, but he'd certainly assumed it before. If she wanted him to word-tangle, he would give her his best.

Her lip curled and she glanced over her shoulder.

"You're a lord now, she said?"

Tyren nodded. "Courtesy of the queen at Lo-*eilania*'s suggestion."

"So, you could theoretically court anyone you wanted to. Most wouldn't entertain a new title of course, but that's merely politics."

She said it so simply, "merely politics" as though the whole ebb and sway of Fae culture was nothing more than an irksome detail she could swat aside because she was a princess.

"I suppose theoretically I could. I'm young though. Not interested in settling down yet, not until I find someone I can be compatible with."

Blossom stepped right in front of him, the tip of her forefinger landing on his chest.

"We could be compatible," she said. "When I visited

the Revel Court, we got on extremely well."

How do I tell her that I was basically told to keep her sweet the whole time?

He couldn't think of a single thing to say, and still he couldn't hear any sign of footsteps in the hall or shouting. He strained his ears for any echo of fighting outside, but all he could hear was the panicked thoughts rushing through his brain.

His silence was apparently answer enough and Blossom stepped back, her features narrowing.

"No? What a shame."

She lifted the orb before he could find any way to placate her.

"Belladonna," she called.

He eyed the open doorway but she lifted a hand without looking and the door slammed shut.

"I have charm, influence and audible gifts," she said. "I can influence items around me, charm the Fae from their towers and hear anything around me. I wouldn't try it."

She could influence the door to stay shut. His best bet was to placate her and use his words. Other than that, he had his protection warding, some basic combat training centred around stage-play and one specific gift he really didn't want to have to use.

"I'm not planning on challenging you," he tried. "But the whole of the Flora and Revel courts will take this as an attack on them."

She smiled. "You're not officially sworn to the Revel Court, so they wouldn't risk it." So absorbed in delivering her spitefulness to him, she didn't notice the orb come alive and project her sister's glowering face against the wall beside her. "The Flora Court might, but they're about to be turned into a battlefield, so they'll be a bit too busy to come and rescue some random lord nobody cares about. Once the battle begins, the Revels have instructions to withdraw and let our side decimate this pathetic excuse for a court."

Tyren forgot about the orb and the projection and even Blossom momentarily.

They wouldn't. I know the lord isn't really keen on the new queen, mainly because of her age and also he thinks he should be king of the entire universe, but he wouldn't side with...

"I send you on one mission, and you're spilling everything!"

The voice ricocheted out of the orb and rattled his ears. He cringed away from the screaming tantrum but kept his warding solid. If fighting had already spilled out, Lolly might not be able to get to the queen or anyone else. She might even be in danger.

He shunted around Blossom as she stood goldfish-mouthing at her sister's irate face and reached through his warding to grab the door handle. But no matter how much he jiggled and hauled on it, the door wouldn't open.

Retracting his hands into the safety of his protection, he twisted to face the enemy.

"-accident, I didn't mean to," Blossom babbled. "She ran out of the door, she must have a speed gift or something, and then I didn't mean to tell him everything, I'm sorry!"

Blossom pointed at him. He had the bizarre urge to laugh, but it wouldn't help him any so be pinned his lips tight together. If Blossom had influenced the door to stay shut, he didn't have much hope other than jumping out of the two storey window. But if she was holding it shut with concentration, he might be able to open it when something distracted her.

He slid his hand slowly behind his back, feeling for the handle.

"Well, he'll have to do," Belladonna snapped. "Is he worth anything?"

Tyren shook his head instinctively even as Blossom's face lit up.

"Yes! He's just been made a lord by the queen, so she has to have some attachment to him, and he means something to Leilania too."

Tyren found the handle and pushed down. The mechanism clicked.

Three... Two... One...

He twisted aside and swung the door open, darting through.

"You didn't lock the door?!" Belladonna's scream echoed after him.

"I did! I influenced it! This stupid court must be working against me."

Blossom's voice bounced after him, but his heart lifted at her choice of words, his steps filling with a fresh spurt of energy. Lolly's court had chosen to let him out even though Blossom was influencing the door. He slammed a hand to the stone doorframe at the start of the stairs leading down.

Thank you thank you thank you.

He took two steps before the sound of feet echoed below him, soft steps slapping fast. A body came at him, hurtling fast with hair flying wild, and he had to back up or risk sending Petra flying back down the stairs.

"Whatever happens, do as you're told," she hissed.

"Wait, what? Where's Lolly?"

She forced her warding around his and he had to let his

meld with hers or be forced small, an odd sensation that felt far too intimate when he'd barely spoken to her before. Blossom appeared in front of them and stumbled to a halt when she saw Petra.

"She's fine," Petra insisted. "If we get taken, say nothing."

Tyren opened his mouth to ask what she meant by that. The words dissipated as several grown men and women appeared beside Blossom, appearing out of thin air as though they'd realm-skipped in.

"She's safe?" he whispered. "What about the battle?"

Petra glared at him. "Yes, now *silence*."

"Hand him over," Blossom said. "You can't fight all of us."

Petra snorted. "I can try."

Tyren twisted around, realising now why Petra hadn't insisted they go back the way she'd come. Three people he didn't recognise were blocking the stairs, and their grinning faces didn't seem to be in any mood to let anyone get past.

"What's the deal then, princess?" Petra asked. "Give him over and you'll let me go? Give him over and you won't hurt him, or me? We both know your sister won't stick to any promises you make, and you're too weak to hold to any."

Blossom hissed at the insult. "We'll take both of you and torture you until he spills every word."

"I don't know anything," Tyren said. "My lord is clearly in league with your lot more than I ever will be, and thankfully I'm not sworn to the Revel Court as you so charmingly reminded me, so he's really not my lord anymore, not after this. Lady Leilania has told me absolutely nothing, and I've spoken to the queen and king consort a grand total of once each or thereabouts. We spent most of it talking about Leilania, actually, and I'm sure you're not that bothered to know about her."

Blossom's face twisted with petulant rage and Petra sighed in resignation beside him.

"I told you to be quiet," she muttered.

But he saw a flash of admiration in her tiny, fleeting smile and that filled him with the last burst of confidence he needed.

"Take them both," Blossom insisted.

Petra pulled a hair from her head and lifted her arm. Tyren flinched sideways when the hair swelled and lengthened into a gleaming sword.

"That is amazing," he whispered. "Can I have one?"

Petra snorted. "I can only make them one at a time, so no. We're not getting away from this but we go down fighting, okay? If I can find a way to get you free, I'll do it. Otherwise, punch, scratch and bite anything that breaks through."

"I can't do much, but I'll do my best."

Blossom stood back as her crew advanced until they hit the warding. Then the attacks began. Tyren winced as each blow hit, some hitting them with swords like Petra's and others throwing super-strength gifts behind punches and smacks. Fingers snared through the warding by his middle and he shoved them away, focusing on letting his strength seal the gaps. Beside him, Petra was sending her sword out with lethal precision, the warding reforming before she had even fully pulled it back. She fought as if possessed and Tyren turned his back to hers, trusting her to handle her side while he protected his.

Most of the group from the stairs were around the front and sides now, but one managed to get both hands through groping for Tyren's throat. Tyren sent his foot out through the warding, catching behind their ankle while grabbing their wrists.

The man's eyes widened as he lost his balance. Tyren held on, mindful of the stairs, but his hands were sweaty from nerves and stress and fighting. The man toppled backwards, arms flailing, and tumbled down with a sickening series of thuds.

Crud, what if he's dead? What if I killed him?

He almost missed someone snatching at his face from the side and shoved them away. Their enemy kept swarming, the stairs full of bodies ready to block their path. They were coordinated, well-practiced at hunting down their prey, and even Petra was flagging against the onslaught.

"Get our backs against the wall," he hissed. "Then we both fight forward. The moment the stairs are clear, we run."

She shook her head. "We can't risk drawing this lot outside, not yet."

She lobbed her sword out and almost severed someone's hand off with a flourish, but the woman staggered back in time. Tyren wanted to ask why but a man reached through their warding and hauled Petra in by the sword. It should have sliced his fingers clean off, but he clung on while leering at her. She had to let go of the sword and reached up for her hair again, her face frantic.

Tyren reached out to slap the man's arms away but too slow. Petra yelled, her tone feral as the man grabbed her around her waist and hauled her away. Tyren winced as her warding tore free of his and he froze, torn between his own warding and charging after her.

A strong weight anchored around his neck and he

gasped as the hold cut his air. Blotches of light danced in front of his eyes as he clawed at the unyielding arm holding him.

"TYREN!"

He heard the echo of Lolly's voice and someone else echoed Petra's name too, but the end of it faded into nothing as a waft of cold air whooshed over him. His strangler disappeared and he dropped to his knees, huffing in panicked breaths.

"Enjoy the cells." Blossom's relief was palpable but he couldn't find energy to lift his head. "You should recognise them, Tyren."

That forced his head up enough to see the room around them. The slam of the door jarred in his spinning head, but Blossom was right about one thing. He recognised where he was.

"You alright?"

He twisted to find Petra beside him, halfway through shuffling backwards across the floor to lean against the wall.

"They're not actual cells," he babbled. "But I know where we are. The lord wanted a place to punish people who disobeyed him, but he didn't want people thinking we were cliched by building actual cells or dungeons."

The room was small, barely even the size of a basic bedroom, and had a toilet in the far corner. But it was clean. The mattress had sheets and a pillow with a blanket. There were even three toilet rolls on top of the cistern.

"Revel Court?" Petra asked, her eyes closing as she dropped her head back against the wall.

"Yep. She admitted to me that my- *the* Lord of Revels is on their side. I promise, if they've been using our court as a base I had no idea. I don't know where they could have been, but there are hundreds of places to hide in the markets. It's like a maze out there."

"It's something the queen feared."

Tyren clambered to his feet to try the door, but of course it was properly locked this time.

"We need to figure out a way to get free. The Forgotten are going to invade the Flora Court and Lolly's there and the queen and the Revel Court aren't going to help and why aren't you bothered? Are you sick?"

Petra lifted her head, blearily opening her dark eyes.

"Not sick. Exhausted. Sit a while. Do you really not think the queen has a plan for every possibility? Maybe not your involvement, but she's not dim."

Tyren inched across the room to the mattress, then held out a hand to help Petra onto one end of it.

"Thanks."

He frowned as he flopped down beside her. If he managed to get through the door, even in his own court he wouldn't get far if one of the Forgotten found him. He needed to rest a while and come up with a proper plan first.

"Are they going to be okay?" he asked.

He worried about Lolly. She was argumentative and belligerent, but her heart was one of the kindest he'd met. She would be more worried about the plants and her people than herself.

Petra snorted, closing her eyes again.

"The queen handled the Forgotten onslaught. She's gained some new skills in preparation, so I wouldn't worry about her. Or was it Lolly you were really asking about?"

There was something in her tone but he couldn't place it, a subtle needling that his brain told him he should take notice of, a teasing almost. But he was so tired and so worried that he couldn't focus on it properly.

"Yeah."

He turned his head in time to see Petra grin.

"She's the last person you need to be worried about."

CHAPTER FIFTEEN
REYAN

The sound of chaos swamped the moment the nether released them into the Flora Court. Kainen looked around in horror even as Reyan threw a warding around them, wincing as something flaming hot hit against it.

"Crud, this is bad," he muttered.

His arms were still wrapped around her while she stood clutching her honey with one hand, the other raised to hold the warding. Strands of Kainen's power wrapped around hers, reinforcing their protection and she sagged against him.

Gifts pinged and sizzled everywhere as people charged in a tangled melee, others fighting by combat. Reyan searched the crowd and saw Demi and Taz back to back nearby, Taz with his wings wrapped around her as she stood with her eyes closed and her arms outstretched.

Kainen tightened his hold even as she struggled to free herself and run to Demi, to do what she had no idea. In a rushing wisp of purple grey, the scene shifted and they reappeared beside Demi. Taz noticed them and said something Reyan couldn't hear, but Demi opened her eyes, glanced their way and nodded.

The air quivered, a strong ripple gusting through the air and for a moment Reyan thought Kainen had realm-skipped them somewhere else. But Demi was still visible with Taz. The ripple waved over the fighting crowd, Demi's face pinched with concentration.

"She's… she can't be," Kainen said.

Reyan glanced up at him. "What?"

He didn't answer, nodding instead toward the revel-turned-battlefield as one by one the crowd started to fold. Knees sagged. Arms dropped. People folded into each other, eyes closing as a chill settled around them.

"I still can't do it without the frost," Demi muttered.

She took a step forward and stumbled, but Taz spun on his heel and caught her from behind, holding her steady.

"You took down a whole court," he huffed. "*Two* whole courts. Stop complaining. Also, I'm so not happy with you right now."

She rolled her eyes and used his arms like a balancing beam to stay upright.

"It had to be done." She glanced around. "Petra's gone after Tyren and Lolly. We need to find them first."

Reyan stared once more at the now still court. If she hadn't heard the subtle snore from the woman nearest to them, she'd have assumed they were all dead. The Eastwicks were still moving on Demi's other side along with the Hutchinson brothers, but other than that, they were alone.

"Any news?" Demi asked.

Reyan guessed she needed a moment to recover before charging after the others. She nodded, managing to bat Kainen's arms away from her waist.

"The Wachala didn't want to tell me much," she admitted. "And it wasn't confirmation exactly, but she mentioned that legends have grains of truth, and there's only one place all legends are recorded. When I asked if it was the Court of Words she went silent, and she was pretty chatty and insistent before that. She also said something about not all stories are formed of words or something, I thought maybe songs instead? Then she gave me some honey and sent me on my way.”

Demi grimaced. “I didn’t realise who she was, I’m so sorry. I didn’t know she was this ancient spirit who steals souls.”

“It’s okay.” Reyan ignored Kainen’s quiet grumbling at that. “Whatever you do if you go there, don’t step over the threshold, stay behind the gate. Also, she’s made of bees I think, like a swarm-spirit.”

“Well still, I didn’t realise, so I’m sorry.” She glared over her shoulder as Taz started poking her. “What, what is it?”

He pointed toward the court buildings and they looked to find Lolly steaming toward them, her hair flying out behind her as she tumbled over the grass.

“Blossom!” she shouted. “Petra’s gone after Tyren, but she had an entourage, she might have them outnumbered!”

Demi’s voice appeared in Reyan’s head before she could process what Lolly had said.

Go to the Revel Court. My instinct tells me there are enemies there. Don’t be seen by any means. Find Petra and Tyren if you can, or anything relevant to the enemy, then report back here.

Reyan nodded. She glanced at Kainen, still glaring at Demi no doubt after the whole incident with the Wachala.

I’m going back to the Revel Court, she told him. *I’ll be careful.*

He grimaced. “Fine but if you need me, skip straight home and orb me, okay? Promise me.”

She nodded but he grabbed her wrist.

“Promise me, Reyan.”

She nodded again. “I promise I’ll skip home and orb you if I need to.”

Satisfied with that, his gaze dropped to her lips

moments before he kissed her cheek.

"For luck. I'll skip you in, you look half-dead as it is."

She didn't have time to reply as the nether wisped around her. She'd had one energy ring as food all day, crossed through several realms and different times since waking, and now she was being asked to creep through the shadows of a court she didn't know to find two people she wasn't sure she could recognise.

Kainen had skipped them right into the centre of Arlen's book stall. Luckily, time had passed and the building was in darkness, as was the deserted street outside.

"Can you get out?" Kainen asked.

She nodded. "Through the shadows I can, or I can skip myself anywhere now. I won't be seen and I'll get through as quick as I can. I'll skip home then orb you to come and bring me back to the Flora Court."

"I don't like this."

She sighed. "I know, but I'm the best bet there is of finding if they're here or not. Now, Tyren is the man Lolly was with yesterday, the dark-haired one, and Petra is Demi's mentor, right?"

Kainen nodded. "Don't risk speaking to anyone either."

Reyan couldn't help grinning. She shook his hand off her wrist gently and pressed her fingers to his chest instead. He looked down in surprise, giving her the angle advantage to reach up and press a soft kiss on his cheek. Even though she was only a fake lady and people had probably been destroyed for doing less to a court lord without permission, she couldn't resist.

His startled blinking as she drew back gave her all the strength she needed.

"Anyone would think you were worried about me," she teased, before dissipating and becoming one with the shadow.

She hung around for a moment longer as Kainen shook his head with a disbelieving chuckle and realm-skipped away with his fingers pressed to his cheek.

Total softie really.

She pushed thoughts of him aside, slipping through the shadows of the shop and out under the door. She'd tried to explain her disassembling before, that she could become shadow like transmuting herself from solid into air, but everyone struggled to get their head around it. She simply became like a dark wind wisping through the darkness, moving her consciousness and the particles of her being along with her.

Without eyes she was down to her senses, but the shadows seemed to form a 'knowing' of sorts in her mind, wherever that technically went in her shadow form. She bypassed the Revel Court boundary at the edge of the market without any trouble, sneaking up the hill and into the large, towering red-brick castle through the kitchen entrance that Arlen had pointed out to her on her first day with him.

Where do I start?

She moved along corridors of the vast castle, twisting and turning, trying to get her senses to keep mind of the turns left and right, up steps and down. Sensing people nearby, she waited. They likely wouldn't notice her but she had a recurring fear that one day she'd come across someone who could see into shadow.

Like the Wachala could see through my glamour.

The buzz of someone speaking caught her attention and she dipped into the nearest available alcove, allowing her shadow-self to form, a faded outline of herself with her head formed for ears to hear with and eyes to look with.

"The fun thing is, we don't need you to tell us anything," a strong voice sang. "Your queen will come sailing in to save you and she'll not be expecting the entire Blood and Bone Court waiting for her."

Reyan thought she recognised the voice as Lady Belladonna's. Her attention moved further down the corridor to where Lady Blossom was pacing. Sourness curdled at the sight of her.

She'd been Kainen's original intended bride, the woman whose appearance had driven Kainen to seek a fake bride in the first place.

I should thank her. Without the threat of her, he wouldn't have grabbed me out of the crowd at all.

That wasn't exactly a flattering take but she couldn't knock the new life it had gifted her either. While Blossom paced, Lady Belladonna strode toward her with her hands wrapped around the wrists of another woman, one Reyan recognised.

"You don't know her." Petra said, holding her head high as she was shoved forward down the hall. "She's smarter than you give her credit for."

Belladonna rolled her eyes. "Oh, she may be smart, but her emotions lead and her head follows. She'll come for you, I have no doubt. Even if we don't crush her today, the delay will give us more than enough time to find the keys to the Prime Realm before she does. With them on-side, and how could they possibly defy or oppose us? None of the queens will be able to stand against the Blood and Bone Court."

Well that's clear enough.

Reyan held her position as Belladonna forced Petra through a door with astonishing strength. She shut the door behind them and Reyan risked creeping along the hall. She wouldn't be able to hear much through the door, but perhaps she could sneak in through the shadows to listen. She had her realm-skipping ability now if by some mad chance Belladonna did see her.

A soul-shattering scream tore through the air. The shadows shivered, absorbing the emotions and Reyan almost screamed with the pain of it. Shadows absorbed emotion much better than anyone would ever assume, and she was sure it was the shadows that linked to the nether and therefore the semi-sentience the courts seemed to develop. Like imprints in sand or warm breath on glass, courts reflected the emotions of their people and their lord or lady, and the shadows seemed to follow that logic too.

The screams were coming from inside the room Belladonna had Petra in, and Reyan didn't dare try to slip inside now, the waves of fear from the ones already in there too toxic to bear.

There's still Tyren. If I can get to him and he's on his own, I can let him know help is coming.

With the excruciating, tortured screams echoing once again behind her, she slipped back into shadow and rushed into the room Blossom guarded so anxiously, taking a risk with her shadow-form.

Tyren looked like hell. He had a split cheek oozing blood into the pillow he had his head on, and his clothes looked rumpled. Reyan risked taking form and made a soft hushing noise to gain his attention, aware of Blossom outside. Most of the Illusion Court knew Blossom had an auditory gift, and she didn't want to risk being overheard.

Another scream rent the air and Reyan clenched her fists to avoid the wash of revulsion fighting its way from her stomach up her throat.

Tyren scrambled up to his feet, hovering in a weird sort

of lean as if he was going to bow but doubting himself. Then he pressed a finger to his lips. Reyan nodded and pointed over her shoulder as he limped past her toward the mirror. He winced as he blew on the mirror, no doubt from pain in his cheek, then he lifted his shaking arm upward to write.

"Petra taken for torture. Need queen. Couldn't orb out, rooms gifted against skipping."

Reyan nodded and wiped the words away for him before blowing on the mirror for her own message.

"Got it. Will take location back Demi. Stay strong and say nothing. We're coming back for you both."

She hoped the neat lines of the tiny letters gave him hope, but patted his shoulder gently in case that helped too and disassembled back into shadow. Tyren wiped a hand over the unharmed side of his face and she didn't wait around to see what he would do.

She slipped past Blossom and whisked down the hall, trying her best to navigate a place she'd never been. She reformed her head and smelled the kitchens nearby, but a wrong turn left her in a dead-end hall with a single doorway she definitely didn't recognise.

I need to get to the market and skip myself home, then orb Kainen to get me to Demi.

She searched the shadows in frustration, then froze as voices echoed from a nearby doorway. Taking her shadow-form fully again, she hemmed herself in behind a huge statue and hoped for the best. She couldn't realm-skip inside the court according to Tyren, but she could dissolve into shadow and flee quick enough back to the market.

Belladonna walked down the hall with a man beside her. Not so much time spent torturing, which was good for Petra, unless…

Reyan suffered the wave of fear at the thought, her thoughts spinning as she recognised Belladonna's companion. Her insides roiled with disgust at the sight of him. Lorens had been a prisoner briefly during the fight at the Nether Court some weeks ago, but Demi had insisted Reyan and Kainen take him away and let him 'escape'. Now here he was, strolling along with Belladonna of all people, his short brown hair and ageless face betraying what she assumed was a ridiculously powerful unknown Fae.

"It shouldn't take long," Belladonna said. "The Lord of Revels is only too happy to please me, as he'll tell you himself."

She chortled to herself as they neared Reyan's shadowed corner and turned through the archway.

"There you are." A whiny male voice floated out. "What news?"

"We should be safe to talk in here," Belladonna said.

Reyan stayed in place, reforming just her ears to hear with. She should be racing back to safety but the thought she could take even more information back to Demi was too tempting to resist. When Lorens spoke next, she recognised his voice and let the shadows rearrange to shift her closer.

"We won't have any luck with Petra. I doubt Demerara is silly enough to share her plans with anyone other than Taz, and we can only hope that the Flora Court revel was a ruse to bring us out. They may even have ways of tracing us back here, so we should be on guard."

"What does it matter if they do trace us back here?" Belladonna demanded. "We're more than prepared for another fight."

"You haven't noticed that half the court hasn't returned

yet?" the whiny male voice said. "We need to be focused on finding a way into the Prime Realm. We have the location now but even if we stormed the human world to get to it, we have no idea how to cross through yet. That must be our priority."

"It's that important?" Belladonna asked.

"The queens have Faerie," Lorens replied. "Even the nether chose sides in the end. We need to weaken them on a personal level and for that we need more Fae and the power that the Prime Realm is said to hold. Now, continue with the plan. I'm sure we all have things to be busy with."

Belladonna huffed at that but said no more.

Reyan shrank against the statue, her heart hammering as Belladonna walked out again with two men. She recognised one of them from the Flora Court, but the Lord of Revels looked decidedly whiny in expression as he darted furtive glances at Belladonna. The other man was shorter and stouter with no sign of hair under a flat cap.

Reyan didn't see Lorens with them, but Belladonna and the others didn't look back once as they disappeared down the hall. Reyan stayed in her shadow-form, creeping toward the archway against her better judgement.

She peeked around the stone archway, stunned to find the wide room empty.

Where did he go?

She couldn't see Lorens anywhere, and no sign of another exit either.

Unless he was using a glamour, or he's spying on me as much as I'm trying to spy on him.

Panic sent her fleeing into the shadow and she raced through the darker hints of the castle corridors until she finally located the kitchen. Not able to knock anything over, she still slowed down to avoid brushing against any of the people rushing around the room until finally she was outside.

Time had no meaning for her any longer. She was exhausted and full to bursting with information that didn't quite make sense yet, so she ignored the lightening dawn sky and sped toward the shadows of the market.

As she reached the street, she reformed her body fully and focused all her energy and thought on home. Kainen's room, which she'd technically spent more time in than her own, formed around her and she dropped to her hands and knees from the effort. The urge to crawl to his bed and close her eyes tugged at her willpower, just for a few minutes.

Only the thought of his wicked delight if he came back to find her asleep curled around his pillow got her to her feet again. Her stomach growled and a wave of nausea swept over her, the hot flush turning quickly to cold chills. She didn't have an orb of her own, but the court sometimes let her use Kainen's multi-way door.

She pressed one hand to the handle and the other to the wood, pressing her forehead against it.

"Study please," she murmured. "Please please please."

She swung the door open and grinned with relief to see the study on the other side.

"Thank you."

She hurried toward the desk and lifted her hand over the large desk orb, opening her mouth to call for Kainen.

"The lady of the court returns." The familiar voice sent a chill over her skin. "How interesting to find you alone for once."

CHAPTER SIXTEEN
TYREN

Pacing the small room did no good. Rattling the door handle and calling out to footsteps passing by did no good. By the time Tyren's stomach was rumbling with gnawing hunger, he'd all but given up. Petra on the other hand sat quiet and still the whole time. She'd used her orb but reached nobody, then tried one attempt at picking the lock on the door with a pin, muttered something about 'tools' and sat back down. But she'd kept him safe against Blossom's crew. He wanted to be on her side rather than against her, even if she was content to do nothing, so mentioning her inactivity wouldn't do him any good.

He couldn't do nothing though so he dropped into a crouch by the door, peering out for the umpteenth time. He recognised the hall outside, the long corridor that led the length of the rooms that counted as cells. Every now and then a strain of noise from the markets below reached them, but he couldn't tell what was going on. Probably a normal day and soon it would be dark. The market stalls would light up like fireflies in the night, the narrow, winding alleyways between buildings glowing like rivers of dancing amber gold.

Even with the delights of his court clear in his mind, Tyren's focus slid back to the quiet beauty of the Flora court.

"Do you think they'll bother coming for us?" he asked.

Petra snorted. "You've met Lolly, right? Well, I'm her friend and you… I'm not sure what you are actually. What are you to her?"

A wholly unexpected turn but Tyren wasn't entirely sure of the answer. Lolly might not consider him a friend, but then she knew Hutch and Harvey's girlfriends well, which sort of made her a friend by association.

"She's a friend for my part," he said. "I know better than to answer on her behalf though."

Petra's chuckle could have meant any number of things.

"She'll be tearing down the courts to find us I reckon. Demi won't let it lie either. She has ways of finding things, so we sit tight. If we have to fight, we fight. Not much else we can do until then."

She had a point. He clambered to his feet but the echo of footsteps in the hall sent him hurrying back to Petra's side against the wall. She was already on her feet and he didn't argue when her warding merged with his moments later.

The air shivered with tension as the footsteps halted and a key rattled in the lock.

"Say nothing," Petra muttered. "Be brave and don't succumb if they torture us."

Tyren grimaced. "Blossom has an auditory gift. Tell me nothing either."

Her eyes widened and he wondered if he should have told her that before. But as the door swung open, she nodded, her face grim with hard-worn determination.

"Well, I bet you never expected to be captive in your own court, Berell."

Lady Belladonna swept into the room, her eyes deceptively innocent in their brown wideness. In stretchy black trousers and a flowing black shirt, she looked more like a sword-mistress of old than a traditional Fae princess. But he noted the small nicks and scars on her hands, and the tight way her honey-blonde hair was tied back out of the way. This was a Fae who fought her own battles when she felt free enough to drop the ladylike charade. She exuded terror, the danger radiating from her in palpable waves.

He'd seen her at the court many times but had been far beneath her notice, unlike Blossom who was only fourth in line. Tyren had learned her family's lineage early; a daughter who abdicated and all but disappeared from Fae society, then Lady Belladonna, Blossom, Taz who had been born of Faerie itself, and finally May who very few people knew much about.

Blossom hurried in behind her sister, mindful to shut the door behind them. Tyren risked a glance at Petra in time to see her keen dark eyes scoping out their enemy.

"You don't answer your betters when they address you?" Belladonna tutted, her smile widening. "*KNEEL.*"

The compulsion washed over their warding and Tyren's knees tried to buckle. He held firm, gritting his teeth against the force of her power. Petra threaded her fingers through his and he clung on, taking strength from her.

"I'm a lord now," he said. "And I don't bow to traitors."

He could almost hear the mental groan reverberating around Petra's head, but he would wear his allegiance with pride whatever the cost.

Blossom hovered behind her sister, her anxious face peering over Belladonna's shoulder. Her jeans and floral blouse put her at odds with what her sister had clearly come to do to them, but Tyren wondered if her worry was something he could use.

"I'm glad you both have some spirit," Belladonna said. "It'll be more fun breaking you."

She eyed her fingernails and flicked out a hand. Tyren winced against the sheer burn that licked over his skin, but he could feel the surge of Petra's will holding firm and cool beside him. All he could do was provide his own meagre skill in support, let her draw from it where she needed it.

We aren't going to survive this. The thought stabbed its way through his resolve. *Even if we hold on, it's only a matter of time.*

The burning dissipated and he gasped a few ragged breaths before doing the one thing Petra had told him not to.

"Why the Revel Court?" he asked.

He waited for some attack, either from Petra or from Belladonna, but he hoped she at least was predictably Fae enough to show her vanity early.

Belladonna rolled her eyes. "Because your lord wants power, and we offer it without the restrictions the new queen and the old queen do. His decadence and desire for excess makes him easy to manage."

Tyren didn't doubt it for a second. His lord was fickle, easily swayed. But what worried him was that he'd had no inkling at all that anything was going on at the court at all.

Did my father know any of this?

He couldn't bear the thought, or face it with the enemy so close. The minute she lost interest, she'd attack again.

"I can believe that. So what, is this a plot to lure out the queen? Or were you going for Lo- Lady Leilania instead?"

Blossom gave him a harassed look, her eyes wide with warning, but Belladonna laughed.

"I heard rumour somewhere that you were smart. At least, I think it was you. No point luring the queen out when I plan to gather infinite strength and resources first."

The Prime Realm. She's hoping to find it and gain allies there.

But Petra was silent beside him, letting him talk. He

didn't dare look her way, holding Belladonna's attention instead. If one of them got free with any kind of information, it could go straight back to Demi.

"Faerie might always be divided," he said. "I doubt the human world will help you, especially not when they realise what your view of their kind is."

"As if we care about humans, or need anything from them." Belladonna's face contorted in outrage.

"They're only in the way," Blossom piped up. "Once we find a way to blast through their world and work out how to get through the gateway to the prime realm-*Owww!*"

Tyren winced as Belladonna's hand arced through the air and slammed into her sister's cheek. Blossom staggered back with the force of the blow, her shoulder shunting into the wall. Cradling her red cheek with both hands, she remained cowed against the wall.

"Now we have to kill them," Belladonna sighed airily. "Don't worry though. We'll make it last, make it hurt. Perhaps your court would like to watch."

Sickening fear curdled like bubbling acid in Tyren's throat, but he inhaled a sharp breath and focused on the warding with Petra alongside him.

"With the current lord leading it, I no longer claim it was my court," he said. "I'm not court-sworn, nor am I bound by any debts. But if you think the locals will want to see one of their own tortured, you think that'll get them on your side, that's your funeral."

Petra's hand squeezed his fingers, a wordless reward. She approved of his bravery at least, even if it was going to be the death of him.

"Very touching," Belladonna sneered.

She glanced around the room, then glared in Blossom's

direction.

"Stay outside the door. Nobody goes in or out. Got it?"

Blossom nodded and Belladonna lunged.

Tyren shouted as Petra's hand tore from his grip. He pulled a warding over himself and tried to grab Petra, but she was already in Belladonna's grasp.

"Time for torture," Belladonna sang. "Ladies first, of course."

Tyren barrelled forward. "Let her go!"

Petra raised her arms out wide and brought them down on top of Belladonna's, trying to break her hold. Belladonna kicked out but Petra was fast enough to dodge the attempt to bring her to her knees. She ducked and twisted under Belladonna's arm, almost free, until Blossom stuck out a foot.

Petra tried to hurdle it but there was no amount of finesse that could have avoided it. She tumbled to the floor with a jarring thud.

Tyren ran. Belladonna ran. Both of them grappling to grab Petra's arms and legs even as Tyren tried to throw his warding wider, to encase her in it.

Petra kicked out and landed a savage blow on Belladonna's wrist. The crack echoed through the room, but Belladonna clung on, pulling her across the floor with indomitable strength. Tyren followed but without breaking his protection, he couldn't grab Belladonna or try to force her to let go.

Screw it.

He dropped the warding and dodged around Belladonna, throwing arms around her neck from behind. He clung on, yanking with fierce jolts to try and get her away. Petra sat up and clawed at Belladonna's hands, scratching and even trying to bite to get herself away. As she slithered free, Belladonna roared and twirled in a circle, the speed sending Tyren's legs flying outward. The sheer force of it slammed through his arms and he had to let go of her, brief moments of weightlessness registering a moment before his body crashed side first into the wall.

Get up. Get up. Get up!

He managed to get his brain talking to his hands enough to get them underneath his body, but when he tried to stand the room spun and he lurched forward, almost smashing his nose on the floor. Through his watery vision, he could see Belladonna and Blossom holding Petra, Belladonna bleeding from her nose.

Did I manage that? He couldn't remember clearly.

Even outclassed, he tried to stand again, his legs slipping about underneath him.

"Pathetic," Belladonna spat. "She'll suffer all the more now because of you. I'll make sure we're close enough for you to hear the screams, low-born brat. Blossom, keep watch outside. No mistakes."

Petra didn't struggle as they towed her out of the room. She used her remaining moments with him to give him a look, and to mouth *"trust the shadows"* before Blossom slammed the door shut.

Trust the shadows? What?

He pressed his hands to his aching head. His shoulder was throbbing now and he wanted to cry. He huffed in sharp breaths in the hope of quelling the burning tears. He tilted his head back, frantically searching the room for something he might have missed. The thought of leaving Petra with Belladonna while he found an escape route was awful, but he couldn't fight an all-powerful royal like Belladonna alone. He needed to go for help somehow.

He clenched his fists as a scream ricocheted through the

air. Gritting his teeth, he found the wall behind him and pushed onto his hands and knees. A few more breaths and he managed to climb up the wall to get to his feet.

"I can kick the door down," he muttered to himself. "I can smash the mirror and use the glass for defence. There must be something I can do."

Another frantic scream tore at his insides. Heaping down, he tried to rest his swimming head under the pillow. Shame at not being able to protect Petra drove him to hide from the screaming that kept on coming. He had no idea whether the Queen would be able to get to them in time. Belladonna likely wouldn't get rid of Petra straight away; she'd want it to last, to hurt a lot.

He let the tears soak into the pillow, the softness of it only dulling the horrific sounds piercing the air in frequent waves.

This time a couple of days ago I was here completely unaware. Now I'm here as a prisoner.

He couldn't save Petra. Couldn't escape. But at least Lolly was safe at the Flora Court. At least she was okay.

Trust the shadows, Petra had said. He frowned, his mind hazy. Did she mean there was a way out? Were the shadows some kind of clue?

As if answering him, a patch of darkness formed in the corner beside the mirror. He flinched and almost fell flat on his back in alarm. The shadows roiled around themselves lines slowly taking form. He wanted to back away, to scream, to do something other than stand there waiting for whatever his fate would be. But his legs wouldn't move as the darkness took the form of a person.

The features settled from darkness, growing lighter until colour began to bleed into the face, the clothes and the shining blonde hair.

Tyren had a feeling he should kneel as he would normally have done, but he was a lord now. He also couldn't do it without the risk of not getting back up again.

Blossom's outside.

The thought echoed a warning in his head as the Lady of the Court of Illusions materialised in front of him, and he pressed a finger to his lips. He ignored her horrified face as she took in the sight of him and he limped to the mirror.

Trust the shadows, Petra had said. If she trusted the Lady of the Illusion Court, he would too.

CHAPTER SEVENTEEN
LOLLY

"I want them found and I want her *dead*!"

Lolly's scream filled the halls as though the court itself had amplified the noise. She knew the court responded to her mother's will, but she had her mother's blood in her and right now every drop was boiling up an apocalypse.

After seeing Blossom and her crew vanish with Petra and Tyren in tow, she'd stormed straight to Demi, then to her mother's office. Her mother listened for a surprisingly long time before trying to calm her down, but Lolly refused to accept the usual placations.

Subtle rumblings underneath the court suggested Arthur was happily joining in on the tantrum, but she'd taken a liking to Tyren too. Lolly couldn't help wondering if Arthur had sensed somehow what had happened, or perhaps someone had tried to attack her mid-battle.

"That seems like an overreaction," her mother said placidly. "Petra is brave and strong. Tyren too by all accounts. Now, I need to see the queen. I've kept her waiting five minutes already for this. You can let her in on your way out."

Lolly stormed to the door and threw it open, but as Demi approached, she stood to the side and wordlessly refused to leave. Her mother sighed, weariness showing in lines around her eyes for a moment.

"My queen. This is extremely worrying."

Lolly stalked over to the window and looked out at the unnatural stillness as the queen faced her mother with a grave face.

"Forgive the excessive methods, but it was better than a battle."

The revel, the crowd of guests and the Forgotten, who'd somehow realm-skipped right into the middle of everything, were all fast asleep. Some slumped over stalls and others had folded into accidental embraces on the ground.

"I won't be able to hold the calm for long," Demi added. "My court will do their best to clear the Forgotten into our keeping, but anyone waking will probably remember and either flee or try to resurrect the fight. It's bought us time though and avoided more fatalities."

Lolly folded her arms and Demi's gaze switched to her.

"Petra was my mentor. Still is in many ways. I know people who are very fond of Tyren too. Once we find out where they are, we'll be going in to rescue them. If there's anything at all you can add, maybe something you've overheard?"

Lolly took a deep breath. Anger would keep her running but she needed to make sure she thought clearly and forgot nothing.

"Tyren and I went up to check Blossom's room." She ignored her mother's indignant squeak. "He found her diary and there were mentions of two human world places-"

"Don't say them out loud," Demi interrupted. "I'll have Milo come see you and you can write them down if that's okay."

Lolly nodded. "Fine. Then Blossom came in with Loudmouth Lyle and called her sister, you know Belladonna, the one who defected? They barely spoke before I saw my chance to leave and I took it. I shouldn't have left Tyren behind though. I should have carried him or something."

Demi smiled sadly. "He's a big guy. He also had Petra with him and she's one of the smartest, bravest people I know."

"Wait!" Lolly froze. "Lyle! We need to interrogate him. He knows everything. Is he still here? Do we need to wait for him to wake up?"

"Leilania, enough."

Her mother stood, her hands pressed to the desk. Lolly shook her head.

"No, I won't sit down and be good this time. I can't. It's one thing to be cautious, to not want to anger people who could hurt us, but they're hurting us anyway! They threw the first punch. They took Tyren and Petra for no obvious reason except to lash out at us. You might want to let it wash past us, but I can't. I *can't*."

She saw the anxiety cross her mother's face. Without her mum there to act as the jolly, sensible go-between always suggesting compromises, they had no way of settling differences, especially not one as serious as this.

"Lyle is in my court's keeping already," Demi said, her voice quiet but strong. "You'll be in no danger with me when we speak to him. He showed some interest in you previously so I've heard. Perhaps he'll talk with you there."

Any other day that would have been a victory, but Lolly couldn't find any glee in it. She'd spent so long being busy then storming about fuelled by anger, that if not for Tyren's insistence on her eating that morning, she probably would have fainted by now.

She glanced at her mother. The Lady of the Flora Court would never refuse the command of her queen, no matter how politely it was worded. But her mother also wouldn't want her near any danger.

"I want protection with Leilania at all times," Lady Flora muttered.

Demi nodded. "Done. The Hutchinson brothers may play the fool, but they're quick and smart where it counts. They're with her until this ordeal is over. The Eastwicks too if you want."

Her mother pursed her lips. "Fine, thank you, my queen. Wait outside now, Lolly."

Lolly conceded that time. She had her orders, to find Milo and give him the human world names, but she didn't want to risk losing track of Demi and the chance to interrogate Lyle along with it.

With the office door closed behind her, she sank against the wall.

Lyle was part of the Forgotten this whole time. Does that mean Claus is too? Is that what they were arguing about outside the greenhouse? Why did Claus warn me away from Tyren? Why did the Forgotten go with Tyren and Petra rather than attack, to lure the rest of us out? They can't have known Demi would be able to send the whole revel to sleep. Either Demi has a traitor somewhere close by, or Blossom panicked and grabbed the first people she could as hostages.

She looked up as footsteps echoed along the hall to find the Eastwick sisters barrelling toward her.

"There you are!" Beryl exclaimed.

Cheryl folded her into a strangle-hug. "We were worried about you."

Meryl patted her on the head.

"What?" Lolly struggled free. "I'm fine. It's Petra and Tyren I'm worried about."

The three of them exchanged glances, communicating without words. Lolly wanted to scream, but she held onto the urge.

Save all your anger for Lyle. If he's on the enemy side, there's no mercy.

"Petra is strong and-"

"Yes, yes, everyone keeps telling me Petra is strong and brave and smart and Tyren is clever. It doesn't help."

Cheryl sighed. "We just need to know where they are."

"Well, we interrogate Lyle for that," Lolly insisted. "Demi said I can go with her."

Three identical grins formed, scary in their sinister similarity.

"We're good at interrogating people," Meryl said.

Beryl nodded. "We're so good, people would rather cave than let us try it."

"Especially if we get Hutch and Harvey to juggle as an introduction. They can go seven straight minutes without dropping anything now. And they're *really* fond of Tyren. They probably wouldn't even try to make us trade for it."

The office door opened before the sisters could tug a smile from Lolly, although she could feel it brewing. With them around somehow the impossible felt possible.

"Right crew." Demi closed the door behind her and clapped her hands together. "Taz, Ace, Hutch and Harvey have Lyle. We get the location of the Forgotten's base from him, and anything else we can squeeze out. Once we know where they are, everyone is on lock-down until we have a plan. No-one is running off to play the hero."

Lolly froze as Demi's gaze fixed on her and she didn't dare say a word. If playing the hero meant disobeying a royal order, she would do it if she had to and take the consequences.

"Where are they, home?" Beryl asked.

Demi shook her head. "We found a very useful guard to help us. Turns out Lyle fell foul of them last night and they were only too happy to help."

Confused looks passed around the group as Demi set off across the conservatory. Lolly hurried after her with the Eastwicks hot on her heels.

"We should find his brother too," she piped up. "I overheard him with Lyle by the greenhouses last night and they were talking about family loyalties. And he tried to warn me away from Tyren."

Demi smiled over her shoulder.

"I wouldn't worry about Claus," she said. "Focus on Lyle for now. If he seems likely to talk to you most, we'll fall back and let you talk to him."

Surprised that Demi was giving so much trust to her, she stepped into the dining hall and halted.

The room was deserted except for a small group in the far corner. Taz, Hutch, Harvey and a boy Lolly thought she recognised as Milo's boyfriend stood around a cowering, quivering Lyle. Above him, hemming him in, was an extremely salivating Arthur.

"Apparently, he tried to cut one of Arthur's vines off to bring you as a gift," Demi said. "Slaying the beast for you kind of thing. Arthur didn't like that one bit."

That explained the tantrum rumbling across the court alongside hers. Lolly would have laughed if she hadn't been so appalled. But her mind was ticking now, and she knew that shouting and insulting Lyle wouldn't get him to open up to her. No, she had to play the person he coveted most, haughty and near the top of the Fae ladder. He would look for ways to get himself out of trouble, so she could offer him deals and consideration to soothe his ego and get him babbling.

Arthur loomed over everyone's heads, snapping her pod-mouth. Lolly smiled but didn't risk stepping close to Lyle.

"Aww, I'm okay," she reassured. "Did this boy try to cut you?"

The pod dipped in a mimicry of nodding. Lolly wasn't sure if Arthur understood actual language or just basics, but she operated on the basis that it wasn't her place to judge and as long as Arthur was happy and healthy, that was enough.

"It dribbled on me!" Lyle wailed. "I'm going to explode any moment, I know it."

Lolly rolled her eyes. "Oh hush up. It won't do much more than sting a while. Why on earth did you think cutting her would be a good idea?"

She stood surrounded by FDPs and royalty, something Lyle's greedy eyes noticed even in his supposed torment. She was all but untouchable, which elevated her in his mind as something desirable. Even while he sat huddled against the wall, he was scheming for himself.

I should take his shoulders and rattle his brain right out of his stupid head.

"You were obsessed with it last night," he whined. "I figured showing you I could control it was a way to get your attention. You danced with my brother but not me."

"Your brother had the guts to approach me. We danced. That was it. But he at least gave me a couple of fanciful warnings, so perhaps it's him I should be speaking to right now."

Lyle's lip curled. "What good would he be? You want information about the Forgotten, right? That's why you're all here?"

"Go on then." Lolly folded her arms.

"What's it worth? The Forgotten will tear me apart for talking to you, let alone giving you actual information. I'm not doing it for nothing. Besides, comfort as the Queen's captive is better than torment as the Forgotten's traitor. Seems like I'm exactly where I should be."

Lolly refused to let that rattle her.

"Then no point talking to you. Thought you'd aspire to more than a prisoner nobody would remember. It's kind of disappointing, but I guess not exactly unexpected. Loudmouth Lyle, all talk and no action."

It was unnecessarily cruel maybe, but it worked. His eyes narrowed and he straightened his shoulders with one eye on Arthur as she twitched her vines in warning.

"Oh please! You all fell into the trap I wanted you to. 'Loudmouth Lyle', nobody can trust him not to blab to the whole of Faerie. While I've been keeping Forgotten secrets for months now!"

"What secrets?" Demi asked.

Lolly glanced over her shoulder, but Demi's eyes were fixed on Lyle.

"Nobody knew that the Lord of Revels is working with Lady Belladonna. He hopes to be her next king when the Blood and Bone Court take over Faerie."

He gasped the moment the words were out. Lolly hadn't seen compulsions at work often, but she guessed Demi was forcing him to answer her questions. Hoping she wasn't overstepping, she jumped in.

"Why take Tyren and Petra?" she asked.

Lyle's eyes widened, darting from her to the others.

"I don't know. That wasn't the plan. Lady Belladonna wanted you. The Lord of Revels suggested it. The plan was to unite you and him to get control of the Flora Court, not that he knew that. He wants Belladonna."

Lolly waited all of one beat. "And where have they taken them?"

A gurgling noise filled Lyle's throat, his eyes bulging as his cheeks turned red.

Demi swore. "They've bound the information against compulsions."

Lyle sagged, his breathing ragged and relief scrawled across his face. Lolly dredged up every element of anger inside her, smiling as viciously sweet as she could manage.

"That's fine," she said. "If he's not of any use to you now, can I keep him? I've been studying some poisons, academically obviously, but I doubt anyone would miss him if I run a couple of tests. Human skin is so fragile yet resilient."

She had no intention of running anything, and the poison study was only for the purpose of her index, not something she'd ever consider testing on anything living.

But Lyle didn't know that. He shrank against the wall as she took a step toward him. Arthur waved her vines helpfully, adding weight to the threat.

"I can't let you strangle him," Lolly told Arthur. "Or chew on him, worse luck. That would take a long time to affect him properly. But I know there are some *artanantaceps* in the woods, and their flowers have really strange properties. Never had an actual human to test them on before."

She word-tangled fearful threats and Lyle started shaking.

"All yours if you really need him," Demi offered. "Can't say we need another one clogging up our court."

"What would happen to me if I told you freely?" he begged.

Lolly glanced back at Demi, who shrugged.

"We'd go through a period of retraining. If it didn't take, you'd be sent to the forever mountains. Otherwise the Flora Court will take you. Can't say I'll pay too much attention to how she treats you."

Lolly read between the lines and almost smiled at the trust implied there. Demi might be saying it to frighten Lyle, but Fae couldn't lie and it meant both of them knew Lolly could be trusted to treat any prisoners of the Flora Court compassionately.

"If I tell you where the prisoners have been taken, you'll take me with you? I don't want to be left here with her, and *that*." He glanced up at Arthur.

Demi nodded. "Yes, but it has to be a legitimate location. Any tricks, word-tangling or Fae nonsense, and the deal is off."

His face scrunched in disbelief.

He honestly thought he could trick the queen of Faerie. Lolly almost laughed. *The arrogance of it.*

"There's a court that's betrayed you, that you know now," Lyle said. "They fought alongside the Forgotten today, and it's their court that houses the new Blood and Bone Court."

Demi appeared beside Lolly, her face grim.

"There is no Blood and Bone Court, only a bunch of psychos who want to resurrect old ways. It will not happen. If you're lying to us, your punishment will be painful and severe. And *long*. If you're tricking us, the same applies."

Lolly took a step back and Lyle looked up at her, hatred swimming in his eyes.

"The Lord of Revels will reward me for supporting the true way of Faerie, as will Lady Belladonna when she's queen. You should go back to your twisted plants and flower arranging. Give up your friends because they'll be mad or dead before you can find a way to them."

Panic reared inside her but Lolly held herself firm. She pulled every element of malice and spite to the fore, letting the ice crystalise in her eyes and the sharp bite filter into her voice.

"Oh you poor, deluded Fae-boy. You think the Flora Court is all flower wreaths and dancing around willows? We are the rock of the mountain, the core of the earth and the forged metal being mined in blistering furnaces. We are the poison dripping from every stem and by my name, your blood will be the first I spill if anything's happened to my friends."

She turned on her heel and stalked away, aware of the Eastwicks following her across the dining hall. Worry for Tyren and Petra pounded through her, putting speed into her feet so that the others were jogging to keep up with her.

"We're all staying in the same room tonight," Beryl called to her. "Us and the boys. We sleep, we eat, we plan. Then we attack. Don't want to miss that."

Lolly stopped and turned so fast they almost tumbled into her. Ignoring their grumbling, she frowned as her mum approached.

"Bad business this," she said. "Your mother isn't impressed by any of it, Lol, but I managed to calm her down somewhat. If you're planning on heading out anywhere with the queen, make sure you let us know before you leave, okay?"

Lolly nodded and settled as her mum kissed her forehead.

"Good girl. I'll keep the greenhouses running while you're away. We've got your notes on the panels, and the others are well up to the challenge."

She's already guessed I'm going after Petra and Tyren. And she's not trying to stop me.

Lolly managed a weak smile as her mum muttered something about food and set off, sidling out of the way as Demi strode past.

"My room. I've asked for food to be sent up and the boys will be with us after they've taken Lyle away. Then we'll see what we're dealing with."

Lolly opened her mouth to protest, to say she wanted to go too, but Demi gave her a weary look.

"I had a feeling about the Revel Court after their lord was absent today, so Reyan's already gone looking there. If there's a way in, she'll find it and report back. They have instructions not to go in without us."

Lolly had to be content with that and slouched after the others to Demi's room. She'd barely set foot inside it before, never having any need to go and see the rooms that were reserved for royal visits. Queen Tavania from the oak line had never bothered to visit, and Demi hadn't been queen long. But as she entered, she had to be proud of the court she came from.

The stone walls were carved with natural scenes and several trees and tangles of bush were strategically placed in pots and planters around the room. Green furnishings softened the stone further, along with muted wooden furniture and comfortable throw cushions for lounging on in the sunken centre of the room.

"I love this room," Demi breathed, her shoulders sagging. "Smells like oxygen somehow."

"That'll be all the plants," Beryl said helpfully.

Demi shot her a look of badly veiled amusement and sank onto the nearest plump green cushion with a hefty sigh. The Eastwicks cascaded down to sit beside her with no ceremony whatsoever, but even the angry, anxious part of Lolly's brain remembered that this was the actual queen of Faerie in her court.

She hovered nearby, warring between offering to be of use and taking a seat alongside her friends.

"Sit here, we need to plan." Demi saved her from having to decide by patting the cushion beside her.

She might have guessed Lolly's reservations, or might have been used to the hesitation of 'normal' folk by now, but Lolly did as she was told. Cross-legged on the cushion, she worried the hem of her dress for a moment before remembering she had her comfortable clothes on under the glamour. With a wave of her hand, she vanished the glamour and hunched over her legs with relief.

"So, trap?" Meryl asked.

Demi nodded. "Definitely a trap to lure us out. They wanted Lolly and got the others instead, but they know Petra is important to me."

"We need to be cautious then. Go in with glamours, tricks up our sleeve," Cheryl insisted.

The air between them wavered for a second, halting all discussion. One moment they were alone, the next four boys were crammed into the small square of space between them.

"Whoa!"

Harvey and Hutch wobbled with their legs flailing high to avoid falling on anyone. Taz didn't bother and fell on Demi, who disappeared into the folds of the huge cushion with a startled 'oof'. Ace, Milo's boyfriend, somehow managed to step clear of everyone and slink to sit beside Meryl without a single misstep. Lolly envied his gracefulness. She'd only met him once before when Milo visited, but he seemed friendly and anyone who became a cherished soul to someone like Milo was worth knowing.

"That was quick." Demi sat up with a grumble, shoving Taz to sit on her other side.

Ace nodded, bracing his arms around his knees.

"He was sobbing when we dropped him off, so we didn't stick around."

Demi shrugged. "Okay, so Milo has Arcanium. We're waiting on Reyan. Once we get her go-ahead, we need to know exactly how to get into the Revel Court and grab them."

Beryl grinned wide and cracked her knuckles, earning her a wince from Harvey.

"So the usual then," she said. "Simple."

CHAPTER EIGHTEEN
REYAN

Reyan inhaled a sharp breath, assessing the layout of Kainen's office as she turned to find Ciel leaning against the door that led out to one of the Illusion Court's hallways.

His blonde hair hung around his ears but he'd grown his beard longer than she remembered, and he had a habit of being so still that she couldn't help but get edgy about when he was inevitably going to pounce. She hadn't always feared him, not like she did now, but then he'd never let her see the real him. Not until he'd proposed to her a while ago anyway.

She'd shut the multi-way door behind her so the chances of escaping through that were uncertain, because it might not obey her and send her somewhere Ciel couldn't reach if she tried it again.

"What are you doing lurking in here?" she asked, her voice unsteady.

He chuckled. "Lurking? I still do the court's bidding, something your beloved lord has forgotten, fortunately for me. But we were once good friends weren't we? Why do you look so frightened? Why, as court lady, aren't I supposed to report to you also?"

He was taunting her. Fears flashed in her mind, that he somehow knew the engagement and therefore her status as lady were a fake. But if he didn't know, she would lose so much respect by acting afraid, especially when he went and told their courtiers.

She lifted her head and forced herself to stare right into his eyes.

"How true. You can go."

He tilted his head. "Imprudent. I haven't finished my task yet."

He pushed away from the wall he was leaning on and took a couple of steps toward her. She forced herself to hold firm despite the urge to dissolve into the shadows and hide. He couldn't catch her and they both knew it; this was a game of wills, his sense of entitlement challenging her authority.

"What did you do with the letter?" she asked.

He stopped in the middle of the room and Reyan slid back a step to rest against the edge of Kainen's desk, aiming to look entirely unbothered by Ciel's presence. The desk reminded her of something then, the letter she'd written to Kainen confessing certain feelings that then went missing. She had assumed Ciel took it, and now she could use it to distract him.

"Letter, Lady?"

She smiled. "The letter I left on Kainen's desk. Are you saying you didn't take it?"

He watched her without answering, which told her everything she needed to know.

"You don't need to worry," she added, with as light a laugh as she could muster. "He knows what happened to it and he doesn't need to read it to know how I feel."

Pretty words, because if she had any say over the unfortunate and rash letter that exposed her feelings, Kainen would never see a word of it.

"As you say, Lady."

She sighed. "So, we might as well get this out of the way now. You and Blossom are friends, I believe. We know she's defected along with Belladonna. How far do your loyalties lie?"

His amusement had disappeared now, leaving a haughty look of anger on his face. He folded his arms but she caught the clench of his fists underneath the elbows.

She slid her hand over the top of the desk, her fingers brushing the cold smoothness of the orb as a precaution.

"No witty answers this time?" she asked. "Oh dear, that is telling. Kainen," she paused. "He'll find that very interesting."

"Assuming you tell him," Ciel suggested.

She nodded. "Assuming I do. Why, is this where we trade in secrets?"

"We could come to some arrangement I'm sure," he suggested.

His eyes sparked with interest and she forced herself to look relaxed, to play along.

"Like what, you tell me everything Belladonna and Blossom are planning and help me out with my reputation, and I do what in return exactly? Give you money, land and favour?"

He laughed. "I have money, I don't need land and as for favour? I am popular enough for what I need to do. No, what I want is something a little more fitting of our court's dark nature."

"And what would that be?"

"Revenge. Kainen dishonoured me, and I want him to feel even a hint of what I've suffered since he stole you." His gaze flicked to the orb behind her on the desk, her fingers now anchored to it. "In return, I would assist you with your reputation amongst the courtiers, find ways to improve your respectability. Perhaps in time, you could even rule alone."

She snorted, all attempt at pretence gone.

"You think I'd willingly betray or keep secrets from

Kainen in his own court, and what, overthrow him in favour of you? You really don't know me at all if you think I give a damn about my social standing over my morals or my loyalty to him. I'd choose him a thousand times over, court or no court, before I'd go anywhere *near* you."

Ciel's eyes had widened halfway through her indignant speech, and she wondered how he could possibly be arrogant enough to assume she'd be so easily swayed by a few scant promises.

"Well, that is good to know."

Kainen's voice filled the air behind her. She flinched and twisted around, bashing her thigh into the edge of the desk as her hands flew to her chest.

"Orbs alive, don't come up behind me like that!" she huffed. "Ouch, the table's taken half my leg off by the feel of it."

Exaggerations about pain were a loophole Faerie seemed to tolerate as part of the 'not actually a lie' category, something she was grateful for now.

She glanced back at Ciel with realisation dawning. The widened eyes hadn't been caused by her admission of loyalty but by Kainen's arrival; he'd been caught red-handed trying to manipulate her.

"Our deal will stand, Ciel," Kainen said. "For now. But I believe part of it was that you wouldn't address or approach my lady without her consent."

Reyan blinked. "What?"

Ciel's gaze flicked back and forth between them, but Reyan had no idea what that meant.

"I was in here already when she entered," Ciel said. "I didn't want to be rude, especially when she started asking questions of me. That would count as consent to talk to the lady of the court, I'm sure."

Kainen laughed, the sound dark and full of warning.

"A fancy loophole, nothing more."

Reyan folded her arms. "You told him not to talk to me?"

Ciel nodded. "Actually, he-"

"Get out," Reyan snapped, at the same time as Kainen growled, "sod off."

Ciel threw open the door to the hall and stalked through, slamming it behind him.

Before Reyan could demand Kainen tell her exactly what he and Ciel had made a deal about, his hands landed firm on her shoulders. He looked her over, his gaze sticking on her face for several moments.

"I can rub it for you, if you want," he offered. "Your leg, I mean. Sounds like the rest of you is more than strong enough to cope without my help."

Through his sudden wicked smile, she could see relief and something else she couldn't place. Perhaps the same something that had her staring back at him, trying so hard not to smile widely. But memories of Petra's screams and Tyren's busted face tainted any happiness she might have felt.

"Never mind that, it'll have to keep." She wiped a hand over her face. "I need to get to Demi now. Tyren and Petra are… they're at the Revel Court but not in a good state, and I have so much rattling around in my head that Demi needs to know."

Kainen wrapped an arm around her waist without another word and she settled her face against his shoulder. She didn't care if it was improper or that she wasn't a real lady. All her previous worries that he was simply playing along to keep the ruse going disappeared as her depleted digestive system let out the most ferocious growl she'd ever heard. She froze but Kainen's weary sigh fluttered onto her head a moment later.

"How many time-skips have you done now?" he asked. "Never mind. The moment we get to the Flora Court, I'll get you breakfast. And lunch. And dinner."

As the nether gathered around them, she kept her face pinned to his chest.

"A lord serving people? What would the court say?" "Scandalous things probably. But my lady's health comes first."

CHAPTER NINETEEN
LOLLY

The queen paced up and down like a whirlwind which was putting everyone on edge. Even with Taz moving back and forth at her side, her irritation was transferring to everyone else. Ace had gone back to help Milo manage Arcanium, the location of the queen's court, and that left Lolly alone. No Tyren, no Petra. Just a stressed royal couple and a collection of her friends huddled together. Lolly had tried to keep herself calm as a representative of the court they were in, but she couldn't shake the anxiety biting at her heels.

The Eastwicks and the Hutchinson brothers were deep in conversation about potential diversions and mad plots that would have taken an army to undertake, but at least it kept them busy. So busy that none of them noticed the Lord and Lady of the Illusion Court materialising in the far corner. Lolly jumped up, drawing their attention.

"Oh thank Faerie," Demi muttered. "Did you find them?"

Reyan nodded. "They're at the Revel Court but it's not good. I overheard some stuff too but I'm not sure if now's the time?"

Demi's arms wrapped around her middle, Taz's hand dropping onto her shoulder immediately.

"You can say anything in front of this lot," she said.

Reyan nodded. "Okay, well Belladonna confirmed that they're looking for keys to the Prime Realm, and that she expects you to act on your emotions and go in for a rescue mission."

"Nothing new there," Taz muttered.

"Then I saw them further down while I was trying to find the way out, Belladonna I mean. She walked into a room with Lorens, that escapee from the Nether Court, then out with two others, and Lorens had vanished somewhere. One was the Lord of Revels and the other was shorter and bald, but I didn't recognise him. At least, he looked bald, he was wearing a cap."

Reyan hesitated then lifted her hands up to remove the hat on her own head as though she'd forgotten about it.

"One of the men, I'm guessing the Lord of Revels, insisted on finding the Prime Realm and said they have the location but no idea how to get through. He mentioned the human world as well, storming it. Sorry, my minds a bit frazzled."

Kainen's arms were still around her tightly and she sank against him as Demi nodded.

"Absolutely, I've asked way too much of you today already, and I'm going to have to ask one more time for you to sneak in and get us an open door if need be."

Reyan nodded even as Kainen looked like he was about to spit acid, darkness gathering around him.

Lolly hunched into her cardigan.

"Are they okay?" she asked.

Reyan glanced at her and the grimace spoke volumes.

"Alive. I heard… well, I never want to hear it again."

She paused as worried grimaces flew around the group. "Tyren is in one of the rooms they use for cells on the second floor. I listened a bit but given how eager Belladonna sounded, I don't think it'll be and instant- well, you know."

Demi seethed through her teeth. "She'll want to draw it

out, make it last."

"I reckon we've got a day to get to them both out then," Taz added. "Knowing her like I unfortunately do."

"We move now then," Demi insisted. "What else?"

Reyan frowned, forcing her mind back over the specifics.

"Tyren said the room had been gifted against anyone orbing or skipping in, but the whole court is blocked to entry. So we'll have to get through the markets and into the court unseen that way, then the kitchens are the best bet for getting up there, but it's too busy everywhere."

Beryl nodded. "Diversion, got it. We can handle that."

"Big explosion in the square to thin the crowd," Hutch suggested. "We still have fireworks leftover from the revel. Or maybe a loose animal. Taz, can you turn into an elephant maybe and rampage a while?"

"They'd tranquilise me," Taz said, horrified.

Demi rubbed a hand over her face. "No risking people getting tranquilised. No separating. Usual formation. I don't care what you do, or how you have to do it at this point as long as you don't hurt any civilians, and get as many people away from the court itself as you can. Taz and I will go in."

"And me."

Lolly prepared herself for an argument. Her mother would never let her and she wasn't exactly a qualified FDP like the queen and the others.

"Alright, but stay close." Demi nodded. "The last thing I need is to explain why the future of the Flora Court is missing. What gifts have you got, so I know?"

Lolly's mouth dropped open. The queen trusted her without even hesitating, believed she could be an asset somehow.

"I have speed and also a frost gift."

She zipped to the other end of the room and waited for the others to locate her, then pulled an element of chill into her forefinger and let the icicle form at the tip.

"Good. Okay, let me think a minute." Demi started pacing again. "You lot are sorting the diversion. Try to get a dual attack if you can, draw the central crowd's attention but also clear the court itself if you can, or our route through at least. Taz, Lolly and I will sneak up to get Tyren and Petra."

"I can speed ahead without being seen to make sure the way is clear," Lolly added.

She managed a tense grimace as Demi smiled briefly at her.

"Then we have a plan." She turned to the others. "How long do you need?"

Harvey counted on his fingers, the others looking expectantly at him. He lifted both hands with six fingers raised.

"A few minutes to get the stuff, then we'll come back here. If we can drop in by the Revel Court kitchens, you'll need to count six minutes from the time we separate and then the coast should be clear."

"I'll send a note to Milo," Taz added.

Everyone hurried off, Taz to the adjoining room, Reyan and Kainen to the kitchens on Kainen's insistence, and the Eastwicks off with the Hutchinson brothers to sort their diversion. That left Lolly lingering with Demi, who looked her way with a weary groan.

"It never gets any easier," she said. "Every time we have to go on these mad rescue missions, I'm constantly doubting myself."

Lolly froze. *The queen doubts herself? What do I say to*

that?

She couldn't remember doubting often. She knew what she knew and took confidence from it. Anything she didn't know, she made up as she went along.

"Oh." She hesitated. "What Reyan said, about the noises. Do you think Blossom's torturing them?"

Demi nodded. "Belladonna will. She'll go for Petra first because she knows Petra is more likely to have information, but she'll want to make it last. Fae *always* want to make it last because of their egos. It's literally the only real advantage we have against their ruthlessness."

Lolly winced at the thought of Petra being in pain. She was headstrong and skilled with her gifts, but the pained look on her face moments before Blossom had disappeared with them earlier, it was one of immense strain.

"You wanted me to write my words down for Milo," she said.

Anything to get away from the awful thoughts of what might be happening to her friends.

Demi nodded. "There's pen and paper on the table there. I can send things to him through my orb so I'll burn them straight away after."

Lolly picked up the pen and checked the ink before scribbling down the two words. It was only then she remembered that Demi had grown up in the human world, only finding out she was a fairy in her teens. She hoped Demi would recognise the words because they were absolute nonsense to her.

She passed the paper to Demi and watched her reaction carefully as Taz reappeared. Demi didn't even flinch as he dropped down beside her and peered over her shoulder.

"Oh my god," Demi muttered. "That's mad."

Taz frowned. "Means nothing to me."

Lolly shook her head when he looked up at her, but Demi was too busy tracing her finger over the two words on the page.

"Right, I need to orb these to Milo and Ace." Demi stood up. "The others should be back soon, so if you need to prep anything or get anything, now's the time."

Lolly frowned as Demi walked into the room Taz had just come out of. After an awkward moment, Taz gave a wry smile and followed her.

What do I need to prep? I could take some potions I suppose. The icalatha sap will cool burns, and there's that vial of concentrated extract from Arthur's pod-goo.

Lolly took to her feet and sped out of the room. Nobody saw her as she rushed past, although she knew from past experience she tended to leave people with unexpected shudders from the cold breeze she left in her wake.

She tumbled into her bedroom and stared in dismay at the mess.

"Mum's right," she muttered, heading for the large display unit in the far corner. "I really need to tidy this lot one day."

She rifled through the wooden cupboards, hissing and cursing under her breath until she found what she needed. She wrapped each vial in its own muslin cloth bag and stowed them in the inside pockets of her cardigan. It was her favourite because it was warm enough to endure the greenhouses and thick enough that she could hold any number of things in the pockets and zip them in safe.

She sped back to Demi's room to find everyone already assembled, although they all spared a brief smile for her as she joined them.

"Okay, usual rules apply," Demi said. "Nobody is left alone. We get what we go in for and come out, no heroics.

Don't challenge anyone you can't face."

"We'll realm-skip and come up through the market," Reyan added. "We can warn Arlen to get people out if needed and check for any traps on the way up. I know where the kitchens are so I'll come find you after."

Demi hesitated for a long moment before nodding and Lolly's pulse picked up. Planning a rescue mission was one thing, but now she was leaving the Flora Court. She'd only left on a handful of occasions and always in the overbearing safety of her mother's company.

I'm with the queen. I can't get safer than that. I owe Petra so much, and I can't leave Tyren to suffer.

She frowned at the thought of Tyren suffering in his own court, but Demi was raising her orb and calling for someone named Trevor.

The air in front of them shivered and Lolly flinched back a step as a troll with an enormous wooden rickshaw glimmering in the firelight appeared in the middle of the room.

"Whoa," she whispered.

The troll smiled wide. "Not often I get such a reaction these days! Ooh, I've always wanted to see the Flora Court. Heard great things about the wood you provide for our rickshaws. Sturdy as… sorry, Demi, got carried away."

His sheepish face suggested he got carried away often, but Lolly welcomed the compliment all the same.

"You're welcome to visit anytime," she offered.

She shuffled into the backseat of the rickshaw and got wedged in by Beryl, Harvey and Meryl. With Taz, Cheryl, Hutch and Demi up front, it was a tight squeeze as Trevor took his place between the handles.

"Okay, Revel Court please, as close to the kitchens as you can get us without making a scene," Demi said.

"Somewhere hidden if possible."

Lolly held her breath as Trevor set off at a run and a wisp of cold air brushed her face. She forced her eyes to stay open, taking in the purple-grey swirl of the nether as the queen's suite dissolved around them and a dark room full of sacks materialised in its place.

"Storage room," Trevor announced. "There's a block on this place and I can get through easily enough, but your orb messages likely won't get through it, so you'll have to leave the court boundary if you want picking up again. Should be able to leave this room though, go left down the hall and you'll reach the kitchens."

Everyone bundled out with whispered thanks, Lolly last out. She smiled at him as the others stood squabbling between themselves, the Eastwicks drawing out what an unnervingly varied collection of swords.

"I meant it about the visit," she said. "Assuming we survive this."

He chuckled. "Trust the queen. She's never led us wrong yet."

Lolly nodded. She hadn't heard a single person outside the enemy have a bad word to say about Demi or her rule so far. She stepped back as Trevor disappeared and took a deep breath.

"Right, I should have asked this before," Demi said, frowning at her. "But can you fight at all?"

Lolly thought back to her quiet, scenic childhood and teenage years sequestered away at the Flora court. While other Fae nobles were going to the elite academies or becoming trainees at Arcanium or going into menteeships at places like Gallows Oak, she had been taught by tutors at home.

She caught Beryl's eye. A moment later, she also caught

the sword Beryl threw toward her.

"Before Petra went to Arcanium, she lived at the Flora Court," she said, spinning the sword in hand to get used to the weight. "She taught me everything I know. Time to repay the favour, I reckon."

Demi's eyes lit up, the blue turning electric with relief and anticipation. Lolly hadn't ever visited the Revel Court before, but she'd heard a few rumours in passing and the odd bits Tyren had managed to tell her.

As she followed the others out of the storeroom though, she was underwhelmed by the narrow, dark corridors that were barely decorated, a court all but crumbling and a far cry from the jovial reputation it prided itself on.

"Kitchen's on the right," Demi whispered. "Looks a bit bleak but I'm guessing they don't bother prettying up the staff areas. I'll start counting six minutes now."

Hutch grinned from a nearby window. "You'll be able to see our masterpiece from here. When the sky turns green, that's your cue."

Lolly watched him speed away with his brother and her friends, leaving her with Demi and Taz. She stood slightly separate, one hand out to keep a warding around her. She trusted her queen, but anyone could explode around the corner or attack without being seen. Taz wrapped his arms around Demi's shoulders and she put her forehead on his chest. It was too tender a moment for prying eyes, so Lolly faced the window with uneasiness swirling in her gut.

"It'll be fine." Taz's voice reached her ears. "They're like a five-person wrecking team and Beryl and Harvey can realm-skip them home now if needed. We just need to get Petra and Tyren, then shore up all the courts against the next attack."

Lolly frowned. She wanted to ask what would happen

to the Revel Court now its lord was a traitor. What would happen to its people? People like Tyren, who she was sure had no idea at all about the enemy plan.

"It's all unfolding but there's a piece missing," Demi muttered.

"A piece to do with those random words?"

"They're not random, they're a place. Which means both sides now know where to go. But how to get through? I have no idea."

Lolly refused to look their way even though she was dying to ask questions, as a mass of darkness curled and took form beside them, materialising into fleshy Fae form.

"Whoa." She couldn't help exclaiming.

Reyan shrugged. "It gets old. I left Kainen in the market. He says if it looks like everything's going wrong, he'll have those of our court we can trust here to fight, and he'll get word to Milo."

Demi hesitated and a look passed between her and Reyan, uncertainty going one way and determined disapproval going the other.

Lolly shook her head and set her gaze back to the sight of the market through the window.

Get the others, get home safe, then we can talk about what'll happen next.

A huge bang rattled the very foundations of the building and the sky lit up with a ray of neon blue. Demi and Taz jostled beside her, but Lolly held her warding still with one hand, firming it tight around her so they had space to see out.

"That's a Hutchwick production alright," Taz said, his face alight with awe.

Demi snorted. "The girls wouldn't like the boys' name going first. Eastinson doesn't have the same ring though."

Lolly waited, squinting as chaos erupted down below. Even though the crowds in the market were swarming into a large central square surrounded by weaving narrow lanes stretched out like a huge labyrinth, aptly distracted by the disturbance, there were still many Fae left in the court itself who stood between her and her friends.

"We're waiting for green," Demi murmured. "But that doesn't sort out… ah. Oh, *orbs alive!*"

Lolly gasped as a horde of silver flashes streaked up from one of the lanes and darted up the short hill toward the court's castle.

"Um… they're headed right for us," she yelped.

Demi grinned. "Good, they're ours. Loyal to Arcanium anyway. Meryl's been working in our Quarantine floor and they seem to have taken a shine to her."

The silver flashes came close enough to the window and Lolly gawped. She hadn't seen a real live Frost cat before, but as they streaked past the window toward the side of the building where the kitchen no doubt was, she heard the subtle tinkle of their icy fur.

The sky exploded in a shower of bright green sparks and twirling lights as her frost gift shivered inside her. She let an icicle form at the end of her finger and Demi noticed, her grin widening.

"If we survive this, I'll get you an introduction," she joked. "Come on. They'll flush the kitchens clear."

"We need to be quick," Reyan added. "The distraction might draw people out but if we're facing Belladonna we're better off using stealth over straight fighting."

Demi nodded. "Lead the way. Lolly, if all goes wrong, use your speed to get yourself clear. You're responsible for going for help, okay? Get out of the court boundaries and use your orb to call for Trevor, he'll come for you."

Lolly grimaced. "I don't have an orb. Never needed one."

She almost dropped the one Demi threw her without warning, a deep green marble with dark swirls through it hanging on a keychain.

"Gift and nothing more," Demi insisted. "It'll work but keep it in your pocket, keep it safe."

"Thank you."

Lolly slid the orb into one of her cardigan pockets and zipped it. She wasn't taking any chances with a gift from the queen, especially not one that could get people out safely.

"This one, uh-oh."

Reyan turned a corner and stumbled back, almost knocking them all over.

"She has an auditory gift." She whispered so low that Lolly almost didn't hear her.

But she knew who Reyan meant. Blossom stood outside a door at the far end of the hall and Lolly's fury bubbled inside her chest.

"I'll get her away," she murmured. "If I go past at speed and drag her, I can probably get her down half a corridor at least then speed back before she knows what's happening."

Demi bit her lip, moments of indecision crossing her face before she nodded.

"Straight back though."

Lolly took a deep breath and dodged her head around the corner for a peek.

"Second door from the far end," Reyan added. "Good luck."

Before anyone could change their mind or stop her, Lolly darted down the hall, snatching out a hand.

Blossom's surprised yelp was lost in the speed as Lolly grabbed her wrist and put all the strength she possessed behind dragging the unsuspecting princess down the hall and flinging her around the corner.

She winced as she let go and Blossom sailed backwards, landing on her behind with a loud squeak. But Lolly spun on her heel and sped back to where Demi and Taz were just through kicking the door in.

"Never underestimate the human approach," Demi said, then, "Bloody hell, you look awful."

Lolly's panic reared and she jostled beside Taz to get through the door until he held out an arm and guided her back.

"Not risking us all getting trapped inside," he said.

Lolly nodded but her eyes were fixed on her friends. Petra was conscious but she had lacerations across her arms and her face was blooming with bruises. Tyren was using the wall to stand and his cheek was crusted with dried blood.

Demi and Reyan had Petra between them already, even though she was mumbling obscenities about being able to walk on her own. Lolly's chest squished and she dodged under Taz's arm, ignoring his indignant hisses for her to come back.

Tyren managed a weak smile but it had nothing in it, a habit and no more.

"You've looked better," she said. "Can you walk?"

He chuckled then, his eyes focusing as he looked at her.

"You say the nicest things to me." Realisation seemed to filter in then and his amusement fell away. "What are you doing here?"

She rolled her eyes. "Rescuing you, obviously. Come on."

He might have argued as she put her shoulder under his arm and manhandled him around her to support his weight, but Reyan's panicked voice drew their attention.

"I can't mind-speak to Kainen anymore," she hissed. "They must have locked down the whole court."

Demi grimaced. "Trevor mentioned that. We need to get out the sneaky way."

Lolly glanced up at Tyren. "Do you know where the boundary of the court is?"

"Yeah, edge of the market. But the court is always flooded with people."

"We'll have to risk it," Demi said.

Tyren straightened up as best he could and took a step toward the door, his arm tight around Lolly's shoulders.

"I'll use what connections I have to get us out," he added. "Might not account for much if allegiances really have all shifted, but many of the locals are anti-court these days because they're not looked after. If we can get out of here and down the hill to the market, you should be able to call your rides there. Did you tell her what we saw?"

Lolly nodded. "She has the words, yeah."

"Good. So before I forget, Blossom let slip that they haven't found a way into the place everyone's looking for yet although they know where it is. They plan to blast their way through the human world to get to it though. Then Belladonna back-handed her. Not a nice girl, no offense."

Taz shrugged at the last part which was directed at him.

"Disowned her when she turned traitor. We should get moving though."

Tyren nodded and took a deep breath that ended in a groan.

"We should. Follow me."

Lolly walked beside him in a three-legged wobble out

of the door, scanning the hall in time to see Blossom running toward them.

"My sister will slaughter you when she catches you!" she gasped, rubbing her wrist with her other hand.

Her horror intensified when Taz and Demi emerged and she halted.

"Tell Belladonna to turn herself in," Taz said, his tone entirely conversational. "You might as well come with her. It's only going to get worse if you keep opposing us."

Blossom's shoulders shook but she held her stubborn head high.

"She'll slaughter every one of you," she said. "She has the court locked down already and there are way more people loyal to the Blood and Bone Court than you'd expect."

Taz shrugged as Demi and Reyan helped Petra along the hall.

"Come on," Demi whispered. "He'll be right behind us, or he'll have me to deal with."

Lolly hesitated but Tyren obeyed. He seemed to be taking strength from them, no doubt relief at being out of confinement.

A loud bang brought them all back around, only to find Taz strolling toward them.

"Couldn't be bothered to argue." He shrugged. "This way, is it?"

He strode past them, leaving Blossom behind still as a statue with her mouth open, eyes wide and a hand lifted.

"Did he freeze her?" Petra asked, lifting her head.

Demi nodded. "He's been having fun with that one. Blame his mad great aunt Mildred for gifting it to him. Keeps running around making people freeze in place. Only lasts about five minutes, but I guess it does come in handy."

"If he can do that to Belladonna, it'd be helpful," Tyren muttered.

They stopped talking as they walked down the stairs and Tyren leaned on Lolly a bit more as three people walked past them. He nodded and smiled.

"Hi, did you hear those explosions?" he asked.

The three exchanged looks and inched closer. Lolly froze and warded both of them.

"We heard rumours," one of the women said. "The Forgotten have taken our court and they're blowing up the market, is it true?"

Tyren glanced around. Lolly's limbs itched to get them moving again, but if they acted too sketchy now, it might draw attention to them trying to escape.

"The first part is. I'd find allegiance to other courts if I were you."

"Does your father know?" the man asked.

Tyren's arm tightened and Lolly squeezed hers around his waist in hope of comfort.

"I'm not sure. I definitely hope not."

The three of them sent him a look of sympathy and the woman leaned close enough for Lolly to inch away.

"We'll do our best to intimate we haven't seen you," she whispered.

As they walked on, Lolly tried to unwind her tense arm from Tyren's waist but he clutched her tight to him.

"Come on, we're not out of the woods yet." He guided her toward the others who were waiting in a side hall.

Lolly sensed the chill before they turned the corner, her hope rising. Sure enough, the moment they turned the corner, they found eight Frost cats blocking the way. The smallest, a lithe female with icy blue eyes similar to the queen's, prowled toward them while her pack stayed in place.

"Are they friendly?" Reyan asked doubtfully.

Demi shook her head. "They're not pets, but their allegiance is to Arcanium so they probably won't eat us."

She held out her hand but the leader stalked right past her. Lolly gulped and let a tip of ice form on her finger.

"Hello," she murmured. "You're like me a bit, aren't you?"

Tyren inched backward, trying to drag her with him.

"Are you really talking to the big cat with the huge teeth right now? Is this similar to the Arthur thing?"

Lolly didn't reply, holding the cat's eye contact and reaching out her iced finger. The cat sniffed it, mewled low and turned around with a flick of her tail.

"That's acceptance, I think," Demi said. "Can you lead us out to the market?"

The leader looked back and winked before gathering her pack and heading down the hall.

"That's a yes," Petra mumbled. "Seen her communicate with them before."

Lolly had no idea who she meant, but she trusted Petra's judgement and shuffled Tyren forward.

"Wait!"

Petra forced Demi and Reyan to stop with her voice alone.

"That voice, I know it."

Lolly heard the mumble of conversation now, further down the hall and coming closer. In a tangle, they darted into the nearest alcove. With a grunt, Taz and Demi pulled a huge fern in a pot in front of them, and Reyan sent out a cluster of shadows to cloak them.

A man walked past that Lolly thought she vaguely

recognised, middle-aged, short and stocky with a bald head, but the second man walking beside him Lolly did recognise. The Lord of Revels looked supremely unconcerned about the explosions right outside his court, and she wished she could summon up a fingertip of ice a blade long to stab him with.

"How do we find them?" the Lord of Revels asked.

The other man frowned. "We don't, for now. Let Belladonna handle it. The Blood and Bone Court is her project and this is technically her court."

The Lord of Revels drew himself up tall, disdain flicking across his face.

"This is still the Revel Court, *my* court, which Belladonna is borrowing with my goodwill. I'd advise you all to remember that. It'd be such a shame if the queen were to discover me and everything I know."

The man chuckled. "Go tell her that and see what she does to you then. As it is, you don't know anything the queen probably doesn't know already."

"The queen is a mere child-"

"The queen is not to be underestimated. She has power enough and Faerie on her side, even if her blood is non-existent. But you wouldn't comprehend any of that, would you? Go play courts with Belladonna, you ridiculous man. I have bigger plans to manage."

He walked away and left the Lord of Revels gawping after him, but nobody said a word or made a move until even the Lord of Revels was out of sight.

"Should have known he'd be here," Demi muttered. "Both of them. I should have attacked, should have taken the shot. He's the one orchestrating all of this."

Taz gripped her shoulder. "We agreed not to, not yet. Come on, let's focus on getting out of here for now. His time will come."

She nodded. "But it would have been so easy."

"We knew he'd be lurking around," he soothed. "We'll get all of them, but with my awful sister trashing half of Faerie and beyond, we need the information more than the retribution right now."

Lolly didn't dare ask, not sure if they were talking about the Lord of Revels or the other man who'd spoken to dismissively to him. It wasn't her concern either, not now they had Petra and Tyren free. She let that steady her as they broke cover and hurried the rest of the way through the deserted kitchens.

"It's a miracle we've made it this far," she muttered.

"It's too quiet," Tyren said. "Even for a diversion, there should be someone in here. Cook would never leave by choice for a mere explosion outside."

His anxious tension was transferring to her, but she couldn't shake him off without risking him slowing down.

Then Demi glanced back and stopped dead. Lolly halted at the sight of fury rippling over the queen's face, and followed Demi's gaze. As Belladonna strode out from a side door with vengeful anticipation shining in her eyes, Lolly drew every essence of her being into securing a warding around herself and Tyren.

Belladonna chuckled, the sound scraping dry like knives on bone.

"Well, turns out he *is* a smart boy after all."

CHAPTER TWENTY
TYREN

Tyren clung to Lolly against his better judgement. She was supporting some of his weight, but he didn't want to risk weighing her down so much that he held her back.

She shouldn't even be here.

Now he stared at Belladonna's spiteful smile and vicious eyes, and the only thing in his head was getting Lolly as far away from his court as possible. He noticed the sword hanging from her hip, no doubt her attempt to be prepared, but what use could she have for sword practice somewhere like the Flora Court? Belladonna would tear her to pieces in two seconds flat. She'd never get to stomp around the greenhouses or see Arthur again. She wouldn't find out what might make the *ithalaca* or whatever it was called speak to her.

He didn't rise to Belladonna's 'smart boy' taunt either. The queen was standing nearby and could handle her in-laws for all he cared. If he could get Lolly to the boundary, he could barter with Iggs at the stationers to get her on the next shipment of banners or whatever and back to the Flora Court. He had favours all over the place he could call in to get her out safely, and he would do it.

Several hardened-looking Fae were filling the background now behind Belladonna, and his chances of getting Lolly out dwindled away in front of his eyes.

"Risky idea to use an established court as your base after what happened in Egloriem," Demi said. "We found you easily, but then I suppose that's what you wanted."

Tyren focused on shuffling Lolly backwards, aiming to get her forming part of the line behind the queen as the Eastwick sisters strode in the side door with Hutch and Harvey.

Demi flicked a weary look at them, enough to suggest they'd disobeyed some part of her orders, but he had never been gladder to see the riot of hair colours massing behind them.

Belladonna sighed. "You seem to think you being queen means you can stop us."

Demi lifted a hand and sent a wave of power out, the energy of it lifting every hair on Tyren's body as it hit Belladonna's warding.

Tyren grimaced. Given Belladonna's pinched face and closed eyes, she was fighting it now with everything she had.

She's strong because the Lord has offered her this place as a base.

He had no idea what possessed him to act, but he thought of his friends down in the market who hated having such lazy, selfish courtiers always lording it over them. He thought of his friends inside the court too, the ones who wanted something to be proud of rather than something that caused them second-hand embarrassment.

"The lord of this court might have offered it to you as a place to use, but its people won't accept you," he called out.

Demi pulled back her attack, her eyes flashing electric as she turned them on him. He thought for a moment she was about to obliterate him, but her power settled, a momentary hesitation to show she was giving him a shot.

Belladonna sniffed, her pride now on hold as she recovered from Demi's attack. Her warding would no doubt keep her and her kind safe for the time being, but Demi was a queen. Belladonna had to understand that she couldn't best Faerie's chosen one, only delay or tire her a while.

But perhaps I can weaken her hold here too.

He thought about how the Flora Court responded to Lolly's will sometimes, tiny things nobody would usually notice. It had chosen her to succeed her mother already, he could see that now. Perhaps the Revel Court would listen to its people over its lord if he tried to believe in it with everything he had.

"The people love this court, but the lord has ruined it and turned traitor. Most of the courtiers and the market will support Faerie and its queens, not an elitist group of entitled Forgotten scum."

He tried to push Lolly aside as Belladonna's glare turned on him along with a scalding dose of power, but Lolly clung on to him. He heard her yelp moments before Demi deflected the attack into the wall with a toss of her head. The wall exploded outwards, the daylight flying in. He had a moment of anxiety about what Cook would do to him when she found out he'd been involved in decimating her beloved kitchen, but the burns still scathing his skin were taking too much of his attention.

"Okay, that hurt," he muttered.

He tried to pull free but Lolly wouldn't budge. Not because she was refusing, but because her entire body up to her neck was encased in a solid layer of frost.

"Give me a minute," she said through gritted teeth. "Then I can give you some *icalatha* sap for your burns."

He shook his head. "Never mind that now. We need to get you out of here."

She actually rolled her eyes as though that was the most

ridiculous thing he'd ever said to her, then she faced forward as the ice-blue hue of her skin faded to rosy and the stiffness of her limbs relaxed around him.

Belladonna risked sending out another attack but Demi reflected it. Then the room exploded.

The Eastwicks separated sideways as a flawless unit, moving in and out of the tables. One had part of the wall tumbling down against the enemy warding and another had metal cutlery dancing into formation and flying like arrows.

Tyren tried to drag Lolly down to hide but she shoved him and pulled the sword hanging at her side.

He stumbled forward as someone rushed them, then stumbled back again in absolute horror.

Lolly's arms moved like ribbons of dancing poetry as she swung the blade with effortless strength, agile enough to force the man attacking her backwards. The man had nothing but his gifts to fight with and Tyren forced a warding around Lolly before the huge hands could grab hold of her. The man bounced off the warding but the sword pierced through it like Petra's had, driving him back.

"Flora Court secret," she shouted back, her face alive with amusement. "I'll tell you later!"

Demi and Taz charged past, Taz holding out a hand to turn a nearby unit to liquid. He tried to encase Belladonna in the swirl but she sent out a pulsing wave that splattered the liquid everywhere. People ducked and dodged as the drops turned back to chunks and splinters of wood, but all Tyren could focus on was keeping Lolly under his warding.

Even Petra seemed to be recovering. She leaned on the counter near the windowsill, her hand waving through the herbs growing there, the stems growing unnaturally fast and reaching over their pots to crawl across the ground toward the enemy. She was suffering, he could see that, but she was determined to protect her own to her last breath.

Tyren grabbed Lolly around the waist with one arm, ignoring her cursing at him as she continued trying to stab at people.

"We stand with Petra, she's flagging," he shouted in her ear.

She stopped fighting him, the worry filling her eyes as she wriggled in his arms looking for her friend. He twisted around, giving her a front row view as Petra winced. She lifted a hand, her chin dropping to her chest, sheer exhaustion covering her face as she turned what looked like a rain of metal sewing pins to petals. Her legs buckled and her knees hit the floor.

"Petra!" Lolly screamed.

Demi's head snapped up nearby.

Tyren buckled as Lolly's elbow found his gut with one firm jab and she tore free of him. Demi was moving fast now but Lolly was beside Petra seconds before an arrow found her chest.

Tyren turned his head in horror to see the bald-headed man from earlier standing in the middle of the doorway to the hall, Belladonna beside him with glee all over her face.

Demi's roar filled the entire court, terrifying enough to rattle the hills around them. The wave of power knocked everyone down, Forgotten and friends alike. Even Taz was on his knees beside her, clinging onto her legs as she kicked and screamed to go after the now disappearing pair. They knew they couldn't best the queen and were retreating, leaving their supporters to clean up the mess. But, sensing their leaders had fled, the Forgotten started pulling back too.

Unaware of anything around her, Lolly had one hand on Petra's chest where blood was oozing everywhere, her other one trying and failing to reach inside her cardigan.

Tyren managed to get himself beside her in time, seconds before his sharp-sight saw her move. Just as Taz struggled to hold Demi back from going after the enemy, Tyren wrapped both arms tight around Lolly's chest and clung on with everything he had. He ignored the scratches and the punches while the Eastwicks were dropping to their knees beside Petra, one of them screaming and the other two trying to stem the blood-flow. Hutch and Harvey were already gone, and Tyren had to trust they'd gone to find one of the healers in the market.

But he knew then that Petra wasn't going to make it. His secret gift told him so, the one he'd never told a soul about, not even his father. The first time had been a pet. The second time, a test of what he assumed was a fluke. The third time had been his mother, full of reassurance.

Now, for the fourth time, he would reveal the one thing about himself that he feared the most, that old tales and Fae superstition feared too.

"Beryl." He put as much bark in his tone as he could muster. She looked up. "Hold her."

He nodded to Lolly, who was still struggling even though her energy was failing and tears were streaming down her face.

Taz managed to get Demi on her knees beside the others and the moment Beryl took charge of Lolly, Tyren slid down beside their queen.

"She's almost gone," he said. "You know it, you can see where the arrow is."

"No!"

Demi shoved at him but Taz had hold of her wrists too fast for her to do any real damage.

"Please, please, wake up." Meryl repeated the same words over and over, her head on Petra's shoulder as though she could beg her back to life.

Tyren bit his lip hard and reached a hand over Petra's eyes. Lolly's sobbing tore at his heart, but he took a deep breath and let his mind settle. He sorted through the chaos of life around him, the tears, the energy, and found the quiet. Coaxed it forward.

He didn't need to open his eyes to see the shadow of Petra rising from her body, pearlescent like an orb call and barely there. But he could hear her words clear as the others fell silent.

"Do I have long?" she asked.

Tyren shook his head. "Minute maybe. I'll give you what time I can."

He felt the ghost of a hand on his head and the subtle memory of lips on his forehead, cool like a soft breeze.

"I gift you my ability to draw swords from hair. Thank you for being loyal. Look after her for me. Please, the rest of you, don't spend ages mourning or anything. I gave what I could and I'd do it again."

Tyren felt her spirit drifting and clung on, forcing his gift as hard as he could to keep the connection to her last dregs of life so she could make all the use of them.

"Lolly, don't be sad," she continued. "You're going to make a great lady, and I believe in you. I gift you my ability to wield nature at will, because I know you of all people will use it well and sparingly, for the benefit of others not just yourself."

Again her spirit drifted and Tyren clenched the muscles in his gut, huffing from the exertion of blocking the path of her spirit beyond.

"Dem, don't let this sour your mind. You're the kindest person I know. Don't let them win by getting to you this way. Revenge isn't the answer, okay? You're stronger than you've ever been. Remember to always be good too. When she was torturing me earlier, she mentioned something about keys and imagery. It wasn't clear, but it sounds like we were right after all. Keep going. I love and believe in all of you."

"I can't hold you… much… longer," Tyren muttered.

Again that calming hand on his head. She understood. She was grateful.

"Be good to each other. Remember what I taught you. Be smart. Don't let Hutch or Harvey plan my funeral. Remember that I love you most of all, M, and I want you to find someone who can love you the way you deserve."

The connection faltered. Tyren tried to cling on that last moment longer, but his gift wavered. It was stretching so thin, so close to snapping.

"Okay, mate," he heard Taz's broken voice beside him. "Let her go now."

So he did. With agony and with deep regret, he moved aside and felt Petra's spirit sail on. He had no idea where they went, whether they became a part of Faerie or dissipated into the nether. He'd heard rumours about the queen being brought back to life more than once, but he knew enough of his gift to recognise that Petra was gone.

It was that split second of realisation that made him move in time to catch Lolly before she kicked Beryl in the shin and tore free. He caught her before she could speed across the floor.

"You can't fight them all," he insisted. "You can't. Grieve, then we do it the sensible way. I'll help you, but you won't win if you go after them now. Be smart, okay?"

She struggled against him but it was the futility of grief that had her now, not the urge for bloodshed. He loosened his arms just enough to let her twist around in them and held the back of her head with a hand as her tears soaked his shirt.

Demi raised her pale face, cheeks streaked with tears, her eyes burning blue with icy fury.

"Show us where we can call our ride," she said, her voice faded.

Tyren nodded. "Follow me."

He didn't offer to help as Hutch and Harvey picked up Petra's body between them, he was too busy holding Lolly and keeping her upright. Taz had Demi under his arm but she walked oddly as though the shock had solidified her limbs. Meryl could barely move she was sobbing so hard, and both her sisters had to support her.

Tyren half expected Belladonna to loom back out to attack them again, but even with wardings and arrows that could apparently pierce them, the enemy wouldn't risk Demi's wrath yet.

They fled knowing it would be carnage if they stayed. Maybe that's what they expect to find in the Prime Realm, people or resources who are strong enough to take on a queen.

Belladonna had suggested as much before. They walked outside and stumbled down the hill until Tyren figured they might be far enough from the court boundary to stop.

"Try here," he suggested.

Demi held up her orb. "Trevor, we need you."

Tyren hesitated, about to suggest they keep walking to the fringe of the market, but then the air shivered and a large rickshaw appeared.

The troll between the handles looked at them with a wide grin, that faded when he clocked Petra. His face shadowed with regret and he reached out a hand to touch her arm as Hutch and Harvey slid into the back with her.

"Take her home," Demi said. "You three too."

Lolly lifted her head from Tyren's shoulder long enough to take a look and produce fresh tears.

"We'll give whatever we can," she insisted. "For… goodbye, or the fight, or whatever. If I have any say, I want them dead. All of them."

Demi nodded, her face still a mask of shock. "She said no revenge."

"She didn't say no justice though," Lolly added, her voice rising. "She didn't say no making things right. Unless you call it first, or Meryl, she dies by my hand."

Tyren closed his eyes tight to dispel the sudden dizziness revolving around in his head. He understood Lolly was grief-stricken, and he'd gone through the same thing with his mother's death, although she hadn't been murdered. But he didn't want her threatening or vowing other people's deaths. That seemed to spark something in the midst of Demi's shock though, her eyes darkening.

"Denied. You don't want that on your conscience or your future. Your threat to Lyle earlier is denied too. That doesn't mean we can't take the chance if it comes though," she said, her voice the rumble of demons. "If we're lucky, we'll all get a turn. But she was right about one thing, we need to be smart. We need to train our gifts. And we need to keep to kindness because without that, we're just like them."

Lolly bit her lip and gave a sudden, violent shudder. Tyren had no jacket on to give her, but he cast a glance over the market just below them, and then the castle further up the hill.

"I should see my father," he said. "I need to make sure he doesn't know anything about what the Lord's been planning."

Demi eyed him. "And if he does?"

Tyren gulped. "Then it'll be a huge judge of my character. I'm hoping not. *Really* hoping. I never swore to the Revel Court officially, and I've renounced it now as long as he's lord of it, but I can't believe my father would have been in on any of this, I really can't."

"You're coming back to the Flora court with us first either way," Demi insisted. "There are things that need to be discussed. Then you can coordinate the court in your lord's stead if you want. He's a traitor, proven by confession of one of the Forgotten's sworn members. His title is forfeit, so the Revel Court is currently leaderless. But we can't discuss that here. I need to get my head around… I can't…"

Her voice disappeared and Taz wrapped his arms around her, holding tight. Tyren looked away to give them privacy but not before he noticed tears in Taz's eyes too.

"You can have a cry on me if you want," he told Lolly. "Or a sleep. I promise not to accuse you of being my fake girlfriend."

He wondered in the moments that passed after if she was going to turn him to ice or scream at him. Now wasn't the time for jokes, but it was all he could think of. Then she snorted a hysterical laugh and pressed her forehead against his shoulder.

"I want to go home now," she said, her voice almost inaudible in its fragility.

Demi disappeared and Tyren held onto Lolly as Taz appeared beside him. As queen and king consort, they could no doubt realm-skip at will, but Tyren still felt the tremor of amazement as Taz vanished the three of them easily and they reappeared a moment later in the centre of the Flora Court conservatory.

Demi was already there with Lady Flora and her wife, but when Tyren tried to let Lolly go so they could hug her, she clung on. He gently turned her around as her mum enveloped them both in a tight embrace.

"You're home now," she soothed. "We'll give you both something to help you sleep. You'll need it, trust me. Can I offer you something also, my queen? Might be best to rest the mind before the next step."

Demi nodded. "Please. For all four of us."

Taz shook his head. "I'll take my chances. We're safe here but I feel like I need to keep watch a while."

She didn't challenge that, merely took his hand in hers and they disappeared off toward the door that would lead them up to their rooms.

Tyren froze as Lolly's mum patted his shoulder and then his cheek too.

"Lol, let him go. He's not a soft toy so you can't take him to bed with you."

A subtle teasing note veiled the sadness underneath. They'd heard about Petra already and would do any grieving once their daughter was sorted. Lolly held onto him for a moment longer and finally let him go, wiping her eyes with both hands.

"Do you want us to call your father?" Lady Flora asked.

Tyren watched Lolly's mum lead her away before realising he was being spoken to.

"Not yet, Lady. There's been a lot of uncertainty, and I want to get my head straight first."

She nodded. "Wise. The Lord of Revels has turned

traitor I hear, which is worrying."

"But not surprising now I think about it. No doubt the queen will choose a new lord for the court, but I'm not sure who that'll be. If you'll excuse me, Lady?"

She nodded, but not before holding out her hand. He stared at it as she unfurled her fingers, palm up to reveal a small leaf.

"Our head greenhouse-keeper found that this morning," she said.

Tyren looked from the bulbous pale blue leaf to her. It looked like one of the *icalatha* leaves, but he couldn't be sure. The Lady's lips twitched.

"Apparently your idea of telling them jokes bore fruit. Lolly was huffing about it to one of the groundskeepers and he decided to test it as an amusing anecdote of sorts. Turns out it worked. See the pink edge to the root? They've begun to communicate. That'll be something Lolly will be able to focus on in all this darkness, so thank you."

Tyren shrugged, uneasy at the way she was smiling at him. It wasn't an overly suggestive smile, nor was it hopeful or eager. It was the absolute lack of anything untoward that worried him, but he was too tired to focus on it.

"Go and sleep a while," she added. "I'll have food sent up to your room. When you're ready to speak to your father, you can use my office if you need and I'll ensure your absolute privacy, from myself and my court included."

He nodded. "Thank you, Lady. I hope… I hope she will be able to cope with everything okay. Has she ever lost anyone before?"

Her face shadowed. "No, she hasn't, and this will be an awful loss to bear. But we'll get through it. When you live as long as I have, you learn to bear grief, to make something from the bad as much as you do the good. Otherwise you don't survive, or worse."

He didn't need to ask what worse would entail, thoughts of Belladonna and Blossom and their companions filling his head. He left Lady Flora in the conservatory and started the long climb up to his room, each step like battling a mountain.

I have to hope my father hasn't had anything to do with this, but if he has, can I really even forgive him knowing what I know, let alone support him?

But Lolly was safe. He reminded himself of that as he finally reached his room, locked the door and collapsed onto the bed. Burrowing under the covers, he let that drag him down into sleep.

She was safe. And the scariest thought was about how much that one thing, her safety, mattered to him.

CHAPTER TWENTY ONE
REYAN

Reyan tried to hold back the tears. She knew she had no right to be crying when Demi and the others had lost someone they'd been close to. Even Kainen had known Petra, but he sat with his arms around her now telling her it would be okay. They'd been forgotten about at the Flora Court but it was more than understandable. In the end, Reyan put all of her effort, what little she had left from the ridiculously long day, into skipping them home. Demi would know where to find them if they were needed, but right now Kainen was her only priority.

She managed to coordinate her focus enough to land them on his bed but he didn't laugh or tease her. He simply rolled onto his back, folded her against his chest and held on tight, so she let him.

He's grieving for a friend. I never heard him mention Petra but she would have been at Arcanium with him, would have known him still.

"Demi will ask you to go to the Court of Words next," he said, his tone despondent. "That's what the Wachala said, wasn't it? She'll want you there."

Reyan nodded. "She hasn't asked, but perhaps she will once she's past the shock."

"Claus rules that domain now, it turns out. The news is that the Lady of Words died recently and her daughter is apparently too sick to rule now. Since there are no other blood-born children, and Claus is her oldest stepson, he's the new Lord of Words."

Reyan frowned. "I don't remember him mentioning that

at the party."

"Because he likely didn't want us to know. Demi mentioned it while you were scoping out the court on your own, before I came here and found dear Ciel trying so hard to get you to betray me."

"He's an idiot for trying. I never would."

That managed to dredge a weary chuckle from him, a tiny blessing.

"Yes, you made that blissfully clear to all involved. Which is why if you do get called in to the Word Court at any point, I'm escorting you. Claus and Ciel are friends and while I've sewn up his ability to betray us quite fiendishly, there's always room for error and I'm not risking it."

She managed a small smile at the protectiveness darkening his voice.

"You make an error? Surely not."

His fingers threaded through her hair and she let her heart skip as much as it liked. They still had so much to talk about, not least the fake engagement and so far supposedly and possibly still fake relationship. But not yet.

"Anything is possible, sweetheart."

She nodded with a huge yawn. She was the one who'd attended a Fae revel, done multiple time-skips across various realms, faced the fabled Wachala, spied on and stormed the Revel Court, all without one jot of sleep.

"How are you finding the wide world of Faerie then?" Kainen asked, his voice softer now. "Enjoying your freedom?"

She snorted. "What freedom? All I've done is run increasingly dangerous errands so far. But yes, it's been good for me to see more of Faerie."

He didn't reply to that. She wondered whether he was

asking for something to say to distract himself from his sadness or if he really wanted to know. Thoughts of his recent affectionate behaviour filled her head. She'd missed him during her three weeks with Arlen in the Revel Court market. Missed the court itself too. Kainen had definitely been happy to see her back, and he'd even taken her suggestion about opening up one of the mountain-side decks for the staff to enjoy as if he saw her as an equal.

Does he still see this as a pretence to be ended, or is there something more?

She couldn't bring herself to ask him, too afraid he'd give her the answer she didn't want.

Would he ever actually consider taking me without a grand title of my own, or at least a posh family lineage? Loads would look down on him for it if he did.

The thoughts warred back and forth, until she closed her eyes and decided that lying on his chest with the subtle twitch of his fingers combing idly through her hair was enough. For now.

"Oh for the love of..." Kainen sat up, his face like thunder.

For one life-altering moment, Reyan assumed he'd heard her thoughts. She froze, ready to apologise, but he was digging in his pocket. He pulled out a small orb on a keychain and held it up so that Demi's apologetic face was magnified in front of them in enormous pearlescent grey.

"I'm sorry, I know I shouldn't interrupt-"

"But you're going to," Kainen interrupted.

Reyan shot him a sharp look. Everyone knew Demi had been so close to Petra and would be distraught still, yet she was obviously still having to work which was bad enough after a fight without the addition of the grief on top.

"Okay, to the point, I get it." Demi sighed. "I just

wanted to say thank you to both of you, and to ask if you'll be able to come to Petra's- to the- you know."

Kainen's face softened. "Sorry, I shouldn't snap. It's been a tough while for all of us but for you most of all."

Demi looked surprised at that, the expression hidden under a ton of weariness and crumpled grief.

"We'll be working through the captives we took from the fight at the revel but there are a lot, so we may have some downtime. I might need to call on you, either or both of you."

"Of course," Reyan nodded, giving Kainen a hesitant look until he echoed the same.

"We will need to get to the Court of Words as well at some point."

Kainen nodded. "Rumour has it Claus is now Lord of Words?"

"Yeah, unexpected. I hadn't even heard the Lady of Words had passed, but Claus insists his sister is too ill for it."

"Stepsister," Kainen corrected her. "And I'd ask her that yourself if I were you, just as a double check."

Demi raised her eyebrows. "Noted. Either way, he's offered to host us when the time comes, but that won't be for a while now."

Kainen sighed. "Which will give the enemy as much time to regroup as it does us."

"It does, but hopefully we can be smarter, get there first. Milo's already dealing with the Word Court so that we can start searching for these Prime Realm keys. Um… the… for Petra, will be at the Flora court in two days. You'll definitely come? Both of you?"

She sounded so hesitant. Reyan's heart went out to her. She hadn't known Petra really but Kainen had. She squeezed her hand around his.

Do you want to? I'll go with you if you do. If not, I'll make an excuse.

He nodded. "We'll be there. Petra was always fair to me, even when I was an absolute arse."

"Okay. Milo will send details. See you then."

Her face disappeared and Kainen flopped back onto the bed. Reyan hovered, torn between being bold and doing the same, and making excuses to leave him be.

She didn't comment as he reached over and grabbed her hand like it was the most normal thing in the world for him, his fingers toying idly with hers as he tugged gently until she flopped back onto his chest. She pushed aside the fluttering in her stomach and focused on facts, needing to keep herself grounded.

Kainen had a reputation at court, one she knew was well earned. She wasn't exactly the sweet innocent herself, but she didn't want to risk him seeing her as a solution to a temporary problem or someone he might be able to chase. He might not have any intention of entertaining her as more than a passing fancy or a beneficial arrangement to be had. Most of her doubted that, but part of her still feared and she couldn't risk it until she was sure. Not now her feelings were involved.

"I'm going to fall asleep right here if I don't get moving now," she tried.

He tensed. "Sleep here? Not like that, but I feel safer somehow knowing you're beside me."

She nestled against him, trying her best to rein in the sudden roar of triumph in her chest. Kainen clicked his fingers and plunged the room into darkness, but Reyan could feel the shadows around them, soothing and calm as they picked up the swirl of emotions. He wasn't grieving exactly, just sad.

"You're assessing me," he said.

"Sorry."

"It's okay. What's the verdict, am I broken?"

She smiled and risked pushing her head up until her cheek was resting against his jaw, her chin fitting into the crook of his neck. He wriggled so that he had an arm underneath her waist to hold her tight and it was everything she could have hoped for.

"No. You're sad but you're not broken. We'll make you smile again one day, don't worry."

"You do, every day."

She blushed in the darkness. There wasn't any hint of amusement or mockery in his voice either.

"I've missed the court the past few weeks," she admitted. "Exploring is fun, but this is home."

His head turned toward her in the darkness but she couldn't keep her eyes open or her attention focused any longer.

"Only the court?"

She smiled. "Meri definitely. The food as well. The library. We do the best parties."

He was silent and she realised he was waiting, hoping for something more. She yawned and let her hand slide across his ribs until it settled over his heart.

"I missed you too."

Then, because she couldn't possibly trust her thoughts that sometimes slipped into his head through their mind-speak connection, she let the last few words drift into his head come what may.

Most. I missed you most.

As she slipped into sleep, the gentle kiss that landed on her forehead sent a tingle through her entire body and a determined reply into her mind.

Mine.

CHAPTER TWENTY TWO
LOLLY

Lolly woke up and it took her a moment for the memories to filter in. Then the screaming began. She sat up, eyes wide open as the sound tore from her throat, convinced she never wanted to close her eyes or sleep ever again. The draught her mum had given her removed any risk of nightmares, but now the whole lot slammed back into her with all the weight of her grief behind it.

Her mum hurried in to find her curled around her pillow, shaking with tears streaming down her cheeks.

"There now," she said. "Better out than in. Do you want hard facts or comfort?"

Lolly sniffed and wiped her nose on the blankets.

"Hard facts."

Her mum nodded. "Okay. Tyren's here and resting, along with the queen and king consort. The queen wants to speak to you but I asked if she could give you time to wake first."

Lolly tried to struggle out of bed but her mum stopped her and she didn't have the strength to argue.

"Her parents have been told already," her mum continued. "Her dad and her brothers are vowing war-"

"On the queen?" Lolly gasped.

"No, on the Forgotten. Lady Belladonna. Her followers and any family who support her. Petra's mother was from the Court of Words originally if you remember, and she has a lot of friends there still. I double checked as gently as I could and her brothers want to see you when you're up to it to thank you for going to fetch her."

Lolly hid her face in her hands. She couldn't bear the thought of seeing Petra's brothers or her parents. To admit she'd failed to rescue their daughter, to take their gratitude when it wasn't earned, she couldn't face it.

"The Lord of Words is downstairs also to give his condolences."

Lolly shrugged. She didn't know a Lord of Words at all and couldn't remember anyone so much as mentioning him. There was a Lady of Words, perhaps she'd remarried, although why any husband would want to speak to Lady Flora's daughter instead of Lady Flora she had no idea. It was a distant court and her mum dealt with any business between them. Unless this random lord had known Petra personally, his condolences were unwanted.

"The queen also mentioned that you'd offered the court for anything she needs?" The question was gentle but probing.

Lolly nodded. "I did, and I'm not going to apologise for it. I'm sure mother can pull rank if-"

"Ah, none of that. We'll honour anything we can offer to help. The queen and Petra's family have asked if we can hold the funeral here among people who knew her. Half of Arcanium will skip in for it, but we're being cautious about timing and skip-ways. We don't want another attack."

It was the right thing to do, to farewell her in the court she'd been raised near.

"They've asked if we can lay her to rest in the woods so she's at one with Faerie," her mum finished. "But we offered the family grounds. I thought that would be okay with you."

"Yes, she is family. She's been like a sister to me."

"There we are then. Are you ready to see the queen?"

Her mum shuffled out of the way as Lolly pushed herself out of bed. She couldn't face showering and preparing herself to receive guests, but then Demi likely wouldn't care either way. She put on fresh clothes and wrapped her favourite cardigan around her body. She could feel the bottles clinking in their muslin bags still and reminded herself to find Tyren and see if he still needed any *icalatha* sap for his burns.

She followed her mum downstairs and walked into the conservatory to find a strange collection of people gathered. Her mother noted her clothing choice and closed her eyes in torment, but Demi and Taz managed weary smiles of greeting. Tyren's gaze scanned over her and she had the oddest sensation of heat in her cheeks. He didn't smile, but she was too surprised to see the person standing next to him to focus on it.

"You," she said with a frown.

Claus bowed low, his smile at least a respectful one for once.

"I can't remember if you two have met," Demi flicked a hand between them. "Lolly, future Lady of the Flora Court, this is Claudius Auren, the new Lord of Words."

It took all of Lolly's effort to keep her mouth shut as shock trickled through her. The Word Court kept to themselves, and she'd never met nor taken much interest in them. She wanted to ask what had happened to the Lady of Words, but her mind got stuck on something more immediately personal to her. Claus was the one who had warned her away from Tyren, and his brother was a traitor.

She folded her arms across her chest, aware of Tyren taking a step toward her then hesitating. She could ask Claus why he didn't introduce himself properly when they danced, or whether his veiled talks with his brother meant he was one they needed to worry about. Instead, she went straight for the one thing at the front of her mind.

"Why did you warn me away from him then?" she demanded, waving a hand in Tyren's direction.

Taz and Demi exchanged a look, but Tyren looked like he was trying not to laugh. Her mother looked like she was having some kind of internal emotional episode and didn't manage to say anything like she usually would.

Claus raised his eyebrows.

"He's part of the Revel Court, who were rumoured in certain circles to be turning traitor. I felt it only right to warn you to keep your mouth shut."

Keep my mouth shut?! Who the hell does he think he is?

The anger must have shown on her face because Tyren smoothly interrupted.

"I was part of the Revel Court. Right now, I don't know where I stand with them. But yes, their lord has turned traitor so he's certainly now no lord of mine."

Claus eyed him dismissively. "But you were here to spy for him originally, weren't you?"

Lolly froze. She'd suspected that in the beginning but conveniently forgotten about it over the past day or so.

Tyren eyed Claus, his eyes sharpening as his expression turned hostile.

"I was asked to 'keep an eye out', and to find out anything going on here that might impact our court. The instructions were vague and there wasn't ever any actual requirement to betray any loyalties to the queen."

Claus scoffed under his breath but Lolly couldn't help the sinking sensation in her gut. Tyren had been forced to hang around with her, and she'd been forced to hang around with him. Then in no time at all she'd come to respect him. She'd thought of him as a somewhat weary friend, one she would go into the enemy camp to save.

But of course, he was just doing his duty to his lord, and him now defying his lord and his court is all because of his loyalty to Demi.

The air grew frosty between Claus and Tyren, but their revelations weren't important in view of everything else.

"You wanted to speak to me?" she asked. "I assume it didn't have everything to do with these two idiots?"

Tyren rolled his eyes at that but she caught the spark of incredulous indignation crossing Claus' face. Demi smiled, weakly and barely there, but she managed it.

She's in as much pain as I am over Petra.

"Not everything, no," she agreed.

Lolly's mother cleared her throat. "I'll leave you to discuss matters, my queen, but you have my full support to offer."

A rush of relief washed over Demi's face and she nodded.

"Thank you."

Demi waited until Lolly's parents had left the conservatory before sinking down to sit on the wall around the fountain with a sigh.

"I trust everyone here, so we can talk freely," she said. "Not that I don't trust Lady Flora or anything, but she knows what she needs to know. The Forgotten have found the basic entrance to the Prime Realm, and now we know it as well. The next step for both sides will be to find a way through. We need to make sure we do it first before the enemy get their claws in."

Lolly wished she'd stopped to eat something before insisting on coming down to see Demi. Her mum had suggested but clearly didn't want to pressure her. Now Lolly wished she had as her stomach growled.

Claus and Taz remained standing but Tyren sat near to Demi and patted the wall beside him, an invitation. Lolly joined him, amused when he pulled out a pastry wrapped in a napkin and handed it to her without so much as a glance in her direction.

"Now, onto the issue with the Revel Court," Demi continued. "I've heard of the seclusion the Revel Court has acted in recently. I also know that a lot of the people who live in the actual market city and the surrounding land have been petitioning for independence as a realm for a long time now."

Tyren nodded. "It's been a huge argument, but nobody has managed to gather enough strength to oppose the lord yet. They need the business he brings in. Or rather, he controls it so they don't realise they don't need him after all."

"I have already offered to re-house the Revel Court in mine as you know," Claus said.

Lolly glared up at him, aware of Tyren doing exactly the same beside her.

"And I've noted your offer," Demi replied, her tone cool with dismissal. "It would add too much uncertainty as you don't appear to have any links with the Revel Court personally, and neither does your family."

"With all due respect, those are things that can flourish over time," he insisted.

He thinks he can argue with her, that if he simply throws his weight around she'll cave. Lolly reigned in the snort of indignation brewing. *He's in for a mighty shock.*

Demi seemed to be thinking the same, because when she scoffed she didn't make any attempt to hide it.

"Your title is a new one. Brand new. I have no proof that your rule is going to be able to sustain one court, let alone two. Besides, to move a court to a neighbouring court, it would have to be one that would both benefit its ethos and its people. Would be much opposition from the people if I released the Revel court from service, or maybe even moved it?"

Tyren froze as Demi looked his way. Lolly wanted to comfort him somehow, he looked so startled.

"I… A scant handful of nobility will argue against it maybe. Many of our court-sworn would consider moving, but to disband it entirely would be such a loss. Despite our- his- the lord's failings, we produce so many good things too. To lose that… people would be heartbroken."

Lolly opened her mouth to argue that disbanding a court was unheard of, a savage punishment when most people hadn't even done anything wrong, but Demi looked at her next and she found herself stuck in silence.

"And what about merging courts?" she asked.

Lolly's mind stuttered. "Eh?"

"Huh?" Tyren sounded just as confused.

Demi smiled. "Merging the two courts. Claus has given me a wonderful idea, albeit not in the way he was clearly hoping."

Claus stared at her, his jaw dropping as his eyes grew wide.

"You can't be suggesting-"

"Can't I? Weird, because I just did. I'm suggesting that the Revel Court would become an arm of the Flora Court, but under your command, Lolly. You would become Lady of Revels while your mother is still Lady of the Flora Court. The Revel Court would move here into the Flora Court's domain and gradually, when the time comes, you can take on your mother's role and the two courts would coincide."

Lolly tried to fathom that. Demi was offering her a court of her own, separate to her mother's and the one she grew up in.

No, she's offering me two courts. One now and one later. Orbs alive, what do I say?

She tried to think of what her mother and mum would counsel, but it was Petra's voice that echoed in her head the loudest.

"Remember what I taught you. Be smart."

"Can I take some time to decide? The last thing I want to do is say yes and let down one court, let alone two."

Demi nodded. "Wise. Take some time. We think we might be onto something with the whole getting into the Prime Realm thing, which means our next journey is to the Court of Words, but if you decide and can't reach me, let Milo know."

Claus bowed his head while fighting to unclench his teeth.

"We're only too happy for our turn to host. We may be distant, but we give a royal welcome."

Lolly rolled her eyes and pushed herself to her feet.

"There's stuff that needs to be finished and finished right," she said, and Demi nodded sadly. "But I'll try to make my decision quickly. If the people of the Revel Court would be willing to consider me as their lady, I'll consider them as mine in return."

Tyren stood too. "I know everyone well enough. If you want a hand, I can introduce you to people, tell you who to be wary of, stuff like that."

Lolly managed a smile then, beyond grateful to him. No doubt he wanted to ensure his and his father's places if the Revel Court endured, and she'd honour his title along with his father's position as long as they were loyal and true to her and to Demi's rule over Faerie.

"How does it work?" she asked. "The enemy will keep the location, but the Revel Court's name will come here? The people might or might not choose to move here with it? What about the people in the market, do I offer them sanctuary if the enemy start lashing out?"

Demi nodded. "Yes, yes, and yes ideally."

"The court has moved twice already in recent years," Tyren added. "You'll likely find that the market moves with it. Perhaps there's a quiet part of this realm that could do with livening up a bit, without upsetting the natural lie of the land of course."

"I'll have a think," Lolly said. "Not that I've decided to agree yet or anything."

Demi snorted. "Of course not. Go on, and I'll get Milo to speak to you about details for Petra's… for when we…"

Her voice faded but Lolly nodded. She understood, and doubted she could say the 'f' word either. She would have to receive Petra's family and try not to impose on their grief with her own. She'd have to listen to their anger and agree to support it, because she *would* support it. She'd meant every word when she said she wanted Belladonna and her lot dead by her own hand, even if Demi had refused to let her swear to it.

Maybe not dead, but definitely somewhere awful so she suffers a lot for the rest of forever.

For Petra had counselled kindness and mercy too, and just this once, she would listen. Demi made noises about paperwork and set off with Taz, Claus storming off in a different direction straight after.

"Well, this is a development at least," Tyren announced. "Nature is a celebration in itself if you think about it, and the Revel Court has become way too much about excess and debauchery, and not enough about gratitude and celebrating what we have."

Lolly rubbed her eyes with a hand before realising she still had jam residue on them from the pastry.

"Very eloquent. Sure you don't belong with the Wordy Lord?"

He scowled. "I don't technically belong anywhere now. I need to speak to my father and make sure he didn't know anything about what the old lord was planning. If he did, well, I'll have to deal with that."

Lolly opened her mouth to suggest something both brilliant and rash, but she caught the shine on Tyren's skin and frowned instead.

"You didn't ask anyone to have a look at your injuries?" she asked.

He hesitated then shook his head.

"It doesn't hurt too much now."

Lolly reached into the pocket of the cardigan she'd dragged on, the same one she'd been wearing at the Revel Court. She pulled out a pot of *icalatha* sap and unscrewed the lid, holding it out. When he hesitated, she huffed and started applying it to the burns on his skin.

"You don't need to- okay, that does feel better."

She chuckled as he stood obediently. He was alright really, when he wasn't haranguing her about absolutely everything.

"I need to ask you something," she said, leaning closer to swipe some sap onto his cheek. "*If* I decide to take on the Revel Court, and *if* your father didn't know anything about it, and *if* you're both loyal to Demi, and to me, I'll make sure you keep everything you had before."

His lips twitched. "Very kind of you."

"I thought so." She stepped back and put the lid back on

the pot. "I was thinking, if you needed something to do, maybe you'd want to be my aide and your father can stay on as a sort of advisor?"

She slid the pot back into her pocket and moved onto fidgeting with the cuff of her cardigan, her cheeks heating.

He'll probably say no. Say a few days with me was more than enough for a lifetime and he doesn't think I'm qualified to run my own court, let alone his. He offered to help in front of Demi, but that's probably because he doesn't want me to run it into the ground. He's a lord himself now technically, so she could have chosen him. Why didn't she choose him?

"Thank you, I'll consider it." He must have seen her expression as he hastily added, "it's a huge honour for me to be asked, but we don't know what you're going to choose yet. Also, I still don't know why you came with the others. I know she was a great friend to you, but…"

He trailed off and Lolly frowned.

"I came for you as well," she admitted.

"Did you? Why?"

Orbs alive, is he really going to make me say it?

She barely even wanted to admit it to herself, let alone him. But the subtle blushing which she'd never suffered from before, along with the feral worry about his safety and also the way she quite liked how his eyes crinkled when he smiled and the irritating way her heart went faster when he looked at her for longer than a few seconds, it all added up to one unfortunate truth.

"I'd have thought it was kind of obvious," she mumbled.

She walked a couple of paces ahead until the fresh, cold air hit her cheeks and she could see the greenhouses. But she also had to finish this stupid admission thing she'd started. He could tell her he didn't feel the same and she could shrug it off then go sulk in one of the greenhouses for a while.

"You like me?" He sounded so surprised she almost laughed.

"Yeah, but it's fine, I don't expect you to return feelings or anything."

He nodded, apparently stunned into silence, which didn't seem positive whichever way she tried to look at it. He rubbed the back of his head and sighed.

"It makes no difference," he said. "You're a lady, twice over if you want to be now. I'm either bound to follow my father's footsteps, trapped in a court's service forever, or I'm a nobody because the Lord of Revels is a traitor."

"You're a lord in your own right now," she argued. "You can be anything you want to be. You don't have to align to any court if you don't want to. Go out and find a job. Make your own path."

"It's not that simple. I'm all my father has, and me following him into service is all he's ever wanted."

How awful is that? She frowned up at him. *I know my mother is essentially doing the same to me, but that's through inheritance. Also, I reckon I could abdicate my role and title if I really wanted, but I love this court.*

She would also grow to love the Revel Court if it actually became hers.

Stressed to the hilt and sick of every single day of my life probably, but I'd love them all the same.

But she couldn't interfere with Tyren's family life like she could to her own.

Can I?

"Uh-oh." He grimaced. "Why do you have that scrunchy look on you face? That always means troub-"

Lolly ignored the not-so-veiled suggestion that she had a scrunchy face and acted without thinking. Tyren needed someone to give him a shove onto his own path, and his father wasn't going to do it. So she would have to. He'd thank her someday. Possibly.

She meant to say something cryptic to annoy him, but on seeing him already all frowny and annoyed, she didn't say a word.

He flinched as she grabbed the front of his shirt and pulled his shoulders down toward her. He didn't fight her, probably stunned by shock, but he stood completely still as she pressed a fleeting kiss to his mouth and let him go.

He blinked at her like a startled fish out of water. Except unlike a waterless fish, he seemed to fit the Flora Court, and she wondered then if perhaps merging the Revel and Flora Courts wasn't the best idea for the people the queen could have come up with. Support for the Flora Court and stability for the Revel Court. A marriage of abundance.

Don't mention marriages straight after kissing him, you'll never see him again.

"Excuse me, I have someone I need to talk to."

She left him open-mouthed and blinking in the cold morning air as she strode back up to the castle with renewed determination. Only once she was indoors and out of side did she risk sliding a hand up to her tingling mouth.

CHAPTER TWENTY THREE
TYREN

Tyren was aware that Lolly had kissed him. He'd been aware of it while it was happening and as he watched her stalk away from him, her red hair flying wild and with purpose in her step. He was aware of it when the king consort sauntered out and headed straight for him.

Perhaps he's seen me standing here and assumed my brain has broken down. Has it?

"Alright there?" Taz asked with a broad grin.

Tyren nodded. Shook his head. Drew in a breath.

"She kissed me."

Taz nodded. "Couldn't help noticing that, yeah. Good thing? Bad thing?"

"I… yeah. Confusing thing. She's a lady. Like an actual born and titled lady, not a new one with a dummy recognition title like mine. She might run both her own court and mine, if I'm even a part of mine anymore. She asked me to be her aide, then she kisses me, as if that's not confusing and infuriating enough."

Taz laughed and started walking back toward the castle. Tyren followed him because it was either that or continue standing there until his toes froze.

"Do you like her?" Taz asked.

Do I? Tyren frowned.

"She drives me mad. Half the time I'm irritated by her and the rest I want to see what it takes to annoy her. And there's literally *no arguing with her*, none."

Taz's laughter turned into a wicked cackle, enough that

Tyren managed a smile.

"Maybe you don't want to like her, but if you do, there's no point denying it," Taz said. "If it helps, half the time I'm literally considering regicide because Demi does the dumbest stuff and I'm tearing my hair out."

"But at the same time, you wouldn't have her be any different," Tyren guessed.

"Yep, that's about it. Talk to her. Take it slow. You barely know each other. Move here as part of your court, support her, spend time with her. It may fizzle out or it might be the greatest love story since a queen took a chance on a lowly prince of Faerie."

"Or it might not, but either way I'll regret it if I don't find out," he finished.

Taz nodded. "Smart. But I'm not here just as the wise man of the woods. Also, please try not to rid us of our future Lady of the Flora *and* Revel courts when I tell you."

Tyren groaned. "For Faerie's sake, what has she done now?"

"She might have called your father."

"She *what?!*"

"Yeah." Taz grinned wider. "Walked past me at speed with his face bouncing off the walls, handed me the orb and said if I wouldn't mind just nipping outside to fetch you. Your father sounded extremely confused and kindly asked if you'd call him back."

That was overstepping the line. Tyren grabbed his own orb from his pocket, ignoring Taz's amused insistence that he'd make himself scarce and go watch the girls feeding Arthur. Tyren waited until he was sure he was alone, then made the necessary call.

"Father?"

The familiar face loomed against the wall of the

courtyard immediately.

"I think some explanations are in order," his father said. "I've had a very stressful visit to the farms on the outlands only to come back and find myself barred from the court, stuck in the market with all sorts of outlandish rumours about our lord, our court, the queen, and you."

Tyren walked through to the conservatory with the image of his father's worried face swinging in front of him. He sat down by the fountain, taking comfort from the gushing of the water.

"It's a long story."

He explained and his father for the most was patient, although he could imagine the paling cheeks when he saw his father's eyes going wide at the mention of his being captured. But Tyren knew his father well, so the first thing he said after the whole story wasn't entirely a surprise.

"So, you're courting Lady Leilania?" he asked hopefully.

Tyren sagged with a weary chuckle. "No. Well… No. Not yet. I don't know. But that's irrelevant now. Did you know anything about any of this?"

His father's brows rose toward his hairline.

"Of course not! I mean, I know our lord- *old* lord, was ambitious, but to betray the crown is unthinkable. To ally our court with traitors and Forgotten elitists, it's abhorrent. All of the work we've been doing, or trying to do, to support the queen's new initiatives for the people has been a good thing. Are you safe at the Flora Court?"

Tyren nodded. "Yes, and if Lolly chooses to lead our court as well as eventually take on her own, we would be moving here. It's beautiful and peaceful."

"Our lot aren't exactly peaceful."

"But we could find a distant part of this realm for them

to be loud in. Let the Forgotten keep the current location and use that arrogance to fight them with."

His father chuckled. "I'm glad to see you embracing something of this at least. Also, I'm sure 'Lolly' is a very nice girl. I would be honoured to meet her once you decide what capacity you wish to introduce her to me in."

Tyren shook his head, resigned.

"In that case, I need to figure that bit out first. Are you safe in the market for now? I can ask for you to be brought here instead."

"No, I stay with our people. I'll put the word out discreetly that there might be a positive move in the near future, one we can trust with our support."

"Okay, that's a start. Oh, but you may not have heard. The queen gave me a title. It's only a dummy lord one for recognition, but it's something."

To his astonishment, his father's face didn't split with absolute incandescent joy.

"Oh, that's lovely. Well done."

Tyren frowned. "You're not pleased? I thought you'd be singing sixteen serenades that this day has finally come."

His father scratched his forehead and during the hesitation, realisation occurred.

"She got to you, didn't she?" Tyren asked, his tone flat.

"Of course not, it's great news," his father said placidly. "I'm very happy for you." Then he sighed. "She *may* have mentioned that you're under the impression I want you to follow my example. That would reassure me that you'll be safe and secure, but I only want you to be happy and have a future, even if aide or service to a court isn't part of it."

Tyren couldn't find any words for a good few moments, the touching sentiments surprising him even more than

Lolly's surprise kiss attack earlier. When he didn't answer, his father chuckled.

"Go figure out how you feel and what you want to start with. Stay in touch, son."

Tyren nodded and dropped his arm to his thigh as his father's face disappeared.

Easily said, not so easily done. Whether Lolly took on the Revel Court or not, that was where all Tyren's friends were. Some might choose to stay behind, but others would follow the new lord or lady wherever the queen deigned to place them. Not all the Revel Court members were tricksters or performers. The court also specialised in creatives who built stages, decorations, costumes, instruments and all sorts of productions and items.

The market would flourish here with so much access to natural supplies. Even those dancing trees at the revel might make new contacts, and I bet a lot of the activities Lolly mentioned could be advertised better to draw in visitors, which would help fund the Flora Court's research.

Lolly's research. It would help fund her index and her greenhouses. Which brought him to the unsettling acknowledgement that he wasn't sure how he felt about her. Taz had made several good points, but facing them meant he had to work out what he wanted to do.

"Which I don't want to do," he muttered to himself.

"Room for one more?"

He glanced up as Demi plonked herself down beside him without waiting for an answer.

"If this is advice-hour, your boyfriend has already filled my head with enough," he said.

She laughed. "Actually, I was going to ask for some, but if you're otherwise engaged…"

"No of course not, it's fine. I'm just… It's fine. How can I help?"

She sighed, trailing her fingers through the water bubbling in the fountain.

"Do you think I made the right choice?"

"Offering Lolly the Revel Court?" he asked. She nodded. "Actually, yeah. If she decides it's 'hers', she'll bend over backwards for it. She'll moan and whine and throw tantrums but she'll put the court first and try to learn everything about what makes it tick, tear the rot to pieces and grow it like a sapling."

Demi laughed. "I'm glad then. I know a lot of people think I'm just choosing young people because I'm young, or because I'm legging my friends up the ladder, but we need change and fresh ideas. We need people who haven't been ruined by the rot of the old pieces."

Tyren smiled. Here he sat conversing with an actual queen like they were old friends. He was a lord, not that it meant anything in tangible terms, but his court was also being saved and his father was in the clear.

"She's a good person," Demi added, wiping her hands on her jeans. "Very similar to…"

Her voice broke and she turned her face away. Tyren grimaced, a stab of anguish hitting him square in the chest and whisking his breath away. It took him a moment to compose himself again.

"I didn't know her, but she was strong right until the end," he said.

Demi snorted and wiped her face before turning back to look at him.

"That was her to the core. She was my mentor."

Tyren nodded. "Lolly's too from what I hear. She… I'm not sure what to do about the gift she gave me. When we were fighting them here, I asked for one but I never wanted… I never assumed…"

"Honour it." Demi's voice sharpened. "Use it for good things. I still can't believe it, and she gave Lolly her nature gift. Fitting really considering she will one day rule the Flora Court. But I suppose that's far in the future. What are your plans now?"

Tyren sighed. A good question.

"Lolly asked me if I wanted to be her aide," he admitted. "If she goes through with taking on the Revel Court."

"A high achievement."

"Yes, true. But I think she maybe offered that because she likes me."

"Likes you likes you?"

He nodded. "And I don't want to risk the role being linked to her feelings, which could change, or anything that might alienate me from my court and my friends there, assuming we end up being given a home."

"The Revel Court will always have a home somewhere. I was being flippant more than anything when I suggested disbanding it, and I wouldn't do that unless the court itself stopped being needed. Courts are homes for people, safe spaces or at least they should be. They celebrate the very best of what Fae can come up with, and revelry is as important as nature or speech or the very fabric of Faerie."

Relieved, Tyren forgot where he was and sagged back, almost toppling into the fountain. It was enough to make Demi laugh a little, as though she'd managed to forget her grief and her unending royal stress for a moment or two.

"I want to stay as part of the Revel Court," he decided.

Demi nodded. "Then consider yourself part of it. I can make it conditional if I have to, but Hutch and Harvey have mentioned how popular you are there so that's probably just a load of paperwork for nothing. Much as Milo loves extra paperwork, I can't stomach it at the best of times. And if Lolly's leading it?"

"If she's leading it, I'll do my best to support her. If she isn't, I'll keep in touch with her. Once I've forgiven her for interfering in my business by calling my father of all people."

Demi smirked. "She cares. Oh, there she is, you can tell her off now."

Demi got to her feet and he found himself doing the same thing, his gaze lifting to Lolly walking through from the courtyard.

With Claus.

Who had an irritating grin on his face.

Lolly had her head turned toward him so Tyren couldn't see her face, but she didn't exactly look tense or tetchy around him.

He caught Demi's overly innocent smile, guessing Taz had told her everything already, but he couldn't lie to himself even if he wanted to.

Jealousy equals attraction. Crud.

"I'd go speak to her," Demi suggested quietly. "You don't have to influence her decision or anything. Just keep the lines of communication open. And be glad it's me talking to you right now, because Taz is really into matchmaking these days and he'll get all sorts of scheming ideas."

She walked away with a soft chuckle and Lolly turned her head to smile at her, enough that Tyren could see her face. She was tired and weary, but she was able to smile which was a start.

Questions warred in his mind as he took slow steps toward her and Claus.

Who was going to comfort her in dealing with saying goodbye to Petra? Did she have friends beside the Eastwicks who would be busy consoling their sister? What would happen to her when the mayhem of the queen's court disappeared and she went back to her greenhouses and her index? If she took over the Revel Court, who would support her and stop her decapitating the more traditional nobles for wanting fake trees indoors instead of real ones?

His feet carried him to her side before he had any idea what he would say.

Lolly glanced up at him with an expectant face, but he caught the subtle dismissive irritation Claus shot his way when she wasn't looking.

He's wondering if he can interest her enough to get potential sway over three courts.

He couldn't imagine Claus being able to tolerate Lolly's single-mindedness about plants, or take any joy in the court. As Lolly frowned at him, Tyren eyed the conservatory one more time and realised that he didn't want to be anywhere else. The Flora Court with its beautifully fresh outdoorsy scent, the calmness in the air, the patches of soil spilled from enormous pots and the constant sound of trickling water made him feel more at home than he could ever remember being.

He smiled sweetly at Claus, silently staking a claim, but resisted the urge to wrap an arm around Lolly's shoulders. She'd probably snap at him or laugh and wriggle away. Or look at him in confusion and he'd have to try and make up some random excuse like losing his balance. Or his mind.

"Are you mad at me?" she asked, not looking remotely bothered by the idea.

He ignored Claus hovering and pretended to hide his

smile with great difficulty.

"Not exactly, but I'd prefer if you didn't overstep those boundaries from now on."

Her face lit up.

"You're not exactly mad? So, you admit it helped a bit?"

He tried to make a disapproving huffing noise but the air got caught in his throat and he almost choked. Even worse, she looked close to laughing and the realisation that he'd managed to cheer her up even for a moment was everything.

"The aide thing would be a great move for me," he said cautiously.

"I'm sorry, you've asked *him* to be your aide?" Claus interrupted.

Lolly shot him an impatient look. "Yes, so?"

"Well, no offence, but what are your familial connections?" he asked. "What experience do you have of managing a court? How much history can you call on? Do you even have any favours stored behind you to trade with for the good of your court?"

Tyren forced his expression to remain impassive as his own inadequacies fired through his ears and a lick of shame curled around him. Claus had a point, and Lolly was still young like him. She might not be making the most sensible choice, especially considering she had feelings for him clouding her judgement.

Then her arms folded, her face crunching with absolute disagreeable fury, her eyes flashing as the air around her iced over. Claus seemed to feel the temperature drop as well, his eyes widening.

"Who are you to question any of this?" she demanded. "You run a court in the middle of nowhere that barely even turned up for the battle at the Nether Court. You personally didn't even turn up at all actually now I think about it, big hurrah for you. For what it's worth, Tyren's family connections are irrelevant because he's friends with most of his court already, and that matters a great deal more than trading on obligated family members who probably don't even *like* you."

Tyren had a vague notion he should stop her before she went too far. Frostiness between the courts was the last thing the queen needed right now, and Lolly might need to rely on Claus and his court one day, which alienating him would only make more difficult. But he couldn't remember the last time someone had defended him so vehemently, and considering it was her doing it, he was enjoying the whole experience way too much to stop her straight away.

"And he's helped manage the Revel court," she continued. "Which is one I will be taking on, maybe, if I agree to it. He'll have all the knowledge I'll need, and who cares if he has favours stored? I'll earn my own."

Tyren couldn't help laughing, even though she turned that irritable look on him next.

"I do have some minor family connections, as it goes," he added. "Not many of note but still. I do also have favours stored, and my father is the current aide to the court and I've been supporting him since I was very small. I might not be much, but I'm the one you need."

The moment those last words were out, he regretted them. He fought to keep the blush from his face, then casually scratched his nose as a ploy to hide the minor glamour he covered himself with to hide it.

Claus took a step back, surprise fading from his face.

"Consider me told. I hope at least our courts can be allies though."

Tyren held his breath, but Lolly nodded and held out her hand.

"Our courts can be friends, for the sake of the queen." A shadow of regret passed over her face. "And for the sake of old friends too."

Claus nodded and left Lolly's outstretched hand unshaken, giving Tyren a quick warning glance before striding out of the conservatory. It was almost an insult to not take his leave politely, but his absence lightened the mood in the air immediately. Tyren guessed he would walk to the edge of the court boundary and realm-skip back to his own court, but out of sight and hopefully out of Lolly's mind.

This is madness, how can I be jealous of someone she's barely looked at? He's probably too old for her anyway.

He flinched when Lolly stared at him, not saying a word, just watching.

"You can turn the deep freeze off now," he tried.

She frowned. "What? Oh, yeah. That happens when I'm irritable. I have to be careful if I'm in a mood that I don't accidently give the plants frostbite. So, you're not completely mad at me? I just thought if I explained he might understand, and that you might not want to hurt his feelings, but he's not going to care what I think."

There was a strange sort of demented logic to it, but he refused to let her off completely free.

"I'm not completely mad. He said he only wants me to be safe and happy, which is good. But I think you scared the nether out of him. I said I'd been made a lord and he barely even smiled."

"Well, that's rude."

"If you knew him, you'd understand how unlike him that is. He didn't want me to think he was pressuring me by being overjoyed about it.”

She frowned. “Hmm. Okay. I’ll trust your judgement.”

“Of my own father? I’m honoured.” He risked a grin, delighted when she laughed a little. “Whatever happens, whether you decide to take on the Revel Court or not, perhaps we can talk and get to know each other a bit?”

She smiled, casting her gaze away across the conservatory.

“Okay. A bit. What do you think I should do?”

“No influence from me, *Lady*.” He grinned as she shoved his shoulder with her hand. “Figure out how you feel and what you want to start with.”

“Are you planning on going back to the Revel Court? To the current location I mean?”

He shook his head, realising that for all their lack of many years, the queen and king consort knew what they were talking about where it counted.

“Not yet.” He didn’t comment on her hand sliding through the crook of his elbow. “I’ll hang around a day or two, assuming you’re not kicking me out.”

He let her pick the pace and the direction, walking alongside her toward the dining hall.

“I won’t. But you probably want to get on Arthur’s good side if you’re hanging around.”

“You said she liked me. I think I’m good.”

She gave him a look that failed to hide the surprisingly shy smile hiding underneath.

“We’ll see.”

CHAPTER TWENTY FOUR
LOLLY

While watching Tyren throw fish for Arthur, who really did seem to have taken to him surprisingly fast, Lolly wondered what she should do. She barely even noticed the Eastwick sisters enter the room, but when she caught sight of Meryl the anxious grief swamped around her again. Meryl's eyes were swollen, her cheeks blotchy and her attention unfocused. Cheryl had an arm around her waist and Lolly gulped as Cheryl steered in her direction.

"I don't know what to say," Lolly mumbled, barely able to look Meryl in the face.

She had lost a friend she'd loved since her childhood, but Meryl had lost something even deeper than that.

"Me either," Cheryl said with a ragged sigh. "There's nothing to say. We keep fighting. We take them down. We stop them hurting people we love."

The spoons on the nearby table rattled and Lolly let Meryl grab onto her arm. She switched the hold to her other one so she could put the first around Meryl's shoulders.

"Are you going to take the Revel Court on?" Meryl asked, her voice frail.

Lolly froze. "I… I don't know. Should I?"

"Mer," Cheryl warned.

"Yes." Meryl nodded. "She believed in you. She told Demi you could do it. Did you thank him?"

Lolly was struggling to keep up. "Him?"

Meryl pointed in Tyren's direction without looking.

"Him. She got to say goodbye because of him. Most would hunt him."

"Hunt him?" Lolly stared at Cheryl in helplessness. "Why would they hunt him?"

Cheryl grimaced. "His gift. Back in older times, it was a bad omen if a child was born with the ability to cling to death. Demi wants to find a way of asking him about it when the time is right, but she doesn't want to look like she's trying to use him for it either."

Lolly almost dropped Meryl in panic.

"She'd better not! He's got enough to deal with as it is with his court almost folding and being kidnapped, and why are you grinning at me like that?"

Cheryl dimmed her smile as Meryl looked her way.

"She won't, don't worry. He's safe. For what it's worth, we all think you'll be great for the Revel Court. What are your negatives?"

Lolly sighed. "None. Except for panic about how I'm going to handle an entire court I don't know, navigate people I really don't want to talk to and handle my current court, which technically isn't mine yet but will be one day."

"But aside from that?"

Lolly sighed, glancing at Tyren one final time. "I don't want to be foolish enough to let him be any kind of factor in my decision."

"Don't do that." Meryl huffed. "If you like him, he'll be a factor either way. You say no to the court because you don't want him to be an influence, that's still an influence. Make good decisions based on what's best for everyone."

She sounded so much like Petra in that moment Lolly had to choke back tears. Cheryl might have noticed as she grabbed Meryl's arm and gave her a gentle pull.

"Come on, we'll see if Ace has come back with Leo yet. He always cheers you up."

"I don't need *cheering up.*"

"Fine, but I have to do something or I'll go crazy."

Lolly watched them go. The room was filling up with people she both did and didn't recognise. A few of her court hurried back and forth with absentminded bobs of the head in her direction, something they tried to remember to do despite the Flora Court being her mother's domain in terms of technicality.

If I do take on the Revel Court, its people will be mine. I'll be responsible for them.

"Yo. We haven't actually really spoken much before."

Lolly looked up to find Harvey Hutchinson sidling into place beside her, his purple hair sticking up on end.

"So you thought 'yo' would be the best thing to start with?" she asked.

He nodded. "Works as good as any. Admiring our young lord?" He nodded in Tyren's direction, grinning when Lolly opened her mouth to argue. "He's great. I'd admire him too, you know, if it weren't for Beryl. And if I was into boys. She'd probably appreciate the break actually, but sucks for her. How's my inane babbling working for you?"

Lolly shrugged. "They sent you to watch me? Are you lot on rotation?"

"Nah. Currying favour. See, none of us are actually sworn to the queen's court because we're FDPs. We have the offer, but we're scoping out our options. We'll support and defend her to our dyi… well, you know. But as for swearing to a court, we're available."

"And you're offering to swear to mine?"

He grinned. "Depends. Do you have one for us to swear

to?"

Remembering that he was friends with Tyren and therefore probably knew the Revel Court well enough, she realised this was a good opportunity to get some proper information.

"What's the one thing the Revel Court needs?" she asked. "What is it missing?"

"Big question for much wiser brains than mine to ponder on. But I think a lot of the locals just want someone who will listen to them. They make most of the stuff we sell in the market, yet they get trodden on by the nobles. Taxes and scary stuff like that."

"So you want a giant suggestion box then."

"Ooh good thinking. We could make it like a monthly thing and read out the funniest ones."

"All of which would be planted by you and your brother no doubt." She couldn't help smiling.

Tyren lifted his head and started frowning in their direction, narrowly missing getting gooped on by Arthur who didn't appreciate the sudden decrease in attention.

Harvey bowed low and grabbed Lolly's hand, ignoring her flinch. He pretended to press his lips to her knuckles.

"My lady," he said, grinning wickedly. "When you inevitably decide to adopt us, we will be ready to serve."

Lolly watched him walk away toward his brother and the others, including Taz, Demi, Ace and Milo all whispering together.

"What did he want?" Tyren asked. "Was he bothering you?"

Lolly smiled. "Not exactly. He was telling me all about the Revel Court."

"You could have asked me."

Do I detect a slight hint of irritation there?

She sighed, realising that as much as she wanted to stay talking to him, she had to speak to Demi first. Because, in reality, there was only one choice she could live with ahead of her.

"I'm going to take on the Revel Court," she told him. "I should probably check with my mother first, but I'm betting Demi's already cleared all of this with her before approaching me. If not, I'll have to learn to trade big favours and fast."

He nodded. "Good. You'll make an excellent lady of any court, but the Revels especially will feel safe under someone as caring as you."

An actual compliment, wow. She tried not to let it go to her head.

"Is the role of your aide still available?" he asked. She nodded. "Then I'll gladly accept. I'm probably best placed to help the court cross over to your leadership and to this realm, as you so charmingly yelled at Claudius earlier."

She nodded. That was the best thing for her new court, to have Tyren who knew how it worked alongside her with advice and contacts.

It also put her in a very difficult position. She took a deep breath.

"In that case, I'm sorry for kissing you. I don't want to make things awkward, especially if we're going to need to get on rather than have all this weird snappy tension. We should agree a truce for the sake of your court and mine. Well, my courts now. Ours anyway. At least, the Revel Court will be mine, but also yours and everyone that's a part of it."

She held her hand out for him to shake. The correct protocol would be for him to take her hand and kneel, then to swear his service and loyalty to her, but she couldn't bear the thought of that somehow.

Her fingers zinged as he closed his strong hand around them and she sucked in a laboured breath. His eyes glimmered with unexpected wickedness and she squeaked in alarm as he pulled her toward him, his arm crowding around her waist.

"What are you doing?" she hissed.

"Truce agreed. Which means I need to apologise in advance for the absolutely necessary deviation from protocol."

She wriggled but he wouldn't let her go. "For the what of the what? What are you going on about?"

"This."

His lips pressed against hers, firm yet soft, and she almost bit through her tongue. Fizzles exploded in her gut, her mind swimming through confusion and the distracting rotation of elation. But with the confusion circling, she couldn't sink into the bliss of it and had to break away.

"Wait, the whole point of the truce was to-*mmmfphh!*"

She swallowed the end of her sentence as he grinned and kissed her again. Refusing to let him win, she shoved gently against his shoulders.

"You need to explain this whole th*nnggggg*."

She hoped Meryl wasn't watching and feeling awful, but also guessed that the wolf-whistling noises piercing the air was half Taz and half the Hutchinson brothers. The thoughts slid away one by one, and by the time he finally decided she'd let him win for once, she had absolutely nothing in her head at all.

"I'm still going to be your aide," he insisted. "If you'll have me. But I'm also your friend and your support who will stand by your side. Not for the sake of the courts because that's your decision to make, but for your sake and for mine."

She smirked, her cheeks burning. "And the kissing? That's what friends do, is it? Am I meant to be going over and jumping the queen, or the king consort, or one of the Hutchinson boys?"

"Orbs no, mainly because Beryl and Cheryl could both easily take you down, and I don't think Taz and Demi are sharing types either. Also because you drive me mad, but I can't imagine enjoying fighting with anyone else other than you. So, if you'll have me, I'm offering to be your everything you need until you decide otherwise."

She couldn't help smiling, properly and wide. The grief wouldn't go away, and she would have time to feel guilty about Petra and to worry about the court she intended to care for. But Petra of all people would tell her to grab the happy moments wherever she could and hold them tighter than tight.

"I'll consider it," she said airily.

He rolled his eyes at her. "Good. I want us to take this slowly though, get to know each other properly and let whatever comes build without rushing anything."

"Agreed. A truce then. Also, kissing someone when they're trying to talk to you is rude."

"Too right." Demi appeared beside them, Taz hovering behind her. "They never listen though. We're going to stay here tonight if that's okay, then home before we have to come back for the… you know."

Lolly nodded. "Good. I'm going to take on the Revel Court."

"Excellent." Demi smiled, relief washing over her face. "I hoped you would. Milo will give you all the details, and I mean literally every detail in the history of Faerie *ever*." Her gaze snapped to Tyren. "Are you staying?"

He nodded. "I'm going to help Lolly take on the Revel Court, go between the two maybe where needed, smooth any ruffled feathers."

"I'm glad." Demi chuckled. "We may need to call on you for things as the trouble with the Forgotten unfolds, but I've told the mayhem crew they're welcome to choose, so you might end up with some or all of them begging for your favour."

Given the grin on Demi's face, Lolly guessed she meant the Eastwicks and the Hutchinsons, but at least they'd make her command of the Revel Court entertaining if they did.

"My court is open," she offered. "Or it will be, when it's officially my court."

Demi nodded. "Officially your court as of now. We'll have to orb in at least sometime soon, announce you to the people and explain the move, but with the Forgotten lurking they'll understand you not being able to go straight to them in person."

My court. Officially my court. I'm Lady of Revels.

Tyren smoothly slid an arm around her waist and she let him, although the temptation to shove him off and keep him on his toes occurred to her.

"My father is already in the market explaining the situation to people we can trust," he explained. "The court will be ready when the moment to move comes."

Demi clapped her hands together and Lolly realised their friends had disappeared.

"Brilliant, that's my cue to go and lie down. My lizard is probably halfway through your greenhouses by now, he eats *everything*."

Lolly froze as Demi turned and ambled off toward the conservatory door with Taz in tow.

"Her lizard is eating my plants?" she asked.

Tyren's eyes lit up. "Oh! That reminds me. Come with me."

He grabbed her hand and pulled her behind him toward the door. She resisted out of habit, even though the excitement on his face had her curiosity swirling.

"Don't drag me about! I'm a lady of an actual court now," she grumbled.

He grinned. "And I'm a lord of nothing at all, it's all the same. Trust me, you're going to want to see this."

She relented and sped up so they were hurrying side by side to the nearest greenhouse. He dragged her halfway down the first aisle, bending at the waist and huffing to himself. Lolly followed him, bemused.

"Aha!" He straightened up and pointed at a cluster of *icalatha*. "There."

She frowned and dropped into a crouch. "What are you— oh orbs! The stems are pink. How are the stems pink? What happened?"

"Your mother told me, said one of the greenhouse-keepers took my suggestion of telling them jokes. Apparently it worked."

Lolly stared up at him, her mouth open.

"I thought you were joking! When I mentioned it, it was because I was telling them how much of an idiot you were!"

"I was joking, and probably am somewhat of an idiot at times. The keeper thought it'd be funny to try though and it turns out I'm somewhat of a plant genius after all."

Lolly warred with irritation that he'd managed so flippantly to stumble on a solution to a problem she'd been agonising over for two growth seasons. But seeing him hovering in her greenhouse waiting expectantly for her excitement, she realised it.

He belonged there. In the greenhouse, in the Flora Court, and in the Revel Court. *Her* Revel Court. Maybe even at her side one day.

He flinched as she launched to her feet and threw her arms around his neck, his eyes wide with surprise as she dropped a kiss on his half-parted mouth.

"I could kiss you!"

He snickered. "You just did, but I don't mind if you want to do it again."

She rolled her eyes but left her arms where they were, settling as his wrapped around her waist in answer.

"So, I'm Lady of the Revel Court," she announced.

He nodded. "You are. And I'm a random lord who will be supporting you the whole way. I wonder if the queen will keep an eye on us."

"I don't know. She might be too busy with this whole Forgotten thing looming." She frowned, sadness waving so harsh she couldn't speak for several moments. "I still owe them payback, whatever everyone else says."

"If that's what my lady desires. We have to find a way to the Prime Realm first though, before they do."

"We have the location," Lolly added, remembering the two random words from Blossom's diary. "Although I've never heard of it before."

He shook his head, gaze softening. "Me either. But that's a problem for another day."

As he kissed her again, all thought of strange location words from the human world drifted from her mind and danced away through the nether, leaving her Lady of the Revel Court with Tyren at her side.

ACKNOWLEDGEMENTS

A huge thank you to every reader who has joined us on this mad journey through Faerie! To those who've shared on social media, done ARC reads or just given me compliments about the book to keep me going.

To my family and also my writing family as always, your support means everything to me – Anna Britton, Debbie Roxburgh, Sally Doherty, Marisa Noelle, Emma Finlayson-Palmer, Katina Wright, Alison Hunt, Maria Oliver, Loz Doyle, Estelle Tudor, Aerin Apeltun, the readers who have caught so many printing blips it's not even funny… writing Twitter, everyone who joins #ukteenchat, the WriteMentor crew, libraries and schools who have taken a chance on this and the Arcanium series, shops that are still stocking these books and giving this indie author a chance to reach more readers, and to the readers who will find these books in the future.

THANK YOU!

ABOUT THE AUTHOR

While always convinced that there has to be something out there beyond the everyday, Emma focuses on weaving magic realms with words (the real world can wait a while). The idea of other worlds fascinates her and she's determined to find her own entrance to an alternate realm one day.

Raised in London, she now lives on the UK south coast with her husband and a very lazy black Labrador who occasionally condescends to take her out for a walk.

Aside from creative writing studies, an addiction to cake and spending far too much time procrastinating on social media, Emma is still waiting for the arrival of her unicorn. Or a tank, she's not fussy.

For the latest news and updates, check the website or come say hi on social media:

www.emmaebradley.com
@EmmaEBradley